THE **JOURNEY** PRIZE

STORIES

WINNERS OF THE $10,000 JOURNEY PRIZE

1989
Holley Rubinsky for
"Rapid Transits"

1990
Cynthia Flood for "My Father
Took a Cake to France"

1991
Yann Martel for "The Facts
Behind the Helsinki Roccamatios"

1992
Rozena Maart for "No Rosa,
No District Six"

1993
Gayla Reid for
"Sister Doyle's Men"

1994
Melissa Hardy for
"Long Man the River"

1995
Kathryn Woodward for "Of
Marranos and Gilded Angels"

1996
Elyse Gasco for "Can You Wave
Bye Bye, Baby?"

1997 (shared)
Gabriella Goliger for
"Maladies of the Inner Ear"

Anne Simpson for
"Dreaming Snow"

1998
John Brooke for
"The Finer Points of Apples"

1999
Alissa York for "The Back of the
Bear's Mouth"

2000
Timothy Taylor for
"Doves of Townsend"

2001
Kevin Armstrong for
"The Cane Field"

2002
Jocelyn Brown for
"Miss Canada"

2003
Jessica Grant for
"My Husband's Jump"

2004
Devin Krukoff for
"The Last Spark"

2005
Matt Shaw for "Matchbook for a
Mother's Hair"

2006
Heather Birrell for
"BriannaSusannaAlana"

2007
Craig Boyko for
"OZY"

2008
Saleema Nawaz for
"My Three Girls"

THE BEST OF CANADA'S NEW WRITERS
THE **JOURNEY** PRIZE

STORIES

SELECTED BY
CAMILLA **GIBB**
LEE **HENDERSON**
REBECCA **ROSENBLUM**

EMBLEM
McClelland & Stewart

Emblem is an imprint of McClelland & Stewart Ltd.
Emblem and colophon are registered trademarks of McClelland & Stewart Ltd.

A cataloguing record for this publication is available from Library and Archives Canada.

We acknowledge the financial support of the Government of Canada through the Book Publishing Industry Development Program and that of the Government of Ontario through the Ontario Media Development Corporation's Ontario Book Initiative. We further acknowledge the support of the Canada Council for the Arts and the Ontario Arts Council for our publishing program.

Typeset in Janson by M&S, Toronto
Printed and bound in Canada

ANCIENT FOREST
FRIENDLY

This book was produced using ancient-forest friendly papers.

McClelland & Stewart Ltd.
75 Sherbourne Street
Toronto, Ontario
M5A 2P9
www.mcclelland.com

1 2 3 4 5   13 12 11 10 09

ABOUT THE JOURNEY PRIZE STORIES

The $10,000 Journey Prize is awarded annually to an emerging writer of distinction. This award, now in its twenty-first year, and given for the ninth time in association with the Writers' Trust of Canada as the Writers' Trust of Canada/ McClelland & Stewart Journey Prize, is made possible by James A. Michener's generous donation of his Canadian royalty earnings from his novel *Journey*, published by McClelland & Stewart in 1988. The Journey Prize itself is the most significant monetary award given in Canada to a developing writer for a short story or excerpt from a fiction work in progress. The winner of this year's Journey Prize will be selected from among the twelve stories in this book.

The Journey Prize Stories has established itself as the most prestigious annual fiction anthology in the country, introducing readers to the finest emerging writers from coast to coast for more than two decades. It has become a who's who of up-and-coming writers, and many of the authors who have appeared in the anthology's pages have gone on to distinguish themselves with collections of short stories, novels, and literary awards. The anthology comprises a selection from submissions made by the editors of literary journals from across the country, who have chosen what, in their view, is the most exciting writing in English that they have published in the previous year. In recognition of the vital role journals play in fostering literary voices, McClelland & Stewart makes its own award of $2,000 to the journal that originally published and submitted the winning entry.

This year the selection jury comprises three acclaimed writers:

Camilla Gibb is the award-winning author of three novels, *Mouthing the Words*, *The Petty Details of So-and-so's Life*, and *Sweetness in the Belly*, as well as numerous short stories, articles, and reviews. Her work has been shortlisted for The Giller Prize and won the Trillium Book Award, the City of Toronto Book Award, and the CBC Canadian Literary Award for short fiction. She was named by the jury of the prestigious Orange Prize as "one of 21 writers to watch in the new century." Camilla's new novel, *The Beauty of Humanity Movement*, is forthcoming from Doubleday in 2010. She lives in Toronto.

Lee Henderson is the author of the award-winning short story collection *The Broken Record Technique* and the novel *The Man Game*, a finalist for the Rogers Writers' Trust Fiction Prize and winner of the Ethel Wilson Fiction Prize. A two-time nominee for the Journey Prize, he is a contributing editor to the arts magazines *Border Crossings* in Canada and *Contemporary* in the U.K. He lives in Vancouver.

Rebecca Rosenblum's short fiction has been shortlisted for the Journey Prize, the National Magazine Award, and the Danuta Gleed Award. Her first collection of short fiction, *Once*, won the Metcalf-Rooke Award and was named one of *Quill & Quire*'s "15 Books that Mattered in 2008." Her stories have been seen recently in *The Fiddlehead*, *Earlit Shorts*, and *Best Canadian Short Stories*, among other places. Rebecca lives, works, and writes in Toronto.

The jury read a total of seventy-two submissions without knowing the names of the authors or those of the journals in which the stories originally appeared. McClelland & Stewart would like to thank the jury for their efforts in selecting this year's anthology and, ultimately, the winner of this year's Journey Prize.

McClelland & Stewart would also like to acknowledge the continuing enthusiastic support of writers, literary journal editors, and the public in the common celebration of new voices in Canadian fiction.

For more information about *The Journey Prize Stories*, please consult our website: www.mcclelland.com/jps.

CONTENTS

INTRODUCTION

Writers select their most polished short stories to submit to journals. From what they receive, the journals' editors choose what they feel are the most surprising and gripping stories to publish, then winnow those published stories again to find those they consider most worthy of inclusion in a national anthology. That's when the packages show up in the Journey Prize jury's mailboxes – this year, filled with seventy-two nuanced, deeply imagined, and sharply written pieces of short fiction.

What a pleasure to read so many stellar explorations of a challenging literary form. What an education, too. And what a terrifying challenge to look at what the best literary editors in Canada consider the best stories, and to try to choose the best of those. The pleasure and education far outweighed the terror, but still it was daunting. Brilliant short stories can be brilliant along any number of metrics – realism or strangeness, elegance or blunt simplicity, tight plotting or sprawling authenticity. Comparison is fraught and dubious at best. All we can do, whether in the role of judge, teacher, or simply happy reader, is to consider what the writer was trying to achieve, how well he or she succeeded in that goal, and how excited the reader is about that success.

One terribly exciting success, in our opinion, is "The Last Great Works of Alvin Cale" by Daniel Griffin. This subtle and complicated story of art, love, and lust moves forward on the grim trajectory of death, but also draws haunting life from its central character, Skylar, and his admission to himself of all he truly feels, and longs for. His son's illness renews their relationship and their uneasy intimacy, full of envy, rivalry, and fierce affection for beauty. Griffin has taken on considerable challenges in portraying the working lives of artists, and has done so with amazing, and heartbreaking, force.

Adrian Michael Kelly's "Lure" is also a story about a father and a son, but Kelly's is an altogether different art, full of the simple intensity of a child's observation. Kelly doesn't trouble the reader with anything but the moment as the boy sees it. The drama inheres in a child's anxiety over pleasing his father, over the life of a frog, and the taste of a sandwich. Although "Lure" does have a climax of adult pain, it is the boy's perceptions and tensions that dominate, and it is to Kelly's infinite credit that this seems not a limitation but an illumination.

To continue with family stories, Sarah L. Taggart's "Deaf" is told from alternating perspectives of a mother and her young daughter, both missing a sense of so many things in their lives. The glittering percision of Taggart's language allows for both the humour of children bickering over ketchup and the quotidian tragedy of adults ground down by both hope and disappointment. Taggart never diminishes her characters' lives of canned tomatoes and Hungry Hungry Hippos, nor does she lionize them or excuse their bad behaviour. She just achieves that incredible literary summit of bringing them to life.

The gift in all of these stories lies in the adage of showing rather than telling. Particularly rich in this regard are those stories that immerse us in specific histories or geographies, making setting integral to and inseparable from the events and emotions of the characters.

Yasuko Thanh's "Floating Like the Dead" takes us into a little-known and painful chapter in Canadian history. Here, the few remaining inhabitants of a turn-of-the-century colony of Chinese lepers off the coast of B.C. spend the last of their days clinging to something as futile as hope. The limits of language, racism, and poverty have already defined their immigrant lives. Their alienation becomes complete as their bodies rebel and repel, and they are exiled to die in isolation. They must use their declining strength to battle a rugged geography they cannot beat. The forest is primeval and eternal and the western breezes across the Pacific can only remind them of the China of their youths. Thanh strikes that difficult balance between depicting bigger worlds and worlds within, and uses the resonances between the internal and external to subtle and graceful effect. This is a story of brittle beauty, which gives as much room to the unspoken as the spoken.

In "Highlife," Paul Headrick similarly addresses imminent death, the silences that precede it, and the sounds that surround it. A husband and wife, together for twenty-six years, become unglued from each other in the face of the husband's illness and the anger that consequently possesses him. He is a lover of music – an academic, a radio host, and a critic – making a pilgrimage of sorts to Ghana with his wife. He is looking to hear highlife music in its original context – buoyant life-affirming sounds – but he and his wife are largely silent companions on this trip; there is little he is compelled to voice aloud. Against the heat and confusion, the dancing bodies and the music, his life – and her life in relation to him – are coming to a painful end. In this case it is the contrast between internal and external worlds, the disconnect between them, that gives the story its poignancy, isolating the characters from each other and the world around them.

What isolates the main character in Lynne Kutsukake's "Away" is the arrival of sudden news that casts her out of her day-to-day life. As in "Floating Like the Dead," "Away" brings a little-known piece of history to light – in this case, the abduction of several young Japanese by North Koreans in the late-1970s to serve as Japanese language teachers for the North Korean Intelligence Service. When this is discovered decades later, the main character is stunned to see a picture of a girl she once knew among the abductees. They had been classmates, volleyball teammates, and had once shared an intimate, if confusing, moment. But then Sayuri had disappeared. Photos of her were plastered throughout the town, rumours about her abounded, and the police investigation brought no answers. In the aftermath of Sayuri's disappearance, the main character had felt drawn to the sea in a way she could not explain. She would stare at the waves and the horizon and think of floating and fish, which connected her to the missing Sayuri in some disconcerting way. Thirty years pass before Sayuri's whereabouts are revealed. But there remain silences and vast unknowns and no real answers. There is only the seashore where the narrator used to stand, perhaps intuiting somehow that Sayuri lived on the other side.

The stories in this anthology are written by authors from across Canada, about people from all around the world, and told from the point of view of people living vastly different lives. Some are set in a Canada few of us are familiar with, notably Jesus Hardwell's "Easy Living" and Shawn Syms's "On the Line," which takes us on a rare and intimate tour of meatpacking and slaughterhouse culture. Reading is an act of empathy. A reader wants to believe and to feel and to share in the memories and condition of another person, however unfamiliar or unreliable the person is, and the writer's responsibility is simply to make this possible.

Memory, with its narrativizing techniques of emphasis and elision, is a fiction writer's third hand. It scrambles just as hard as the left and right to make sense of disconnected things. And a great deal of fiction is taken up with an exploration of this unseen hand's dexterity. Memory is a common theme. While a writer's ten fingers type, the third hand caresses the keys of synapses and shifts faraway-driven thoughts to the front of the mind. Memory, drawing from life, grasps what the technology of language tries to articulate – experience. Memory prompts the other hands to work, and sometimes makes its imperfect self the subject of the story, as it does in Fran Kimmel's "Picturing God's Ocean" and in Dave Margoshes's "The Wisdom of Solomon," in which the narrator's humble, ever-worried father finds himself writing an advice column for a Jewish newspaper in Cleveland after the First World War. For its voice, "The Wisdom of Solomon" is an astonishing work of memory guided by the very different voices of two generations. Stirred by thoughts of the narrator's father, the story at once inhabits the melancholy and reflective voice of the son and the eager, worried voice of the father, so that he, the Jewish Diaspora, and the glory days of newsprint are rendered with such unerring clarity that the narrator and his father will both endure in the reader's own memory in great detail.

A great story, by this metaphor's definition, has got superb third-hand coordination, but a story is also more commonly said to *have legs*. When the premise and the language, and especially the characters, are all so exciting to read that you re-read, and tell your friends to read, then a story has legs. It will endure. Included in this selection are two very different stories that have remarkable legs and that also happen to be about characters on the run, physically and psychologically. Alexander MacLeod's "Miracle Mile" is about a runner on his last race in a tragicomic tale of jockdom gone awry. "Miracle Mile" shows us that in life there can be fitness without health, and commitment without honour. Sarah Keevil's story "Pyro" is about a dishonourable young woman running from one bad relationship to another – out of the frying pan and into the fire, as it were – as she finds herself involved with a fire-starter. "Pyro" depicts a narrator fleeing from responsibility who would rather burn away memories and start fresh than face herself and her mistakes.

How many great short stories were published in Canada this past year? Twelve? No way, far more than a bundle of twelve. Journals are still the best first place to fish for examples from our burgeoning literary talent pool. These twelve pieces are highlights from the many discoveries made by Canadian literary journals during the previous year. Readers of *Grain* and *PRISM*, *Vancouver Review* and *The Dalhousie Review*, *Exile* and other literary magazines already know that the country's literary efforts are well beyond the meniscus; this is only a sample. The three of us spent all day talking about our choices, and once the selection was made, it felt like the conversation ended too soon. Short stories have a contemporary urgency to them that makes you want to talk about their implications. That's why once you fall in love with the form, with all that a short story offers in a too-brief amount of space, the possibilities for characters and premises, from then on all you can do is read them as they come, and tell others, "Here, check out *this*."

Camilla Gibb
Lee Henderson
Rebecca Rosenblum
June 2009

THE **JOURNEY** PRIZE

STORIES

ADRIAN MICHAEL KELLY

LURE

On their way down to Ecky's for an oil change and filters his father pulls into Canadian Tire. Stares at the lures as long as his hand. Shimmering eyes and thick as sausage – the long wicked dangle of treble-barbed hooks – they look like specimens bungled by God. Or something older than God. And crueller.

As his father slides a box – it says HEDDON'S COBRA – from one of the long jutting prongs, the boy slips round the end of the shelf. Walks past the spinners and the hairy buzzbaits to the display of shiny spoons. Sees the Red Devil. Notes the price. Moves down the aisle. Stands on tiptoes – his father is reading the back of the box – then scans the display of rods and sees the one his father got him. Checks the tag. Then the selection of open-faced reels. Finds one like his then does the sum. Knows they are not poor. But knows they don't have heaps. And feels the weight of forty dollars.

His father says Son?

The boy scoots back and says I'm here.

Suppose we should be going.

Gonna get that one?

Thought I might.

Maybe it's the charm.

Over the box his father makes a jokey cross and says Hope so.

They walk to the cash and his father pays half with Canadian Tire money and half with real dollars. Then they drive to Ecky's. Pull up in front of the service bay. A car in there with its hood way up. The boy's father rolls down his window. Leans his head out and makes a bullhorn with his hand. Weren't you fixing that one last week?

Ecky leans around the hood and says You're next.

Only kidding, Hector. Take your time.

His father turns off the car and says Shall we pop up to Wing's?

And the boy says Sure.

They get out and his father tosses the keys in the car. They bounce beside the bag with the lure in it.

Up at Wing's they sit at the counter and his father nods hello at the men always there. The waitress named Mary is down near the end talking to a guy in a Roughriders coat. She puts down her smoke and says Hey Morris, tea?

The boy's father says Coffee I think.

And then Mary looks at the boy. He looks at his father.

Tell her what you'd like, lad.

The boy looks back at Mary and says Root beer?

Fountain or can.

The boy says Can. And then he says Please.

Mary serves them and says How's Carol?

And the boy's father says She's well.

Good to hear, says Mary, and she looks down the counter.

The boy's father says Back on the fags?

Hard when you work in a place like this.

Hard anytime.

You want a menu, Morris?

Fine just now, love.

Back in the kitchen Wing hits the bell and says Pick up pick up. Mary goes back to get the order. The boy bends his straw and watches his father pour cream in his coffee and stir long and slow as he looks down the counter and joins in the blather – jokes, the weather, Trudeau, and who's died. The boy drinks his Hires. Turns on the stool. But only a little. Nibbles his straw. Closes one eye and looks in the can. His father turns back and says You peckish?

The boy looks up and says French fries?

His father nods. Orders a plate and they share. With malt vinegar.

Not bad these.

Mum's are better.

So I'll have the last one.

The boy looks at it. His father says Yours. And slides two bucks under the edge of the plate. They get up to go. Wing comes out for a swallow of Pepsi. Wipes his shiny forehead with the length of his arm and says Hello Morris, how are you how are you?

Good, Wing. Yourself?

Oh busy busy. Plan for weekend?

Fishing, Wing.

This time of year? Weather no good.

Perfect for muskie.

A couple of men at the counter look over and Wing stops drinking his Pepsi. Looks at the boy and says You go?

The boy only nods.

And Wing says Wow. Then he spreads his arms wide and says Big fish.

The boy nods again.

And Wing says Be careful he no eat you.

The men at the counter laugh and the boy looks at Mary. She blows out smoke and smiles softly at him. The boy looks down. His father waves bye to her and to Wing and Wing says Bye, good luck good luck!

A man at the counter says He'll need it he'll need it. And he laughs with the others as the bells on the door – three of them on a shiny red ribbon – bounce and clang and rattle behind the boy and his dad.

Up at Ecky's the car isn't done. The boy and his father stand in the bay. Grease stains and tools. Sunshine Girls all over a wall. And on the wall opposite a huge stuffed muskie – Ecky says lunge – on a fancy piece of wood with a brass plaque on it. The boy's father has another look and shakes his head. Forty-eight pounds, Hector.

Under the car Ecky says Yep.

Must have been a fight.

Ecky slides out and looks at the fish but doesn't say anything. Slides under again.

The boy's father says What did you use?

Ecky says Eh?

His father says Bait.

And Ecky says Frog.

The boy's father crouches and looks under the car. Plastic? he says.

Nope, says Ecky, real.

Can't say I've tried it.

Hardly use anything else. For muskie.

Never jerk bait?

Ecky slides out and stands up and says You know why they call it that?

I think I hear what you're saying, Hector.

Ecky wipes his hands on a rag and says Don't mind my sayin –

Go ahead.

Saw that eight-dollar gizmo on the front seat.

The boy says Really it was four.

Yeah, well. You're goin up to Crowe, right?

The boy and his father nod.

Lotta shoals out there, Morris. Weedbeds – right between the islands there – perfect.

The boy's father nods and says That's where I trawl.

Had a follower?

Earlier this fall. I could *see* it, Ecky. Not ten feet from me. It *nudged* the lure. Like it knew, the bugger.

It won't nudge a frog.

How does one –

'Tween the islands there. The ones closer to the western shore. Lob it out on the lily pads. Let it sink a little. Jig it a bit. Don't reel too fast.

What sort of hook?

Big one, laughs Ecky. And he hooks his finger – his filthy pointed nail – beneath the boy's chin. Put it through here, he says. Or here. Then he turns out his leg like a Sunshine Girl. Points near his' crotch and says The meaty part. It'll kick. Bleed a little. Hello, fishy – he nods and smiles – that's what you want.

Where will I find live frogs this time of year?

Place outside of Marmora. I know the guy. When you goin.

Tomorrow first thing.

I'll call him.

Thank you, Hector.

No bother.

The boy's father turns around and looks at the muskie again. So does the boy. The snout on it. The teeth. The boy's father says One hell of a fight.

And Ecky says Why it's on the wall, Morris.

Can one man land it?

Ecky points at the boy and says He goin with you?

His father's hand on the boy's shoulder. Yes, he is.

Ecky horks in a grease stain – it jiggles and glistens – and looks at the boy. Guess, he says, you get to gaff the whore.

At home as they pack the car the boy's father hefts the big pole hook and says Like this, son. Through the gills. Then you lift it in the boat and if it's still fighting I'll bash it with the truncheon. Try.

The boy takes the hook. Looks at the horrible barb. Tries to picture the fish. Grips the pole hard. Behind him his mother opens the door to the kitchen. The boy swings the hook.

Morris, says his mother, what is he doing with that?

He's doing fine is what.

Dad, I don't think I'm strong enough.

Son, with my luck you won't need to be.

The boy looks at his mother. She shakes her head and says Supper.

The boy and his father quickly wash up and then they sit down in the kitchen. It's mostly leftovers. His mother says she'll make sandwiches with the rest of the roast and wrap up the last of the cake as well. Then she goes to her room while the boy and his father wash the dishes. After that they finish packing the station wagon and the boy watches as his father hitches the trailer and backs out to the end of the drive so there won't be so much noise in the morning. They go back in and his father says Make an early night of it. The boy walks down the hall but the washroom door is closed and he can hear his mother having a bath. He walks back to the living room but his father is not there and then the boy hears the scraping of the chair on the floor in the basement and knows his dad will be there a while. Sharpening hooks. Or doing maths. Or just sitting there.

In his own room the boy sets the alarm on the clock just in case his father sleeps in. Then he gets on the bed and kneels at its edge. Imagines the gaff in his hands and swings it. Then he lies back. Stares at the ceiling. It has a new crack.

The release of the lock on the bathroom door. His mother's footfalls. He reaches over his nightstand and opens the door a little. She still knocks. He says Come in. She smells of steam, and coconuts. A towel on her head the way women twist it. The boy sits up. His back against the headboard. She sits on the edge of the bed. Looks around his room a moment. He says All done in the washroom? She nods. He says Have to get ready for bed.

All right, says his mother. Just came in to say – hope you have fun.

We will.

You don't have to do anything you don't want.

The boy looks at his feet and says The presents said from both of you.

His mother says nothing. Then touches his knee. And she says Wear your lifejacket. Starts to stand up.

But the boy says Promise.

And she leans toward him. Her bathrobe bulging at the top. The boy can see down it to the diagonal scar but he looks away and they hug hard and the boy says It was good on my birthday, Mum.

She stands and sniffs and says I'd best make your sand-wiches.

In the bathroom the boy swipes the mirror and does behind his ears. Then his teeth and a gargle and he splashes the sink clean. Gives the taps and faucet a shine with the face towel.

On the way back to his room he sees his mother standing at the counter with bread and wax paper and the rest of the beef. She's holding a knife that has butter on the end and she's looking out the window. And humming.

In his room he lies down and puts his hands behind his head. Hears his mother finish up in the kitchen and go to her room. Listens for his father coming up the basement stairs. Then lets his eyes close.

When they open again it is dark and his arms are numb. He slips them out from beneath his head and flops them down one at a time and they go pins and needles as he rolls over and squints at the clock – a quarter to one. Hum of the fridge. The heat coming on. Moon on his pillow. He turns the clock face away. Breathes out his nose. Falls back asleep but keeps seeing the frog. As though from beneath. Up through the murk. Where it kicks and kicks in the warm and the light. He rolls over again and hears the pulse in his ear then opens his eyes and gets out of bed. Kneels at the foot. Head on his fists. And his lips move but he's not really talking. Doesn't know what to ask. Then he sits on his hands at the edge of the bed. Looks at the moon. Then closes his eyes and tries to think nothing until he hears his father trying not to make noise in the kitchen. Running water. The kettle on. *K-tunk* of the lid on the tea canister. Three heapers in the tall orange thermos. The kettle unplugged before it starts whistling. Water filling the thermos and then his father screws on the lid and gives it a shake. His footsteps in the hallway. 5:01. A knock on the door with just one knuckle and then he pushes it open and takes a step in and stops short when he sees the boy standing.

I'm ready.

Shhh.

The boy nods and follows his father to the darkness of the kitchen where they share a glass of apple juice and lean against the counter. His father hands the boy the glass and nods at what's left. The boy gulps it down. Puts the glass beside the sink and looks at the new pink J Cloth draped over the faucet. His father unscrews the thermos cap and lifts out the tea bags – four of them – by their corners like the tails of small steaming fish. Drops them in the sink – it still smells like Ajax – and screws the lid and the cup back on and reaches for the cooler on the counter. But the boy says I've got it. And follows his father like a thief through the hush of the house. By the door they step into shoes and his father nods at the boy's windbreaker hanging from the middle hook and then he opens the door. Birds. The pale moon. And there are still crickets.

The boy puts on his windbreaker and shivers on his way to the wet-gleaming car. The engine idles smoothly and the boy's father says Well done, Hector. And the boy remembers the fingernail. The little notch it made.

As his father reverses the boy looks at the blinds on his mother's bedroom window. Thinks he sees a chink. Waves a little. His father doesn't notice. Doesn't speak. Just drives. North. Highway 28. Then east on 7. The car very warm. The boy's eyes heavy. His head bobs. He resists. Then doesn't. Feels between his ribs sometime later the thumb of his father. Opens his eyes and looks where his father is pointing. Sun coming up. Sky the same colour as a splayed lake salmon. But the boy says Beautiful. Then blinks hard and gives his head a shake. Looks around. They have left the places that feel like places. Here is like pictures in Art and Geography. Granite. An esker. Jack pines. A river.

Much further?

His father says No. Turns on the radio then hits the middle button and twists the knob a bit. Mostly cloudy, a high of six, chance of showers in the late afternoon, some gusting. His father says Good. Then turns down the volume. People talk about the hostages in Iran and then the boy sees a homemade sign – LIVE BAIT 1 M – on a telephone pole. He looks at his father. Looks up ahead. Sees a small shop and says Looks closed.

Could be, says his father, we'll just have to see.

They pull in. Tall weeds and a camper beside the ram-shackle shop. His father turns off the car and gets out. A cat the colour of butterscotch candy – and with only three legs – comes round the corner of the camper. And then the camper's door swings open and smacks the camper's wall and a man with messy hair and his shirt untucked steps out and zips up his jeans. Looks at the car and at the boy's father. Nods when the boy's father says something and walks to the shop. The boy's father follows. So does the cat. A hand – a woman's hand – and arm in the camper's doorway. Groping for the door. Then pulling it shut. At the door to the shop the man takes keys out of his pocket and shoves the cat with his foot. Opens the door and turns on a light and before the boy's father closes the door behind him the cat scoots in and the boy sees on the wall at the back of the shop a display of tackle and above it the stuffed head of a buck and its fortress of antlers. Then the door opens a bit and the man leans out and tosses the cat. It lands okay then turns around and watches the door. The boy shifts. Adjusts the rearview. Looks at his eyes and then at the rods and the net in the back of the car. The truncheon. And the gaff. He readjusts the mirror then rubs his eyes and looks at his hairless forearms. His spindly hands and broomstick wrist bones. Then the door of the bait shop opens and his father – facing into the shop – nods goodbye and turns around and walks to the car with a white plastic pail and in his other hand a pair of Dr. Peppers. He sets the pop on the roof of the car. Opens the door and leans in a little. Hold this, will you?

The boy takes the pail and puts it between his legs. His father reaches for the pop and gets in and hands the boy a can.

Are we drinking it now?

Why not.

Thanks.

They peel the tabs and drop them in the ashtray. Then they drink.

Cold, says his father.

The boy nods and burps out of his nose. How many did you get? he says. And he looks at the bucket.

His father says Three.

Need that many?

How would I know?

The boy shrugs. And his stomach squelches.

His father says Hungry?

The boy says A little.

As am I. Not far now.

His father starts the car and pulls back onto the highway and the boy looks at the pail. Can hear them knocking against the sides. He puts the pail on the floor between his feet. Has half a can of Dr. Pepper left. Doesn't drink any. His father flicks the blinker and they turn down a gravel road. Then the gravel stops and there is only dirt and potholes. The birch trees gather in like a crowd round a body. In the rearview on his side the boy watches fallen leaves leap and wrestle then fall back to the road. They pass rutted laneways – a crow on a gatepost – that lead between big evergreens to cabins boarded up for winter. Then a dip and a turn and there is the lake. The colour of blackboards. Here and there on the far side a few cottages but not a boat on it.

It'll be just us, Dad.

His father says nothing but his face is all calm. He slows down and pulls onto a widening of the shoulder where there's a green public waste bin and then a boat launch between dried-out cats-o'-nine-tails. He swings left a little – there's a small yellow cottage across the road – then backs the trailer down the slope. Around the corner of the cottage run two dogs – a small black Scottie and a big white sheepdog – and they stop at the laneway and bark.

Pay them no mind, son. They carry on like that.

The boy and his father get out and as they're putting the boat in the water a big man with a thick black beard comes out of the cottage and calls to the dogs. They stop barking and lope back to the cottage but look back a few times like they're saying We're watching. The boy's father waves and the man waves back and lets his dogs in.

You know him? says the boy.

Not really. Spoken to him a couple of times I've been out here. Decent bloke.

The man stands on the stoop as the boy and his father unpack the car. The boy takes the gaff and says Where does this go?

Out, says his father, of harm's way.

Along the side?

That'll do. Frogs?

Oh, says the boy. Then he gets the pail. Here okay?

That's fine. Right, lifejacket.

The boy bows his head and over it his father pushes the fat orange collar. Wraps the ties and knots them.

You wearing one?

No.

Water's kind of choppy.

I'll be all right. Now. The most important.

The boy looks in the boat and says What.

And his father nods at the car. That tea and cooler, he says, I'm famished.

The boy says I'll get them. Sees that the man has gone back inside. Gets the cooler and thermos and says Lock it, Dad?

If you like.

The boy locks the car and gets in the boat and sets down the thermos and cooler. His father says Sit down – the boy does – and then leans and pushes.

Mind your hip, Dad.

I'm all right.

His father heaves and hops and they're floating and the bow slowly turns counter-clockwise. His father takes an oar. Pushes off. Stands up. I'll just get by you, son.

The boy leans.

Ta, says his father. And he sits by the motor. Paddles a bit and then he just looks. So does the boy. Straight ahead about two hundred yards a pair of smallish islands. Like the Group of Seven but realer and more sad.

His father primes the motor. Third pull it starts. He opens the throttle but not so much and the bow rises only a little. The boy leans on his knees and blows on his hands. Thinks of his mother and wax paper and cake. The islands get bigger. His father veers toward the one on the right and ahead the boy sees weeds in the water like exotic dancers in slow motion. His father cuts the motor. Trees lean over the islands' edges like they're exhausted by their own reflections. To the left are lily pads. They drift nearer and the boat's bow turns a little. His father hefts an oar and turns around the boat completely. The boy looks over his shoulder. His father says Best you cast away from the weeds. Into the deeper water.

The boy says Okay.

But first, says his father, give us that thermos.

Here.

Ta. Oh.

What.

Should have brought another cup.

Mum probably put one in.

His father opens the cooler and says Indeed she did. Now, what's this?

The boy looks in the cooler – cake in Tupperware and the wrapped sandwiches – and his father says She's written *S* on these ones. Salmon?

The boy taps his chest and says No, me.

Eh?

They're for me. No butter.

Ah. Right. Well. Your sandwich, sir.

Loin and mushrooms.

Cold roast beef will have to do.

And cake.

At lunch. Give us your cup.

His father pours tea – Get that in you, lad – and then they unwrap their sandwiches. The boy tests the tea against his lips. Sips and swallows. Heat in his throat and chest. Then they bite and chew.

She used, says the boy, the posh mustard, Dad.

His father nods and swallows. About halfway through their sandwiches – the beef's a little tough and tires out your jaw – he says Let's get ourselves set, son. We can eat and fish. Then he puts down his sandwich and reaches for the tackle box and says Give us your rod. The boy hands it to him and then his father says Watch. Fixes a leader and then ties on the Red Devil. This, he says, is a classic lure, son. Catch just about anything.

Muskie?

If your line held. It's just ten pound.

What's yours.

Thirty.

That muskie at Ecky's –

Bloody monster, I know. But most muskies round here are perhaps thirty pounds.

That's still big.

Not as big as you. Not nearly. Now, this reel isn't like your old one.

Open face.

Yes. More control of your cast – with practice. See my thumb?

Yes.

Holds the line. Then the motion like so – lift your thumb – it's away.

Do one.

All right.

The boy watches the lure wag in the air as the line and reel whirr. Then *plish* the lure lands and his father starts reeling. Neither too fast, he says, nor too slow. You don't want it to sink and then snag. Keep it moving and then – he flicks the rod this way and that – try that to give it a nice switching motion.

The boy nods. Watches the wake of the lure as it gets nearer the boat and skims the surface then lifts. His father reels in a little more then hands the rod to the boy and says Try.

The boy releases the catch on the reel and the lure drops.

His father says Thumb first.

And the boy reels in. Holds the line. Releases the catch on the reel. His father leans back and points and says *That* way.

The boy casts.

But the lure flies off to the right and plops in the water.

Less arm, son. More wrist.

Okay.

Reel in. You'll snag.

The boy reels in. Tries again.

Much better, son. Well bloody done.

Thanks.

The boy reels in and jigs – Like that? he says and his father nods – and he imagines the tug and the sudden bending of the rod and the high-pitched zipping of the line and he would land it he swears he would.

You're all set, says his father. And then he starts to prep his own line. The boy looks back. Sees the hook his father chooses. Like a baby gaff. Then his father picks up the pail and pops the lid and the boy looks away and casts again and starts to reel. And has to look back. His father reaches in the pail and then there is a frog in his fist. Puffy chin. Blackbead eyes. The dangling legs. His father holds the hook between his thumb and two fingers and then – Little bastard! – the frog squirts free and hops onto the seat beside the boy.

Grab it, son!

And the boy does reach but not very fast and the frog hops over the side then *ploosh* the boy watches it kick out of sight. Looks at his father who says That little bugger!

And the boy tries not to laugh.

Mind, says his father, your lure.

The boy reels in.

Jumped right out my hand it did.

I saw it, Dad.

I said mind your lure.

The boy reels in and casts again and watches his father reach into the pail and say This time.

The frog does nothing – no sound no squirms – as the hook slides then pops through its chin and its mouth. The boy looks away. Looks back. His father lets out line then lobs the frog – *plash* – over the pads and plays it across and just under the surface. The boy looks at his half-eaten sandwich. Swallows tea. Casts again. Watches the dangling frog as his father finishes reeling.

How long will it last, Dad.

What last.

The frog.

About as long as my patience. Tricky work this.

His father lobs the frog a second time and the boy casts again – his hands getting cold and his wrist kind of tired – and reels until he can see the lure. Then he just lets it lie. Wind picks up. The small boat drifts. Massive clouds pass over the sun and the light on the lake changes like a big dimmer switch. The boy looks across the water to the car and beyond it to the cottage and its smoking chimney and if they started the boat now they could be on shore in no time – he knows this – but this place feels far from everywhere like places in dreams that you know but do not know and that feeling that he and his father will always come back here and everything will be as it is just now. The slateblack water. The fishscale

sky. But his father. His father is whistling softly – very softly –
Glen Miller music and the boy watches him switch the rod to
his left hand and reach inside his jacket and take out the silver
flask with his initials on it. He unscrews the cap and takes a
nip and then pours some in his thermos cup. Swirls the spiked
tea and has a big swallow then whistles some more and the boy
remembers his mother – bagging her old dresses. Slowly he
jigs his rod and watches the lure rise into sight and sink again.
Rise into sight and sink again.

After a while he sees weeds and looks around – they've
drifted between the islands – and then at his father. He
doesn't seem to be fishing. Just sitting there. The boy lets
him be. Looks toward the open water. He'll need a real long
cast. Stands – his father doesn't notice – then whips the rod
behind him. It bends in the wrong direction and then his
father screams.

The boy turns round. Drops his rod. Stares lockjawed at
the lure – hanging like a leech from his father's left cheek.

Fucking hell, boy!

Oh God I'm so sorry!

His father – eyes closed – sits very still and breathes
through his nose. Barely opens his mouth and says Son, sit.

The boy – hands shoved in his hair – breathing fast and
shallow says I'm –

And his father says Sit.

The boy does.

Now. Come here. Slowly.

The boy scooches toward his father.

I need you to look.

Okay.

Did all three catch.

No, says the boy, just one, just one.

Is it through?

Through?

The skin.

No.

Settle. The tacklebox. See it there?

Yes.

Open it.

Okay . . .

Pliers.

These?

The blue handles. Yes. Hand me those.

His father breathes out and cuts the line and then he says Now, pass me a hook.

Which one?

Any fucking one.

Dad, it's bleeding.

Pass me a *hook*. Right – now, watch.

His father puts the end of the hook between the pliers and snaps it off and says See?

The boy nods.

I need you to do that, his father says – and he holds out the pliers – but first you'll have to push it through.

I can drive.

What?

The boat. We can go to the hospital.

We are – listen – an hour away from the hospital and I'm not driving there with a bloody fucking lure hanging from my face.

The boy wipes his nose with his wrist and says Dad I can't.

His father breathes out. Softly prods around the hook. Give us, he says, the pliers.

Are you sure?

He nods. Takes the pliers. Holds his breath and snaps off – grunting – the other two barbs. Takes out his flask. Closes his eye. Pours liquor over his cheek and the nose of the pliers and his fingertips. Then he drinks the last of it. Tosses the flask toward the front of the boat. Applies his thumb to the curve of the hook. Breathes in. Then leans to the right and tries to sick over the side but it's half in the boat and the smell of it.

The boy clamps his teeth.

His father says Son, you'll have to do it.

My hands, says the boy. And he looks at their shaking. His father holds the left one then places it against the top of his head and leans hard against it and says Just pop it through.

Okay.

The boy pinches the base of the hook and – his father growls – pushes like he's threading a lace through an eyelet. The hook pops through. His father breathes out. Grabs the pliers and leans his head toward his shoulder. Feels with his fingers and lays the pliers along his face and crimps off the barb. It shoots away like a tiny silver wasp and then his father slides out the lure. Looks at it in his hand for a moment. Then tosses it in the water. Leans on his knees and breathes like a boxer who can't answer the bell.

The boy pushes the back of his wrist against each eye and blinks and looks at his father and then – it jitters – at his father's fishing rod. *Dad*, says the boy, and he points just as the rod starts rattling along the side of the boat.

Then the boy lunges. Grabs the rod's handle and gets to his knees and the rod bends nearly double. But the boy holds on as the reel spins like a tire on ice. His father reaches round him and holds the rod as well and says I've got it, son, I've got it! The boy lets go. Leans back with his father as he reels and pulls. Pulls and reels. Duck under, says his father. But the boy only watches as the big fish – like the lake spat it out – writhes in the air then splashes and thrashes then dives again as the boy's father says Blood and fucking sand!

Then the line goes slack and curly.

And everything is very quiet.

And the boy sits between the arms of his father staring at the spot where the monster fish was. And then his father's right hand lets go of the rod and when the boy turns around his father is looking at the blood on his fingertips. And then he touches his cheek again and looks at his fingers as though they had lied. Then he wipes the blood on the leg of his pants and says to the boy Go have a seat, now.

The boy moves up the boat and sits and watches his father reel in the slack line and look at the end of it. Wonder, he says, if it swallowed the lot.

The boy looks at the water and imagines the mangle of frog-and-hook in the muskie's mouth. Then he shrugs and says We should go, Dad.

His father's eyes – wide and glassy. But he puts down the rod and turns to the motor.

And on the way into shore he reaches for the pail and tosses the last frog over. An old green pickup passes the launch and the boy's father waves it down. It turns into the laneway of the yellow cottage and stops and the man with the beard gets out. Meets them at the launch. The boy's father cuts the motor and the man says How did it go? Then he notices. The boy looks down and his father says Bit of a mishap. The man leans forward and grabs the bow's handle and pulls and the boy steps out and helps him. Then his father steps out too. A little wobbly. The man looks at his face. Fish jump up and bite you?

The boy's father laughs but not really and the boy says It was my fault.

The man says You wanna come in? We got ointment.

The boy's father says If there's a hospital nearby –

And the man says You know Glanisberg?

Heard of it, yes.

Go down number 7. Turn left on 30. Half hour tops.

That's what we'll do, then.

I'll watch your boat. You go on.

Very kind of you.

No bother.

The boy's father drives with one hand and holds Kleenex to his face with the other. The boy's mother keeps a box in the glove compartment. They use most of it and in Glanisberg see a church letting out. His father pulls over. The boy runs across the street and asks a lady in an old-fashioned hat for directions. Follows his father into Admissions then down to Emerg but they won't let him through so he sits in the waiting room beside the ambulance drivers' office. Hears the static and garble of the radio. Football on the television. He glances at the tired- and sick- and sad-looking people and shuffles through old magazines about hot rods and hunting and jet airplanes. Looks up and sees his father in the doorway. Gauze and tape on his face. The boy follows him to the car and the drive back to the boat feels like ages.

He put it back on the trailer, Dad.

Bloody good of him.

The boy's father gets out and walks toward the laneway but here come the dogs. He stops. Waves. Gives a thumbs-up. The boy looks at the cottage and sees the man in the living room window waving back.

They quickly pack up and while his father hitches the trailer the boy gets in the car. In the rearview he watches his father turn for a moment and look toward the islands. Then – as they pull away – his father says Some fish that.

And the boy says Massive.

Then they don't talk until Highway 28.

Dad.

Yes.

Will it mend?

Son.

Yes.

Shush now.

The boy looks out the window and presses his trembly lips together.

In his room he can hear their voices but not their words. Outside the light is fading and the moon is already there like a blind eyeball. He sits on his hands at the edge of the bed. Can smell the mince and 'nips. After a while his mother knocks and comes in and sits on the bed beside him.

Sure you're not hungry?

The boy looks at the floor.

We're not cross with you.

The boy looks at her. Then down again.

It was, says his mother, an accident.

What if it was his eye.

It would still be an accident.

He'd be blind.

Well. Half.

It's not funny.

Suit yourself. Supper's there if you want it.

The boy lies down. Curls toward the wall. His stomach growls and he gives it a whack. Footfalls again – his father's this time. But they go past the boy's room. Down to the basement. The boy lies there a little longer and then gets up and walks softly to the kitchen. The dishes not done. His place still set and a glass of milk. He peeks into the living room. His mother on the chesterfield. One finger tap-tap-tapping the arm as she looks at the turned-off television like an old movie – the kind that makes her sad – with singing and dancing and natty dresses to die for.

LYNNE KUTSUKAKE

AWAY

After Sayuri disappeared, her picture was everywhere. She stared at us from the windows of Murakami Bakery and Mrs. Nakamura's noodle shop, from the sliding glass door of Yoshimoto Drugs, and of course from the giant poster in front of the police station. It was impossible to go anywhere without seeing her. Iwata Supermarket and Mori Grocers pinned her picture next to their checkout counters, and smaller versions of the poster were wrapped around all the bus stop poles in town. *Do you know this girl?* the poster asked. *Have you seen Sayuri?* It was always the same photograph, the one taken at the beginning of that term. Sayuri was wearing our high-school uniform, a dark navy tunic over a white blouse. As the years passed, the whiteness of the blouse turned grey and blotchy and the tunic faded to a metallic green. But despite the graininess of the photograph and the weathering of the elements, Sayuri's eyes stayed the same: shiny as new marbles, full of hope and mischief.

Have you seen me, I heard Sayuri say every time I looked into her eyes. *Do you know me?*

———

Sayuri disappeared thirty years ago from the small town in Shimane where I grew up and where she and I went to high school together. The town is in decline now but it used to be a big fishing port, and boats went far out into the Sea of Japan almost halfway to Korea and China in search of their catch. Over time, though, many young people moved away seeking white-collar jobs in big cities, and I was no exception. I came to Tokyo and started a new life, eventually marrying the man who was my supervisor at Tanaka Electric and becoming a full-time housewife and mother. I rarely went back home, and after my parents passed away, the severing of my ties to the town was complete. There was nothing at all to draw me back to that place or to that period of my life. And then I saw her. Sayuri's picture appeared on the evening news along with a dozen other young Japanese who had been missing since the late 1970s. Apparently they had been kidnapped and taken to North Korea.

Lost and then found. I could scarcely believe my eyes.

———

We were eating dinner in front of the television when I felt my throat stiffen. "I knew her," I whispered hoarsely ten minutes into what promised to be lengthy coverage of the startling discoveries.

"Who?" my husband, Masayuki, asked.

"One of the abductees they're talking about. One of the girls who was taken to North Korea. Sayuri Yamazaki. We went to high school together."

"You're kidding." Sayuri's photograph appeared on the screen again. "You never told me anything so dramatic happened at your school."

"At the time we didn't know things like that went on. It was like she vanished into the air."

"Well, the whole thing is unbelievable." Masayuki stabbed his chopsticks in the air. "If she was kidnapped while walking on the beach, like they say, you'd think someone would have noticed something. A young girl being dragged away like that."

"We didn't know. Everyone thought she ran away."

"I wonder why they picked her?"

"I don't know." I shivered.

"Poor girl was in the wrong place at the wrong time, I guess." Masayuki answered his own question. "Good thing you weren't walking on the beach then. That could have been you."

My husband turned toward our son and suddenly made a silly swooping movement with his arms like a large crow flapping its wings. "Snatched by the North Koreans. What do you think of that, Tatsuo? That could have been your mother."

My teenage son's head was bent over his food and his long bangs covered half his face. "So when *was* all that?" he mumbled without looking up.

"Many years before you were born," I said. "All that time we never knew what had happened to her."

———

For a long time after Sayuri vanished, I would go after school to my secret spot, a hidden cove almost a kilometre up the coast from the main harbour. Sometimes I would stay for over an hour just staring out at the sea. At the thick waves slicing up and down, at the thin grey line where water met sky at a distant horizon. What drew me to do this was an utter mystery. Back then, none of us in our wildest dreams could have imagined that Sayuri had been taken across the Sea of Japan, spirited away like in a spy novel. To think about it now gave me a queasy feeling: what if I had been looking in the precise direction where she stood on a distant shore? What if she too had been staring back across the same expanse of sea? Would she, I wanted to know, have been looking for me?

At the time, though, I was only fifteen, and if you had asked me then why I came to this spot, why I stood for hours looking at the sea, I could not have told you. And I would not have been lying or pretending. All I knew was that something about the dark swells of water made my insides tighten in a way that was both strange and pleasurable. Sometimes I thought I saw Sayuri's face rise in the curling water. Floating face up, her eyes closed, the trace of a smile on her lips. Could she have fallen in, I would wonder, or might she have jumped? I thought of how fish and other creatures would swim so close they could press their smooth oily bodies against her.

We saw a lot of each other that year, the year she disappeared. Not only were we in the same class, we both played on the school's junior volleyball team. Our new gym teacher, Suzuki sensei, who doubled as our volleyball coach, was young and pretty and full of great hopes for us. We really weren't that good, but Suzuki sensei wanted us to aim for the regional volleyball championships, and her enthusiasm was so infectious and our desire to please her so strong that we thought nothing of practising every day after school and even on weekends. We were always in motion, our running shoes squeaking high-pitched on the dark wood floors, always rushing past each other in a blur. Then Sayuri vanished and a new stillness took over me. Even as I bounced on the court amid all the shouts and noise, I felt on the verge of a great mute void. Just ahead a cliff to plunge over, a waterfall frozen mid-fall.

———

When Sayuri disappeared, there were lots of stories. One rumour circulating through our school was that she had run away with an older man she'd met in a bar. He'd forced her to go with him to Tokyo where he made her work as a sex slave in his Shinjuku nightclubs.

Another rumour was that Sayuri had a secret boyfriend and they'd run off together. We pictured her boyfriend as handsome and tough, the type who wouldn't take no for an answer. He would ride a motorcycle bare-headed, the wind driving more wildness down into his skull, the wind pummelling Sayuri's shoulders and whipping her hair and skirt into a passionate frenzy. We imagined her living a new grown-up life somewhere else, somewhere far away. It sounded good, and Hiroko and Emi said they wished they could live like that. If they had the chance, they said, they'd like to get out of this dull town. They'd run away, too.

We came up with these stories, I suppose, because we couldn't – refused to – imagine her dead.

The police asked to interview each of us on the volleyball team. First they talked to us as a group and explained the importance of even the most insignificant detail about Sayuri. Anything at all might serve as a clue. Then they called us one by one for questioning. I was the last. I was taken down a long corridor and ushered into a small, beige, windowless room. But before I reached the chair I was to sit in, my knees suddenly buckled, my head spun blackness, and I sank to the floor. When I opened my eyes there were two sturdy police officers, one male and one female, hovering over me.

"She's all right." The man's voice sounded relieved. "She's all right," he repeated. "Get her some water."

They began their questioning, but I had nothing to tell them. The last time I had seen Sayuri was at the volleyball game. No, she hadn't seemed any different. No, I didn't know if she had a boyfriend. No, I'd never seen her with a boy.

"Come on, now." The policeman leaned forward across the table and smiled slyly. His front teeth were yellow and one was badly chipped. "I bet you and Sayuri talked about boys. All girls do. Which ones you like, which ones you don't."

I shook my head and stared at the tabletop. His breath smelled of stale cigarettes and peppermint.

How could a girl just disappear without a trace? A girl with homework to do, volleyball practice, piano lessons. The stories my classmates came up with to explain Sayuri's vanishing got wilder and more absurd. Someone started a rumour that she had been pregnant with the music teacher Mr. Yamada's baby.

If you'd seen Mr. Yamada you would realize how ridiculous this idea was. He looked like a frog, short and bald, with long dangly arms and a squashed-in kind of face.

―――――

The families of the abductees were on television almost every day. Sayuri's parents appeared with the mothers and fathers of the other missing young people. They said they had never given up hope that Sayuri would be found, they had always known she hadn't run away on her own. They joined the other parents' pleas to the North Korean government: Give our daughter back. Give Sayuri her freedom, and let her come home.

I could barely recognize Sayuri's father. His once thick hair had receded to reveal a high, bony forehead, and a nimbus of grey tufts rose behind his ears like fine bonito shavings. Sayuri's mother, on the other hand, wore her hair in exactly the same style as I remembered from back then. It was as black as ever but much thinner, so thin that as she sat with her head bent forward, I could see patches of pale scalp between the stiff curls.

On an interview program, Sayuri's mother burst into tears after she was asked what she would do if it turned out that her daughter was no longer alive. The camera pushed closer, hovering over the top of her head, then swinging down to her lap to show the shredded ball of tissue clutched in her hands. *Understandable, Mrs. Yamazaki, such terrible stress, dredging up powerful emotions,* the talk show host's lilting voice rose over the hiccupping of sobs.

Sayuri's mother looked so familiar and yet so different. I couldn't put my finger on it at first and then I realized that it wasn't simply that she had aged – somehow she had shrunk, too. She reminded me of a dry leaf that has begun to curl up at the edges, pulling tighter and tighter into itself.

She wasn't like this when I was young. Unlike my mother and the mothers of all my friends who wore baggy pants and cheap polyester tops, Sayuri's mother dressed in tailored skirts and crisply ironed blouses. Her hair was always set just so. Sayuri and her family had moved to our town less than a year before she disappeared. Shortly after their arrival, my mother pronounced Mrs. Yamazaki a snob. Sayuri's father, who had been transferred here to manage the local bank, wore a navy suit and white shirt, his hands were smooth and clean. My father was a fisherman. I worried that the odour of dead fish filled the very air I breathed at home, and that Sayuri's mother could smell it on me. Sometimes I could swear that she wrinkled her nose when I came too close.

Sayuri was the opposite of her small-boned, compact mother. She was tall for a Japanese girl, and she had a loose-limbed gawkiness that I now recognize was the result of a sudden growth spurt. It was as if her body hadn't quite caught up with her. People who saw her from a distance always assumed she was much older than she was because of her height, and it was only when you got up close that you could see she was just a teenage girl with thick unplucked eyebrows and a little gap between her front teeth. In class I sat one row over and two seats behind Sayuri, a good vantage point for observing her. She had a big dimple on her left cheek and I used to watch the flesh of her smooth skin fold and dip every time she smiled or sucked on the end of her pencil. Sometimes she giggled with Hiroko or Keiko, who sat on either side of her. Sometimes she leaned forward and whispered into Yoshiko's ear. Occasionally she turned around to look at me. Usually it's hard to be the new student at school, but Sayuri never had any problem. Everyone wanted to be her friend.

When Sayuri tried out for the volleyball team, there was no question she would be accepted. At first she looked a bit clumsy to me, but she quickly gained confidence and her long arms and legs gave her a clear advantage on the court. Suzuki sensei's delight in her newest recruit was unmistakable. This year, for sure, we can aim for the regionals, Suzuki sensei kept repeating.

———

It was Tatsuo who made me look for my high-school yearbook. At first I tried to ignore him, but he was so persistent I finally gave in and dug out the boxes I kept in storage. The yearbook was at the bottom of the last box, wrapped in tissue paper to protect its white leather cover. I could feel my heart tapping lightly under my ribcage as I turned the pages until I came to the picture of our volleyball team.

"Well," Tatsuo paused.

"Can you find me?"

After a moment he wrinkled his brow and shook his head.

"No? I'm this one," I said, pointing to my broad, serious-looking face. We were wearing gym shorts and school T-shirts. Our exposed white thighs gleamed like smooth rice cakes.

"Which one is the spy?" Tatsuo asked.

"What do you mean spy? Sayuri?"

"Yeah."

"She's not a spy," I said sharply. "She was kidnapped."

Tatsuo shrugged. "Whatever you say. But don't you think the whole thing sounds like it's made up? Like a movie."

I didn't say anything even though I agreed. It *was* like a movie, a bad, stupid movie.

"This is Sayuri," I said tapping my index finger on the page. "She's here." Sayuri was in the middle of the back row, the tallest girl on the team. The light of the camera flash had struck her forehead at a funny angle, casting a luminous glow over her face and throwing the girls next to her into shadow. Suzuki sensei stood behind our team, her head peering over Sayuri's shoulder, close enough to rest her chin on Sayuri's collar. I'd forgotten how young our teacher had been, how young all of us were then.

Tatsuo and I looked at the photograph in silence.

"If I suddenly disappeared, what would you do?" he said.

"What are you talking about? I'd look for you. I'd search high and low till I found you."

"No, I mean, if I disappeared for good. Like her."

"Don't be ridiculous."

Tatsuo flipped back and forth through the yearbook, stopping every so often to examine a photo or caption. Finally he handed it back to me. "How come you never looked for her?"

"I did. We all did." A burning sensation rose in my chest, like a lump of something hot was struggling to get out. "We looked all over but we couldn't find her."

———

The day before Sayuri disappeared, we played against Nishiwaki High. It was just an ordinary intercollegiate game, but lately whenever we played any other team, Suzuki sensei would get quite worked up. She made me nervous with all her exhortations. "Remember, girls, we're going for the regionals!" Her cheeks and forehead would glow and her short, wiry hair would stick up like it was charged with electricity. That day was no exception.

Our opponents arrived by bus before noon. In the previous season, Nishiwaki High had been ranked in the bottom quarter of the league, so we weren't expecting too much; and in fact they looked like typical farm girls, short and stocky with broad shoulders, sunburned necks, and thick bowed legs. Suzuki sensei greeted them politely, but as soon as they were out of sight she turned around, gave us a big grin, and made a complicated hand signal as if to say we had this game in the bag. I remembered how Sayuri smiled back at her.

The Nishiwaki girls, however, were by no means as clumsy as they looked. They moved with remarkable speed and coordination like one large, nimble spider. It was as if they had spread an invisible net on their side of the court that prevented every ball that came their way from touching the ground. We began making mistakes, and I could feel my arms ache with each volley. Then Sayuri fell. She stumbled as she ran to make a save, and for a few seconds she lay face down on the floor. Suzuki sensei rushed to her side, but Sayuri got up by herself and waved her away. "Enough," I heard Sayuri mutter under her breath. Suzuki sensei's face turned as dark as red bean paste, but she didn't say anything.

Needless to say, we didn't win, and in the locker room afterwards, hardly anyone said a word. Suzuki sensei came in briefly and said the usual. How we'd done our best, how it was just a game.

We showered quickly and changed in silence. "Good try!" Tomoko shouted with fake cheeriness when she left. The other girls didn't say anything, though, not even goodbye. I had almost finished changing when I realized that I hadn't seen Sayuri. I paused and heard the sound of falling water; someone was still in the shower. To save money, our school had very small hot water tanks, so by now I was sure there was no warm water left at all.

I went back into the shower area and found Sayuri in the last stall, crouched on her haunches in the corner. Her head was between her knees, her thin shoulders shaking. Whether she was shivering or crying, I wasn't sure. I reached over and turned off the water. It was cold as ice.

"Hey," I said. "What's wrong?"

Sayuri didn't look up. She made a faint squeaking sound like a mouse.

"You're not thinking about the game, are you?"

She continued looking down.

"It was just a stupid game. It doesn't even count for that much." I tried again. "It's not Suzuki sensei, is it?"

She shook her head violently.

"Honest?" I looked at Sayuri's spine, its small pointy knobs, a delicate track from her neck down to her bum.

"You'd better get up," I finally said. I moved directly in front of her and reached down to grab her left arm. It felt soft and slippery. That was when I noticed the blood. There was a thin pink trickle that slithered down her thigh, across her feet and into the drain. At first I thought it was her period, then I realized that the blood was coming from her hand – she had torn the nail right off her middle finger. The spongy tissue at the tip looked like a squashed tomato.

"You should go to a doctor," I said. "Does it hurt much? Did you show Suzuki sensei?"

"It's my punishment," she mumbled, "my shame."

"Get up," I said. "You're going to make yourself sick."

I put my hands in her armpits and pulled. Sayuri was as limp as a wet noodle and it took quite a bit of work to get her to her feet. As soon as I did, she refused to stand up straight and toppled toward me.

"Whoa, stand up, would you."

Sayuri was a full head and a half taller, so when she flopped against me it was all I could do to keep from falling backwards. We stood in this awkward embrace for a couple of minutes, and I held my hand on her back to steady her. I could feel her soft, wet, barely-risen breasts through my blouse. Her shoulder was against my face and I could see little goosebumps on her pale flesh.

"I'll help you," I murmured, "I'll bandage your finger." To my own surprise, I then pressed my lips against her shoulder and flicked the tip of my tongue over her skin. She tasted of soap.

Sayuri pulled back. She looked me straight in the eye, a dark searching stare that might have been asking if I was making fun of her. Then she scrunched her eyes shut, bent forward, and pushed her lips against mine. I think I was supposed to shut my eyes, too, but I didn't have time to react. Her lips were very cold and a bit rubbery.

"Let's get out of here," Sayuri said abruptly. "I'm freezing."

Before she turned her face away, I thought I saw a faint smile on her lips. It pleased me, but it also confused me.

I wanted to explain to Sayuri that what I'd done to her was not a kiss. Not a real kiss, not like the way people were supposed to kiss. What had happened between us was too fast, too haphazard to count. But I didn't say a word. By the time we'd finished dressing, I even began to think that maybe I'd imagined the whole incident.

Sayuri put on her clothes and I wrapped a clean handkerchief around her finger and tied the corners tightly so it wouldn't fall off. I changed my blouse because it had become so wet. As I didn't have a spare set of clothing, I ended up putting my gym top back on. My skirt was damp, too, but I figured it would dry in the air on the way home.

By the time we left the school building, everyone else – all our classmates, the other teachers, even Suzuki sensei – had gone. We walked down the deserted hallway to the back exit and together pushed the heavy door open. When it banged shut behind us, it made a hollow metal clang.

Although it was almost dinnertime, the sun was still shining and felt warm on the back of my head. We walked as far as the grocery store at the second intersection and then paused. Neither of us had said a word, and I was afraid to look at her.

My heart was pounding. Our homes were in opposite directions and we had reached the place where we had to part. I didn't want to tilt my head back to look up at her – somehow that felt rude – so I ended up staring at her neck. The spot where I had put my lips was buried somewhere under the strap of her backpack.

"We did our best," I said.

"We did our best," Sayuri echoed.

"We'll play better next time."

"Yes," Sayuri said, so softly I could hardly hear her. "Next time."

I turned around once when I was part-way home, half hoping I might find Sayuri following me. But the road was empty, a long dusty stretch of asphalt, lined on either side by trees. In the distance, a shimmering wave of heat rose like the fluttering wings of dragonflies. I pictured Sayuri at the other end of the road, hidden in a low dip just out of sight. Somewhere beyond.

That was the last time I saw her.

———

"I don't get it. Why didn't they just hire their own language teachers? It doesn't make any sense." Masayuki shook his head repeatedly in front of the television. "I can understand spying, but this is too bizarre for words."

According to the news, the abductees had been forced to work as Japanese language teachers for the North Korean Intelligence Service. I tried to imagine Sayuri as she stood in front of a class full of dark-suited men and pointed at words on a blackboard with a long wooden stick. It was hard to believe that anyone would want a fifteen-year-old to teach them.

A photograph of Sayuri, older, sadder, very tired looking, began appearing in the weekly tabloids. It didn't bear much resemblance to her, no matter how much Sayuri might have aged. There was nothing of the girl I remembered from high school, nothing of the Sayuri I'd known, or thought I'd known.

The woman was standing next to a very tall, thin man, supposedly her husband, and flanking them on either side were two small girls who looked like they were carved of wood. The family stood in front of a dingy pink studio curtain. Above their heads hung a large framed portrait of Kim Jong-il.

"Now they're saying that everyone could be dead, you know," Masayuki said. "If they find any graves, the government is going to ask for DNA testing or some such thing, but I can't imagine that will ever happen. Nobody knows what goes on over there."

I tried to picture Sayuri's grave, but it was pointless. I knew it would be empty, a hollow wooden box filled with stale cold air.

I got up and went into the kitchen. Behind me I could hear Masayuki rapidly switching from one channel to another, the background voices breaking up into flecks of sound.

I pushed open the big window over the sink and leaned out as far as I could. Everywhere I looked there were apartment buildings, row upon row like a vast army of giant grey dominos marching toward me. The breeze was hot and dusty. Not a hint of rain, and the sea was far away.

JESUS HARDWELL

EASY LIVING

So long as you didn't try to burn it down, or annoy your fellows with a knife or something, they left you alone at the Beacon. It was cheap, the bar made deliveries, and the shower worked. The Cuban guy at the desk would close his mind like a bag over his face – you could watch it happen – and turn to stone. He was called Jonah because he had worked on a ship, before he jumped. He was ill in some way and given to rages, but was mostly all right, and he'd let you in for free on occasion if you'd share, so generally I did when I'd had enough. It was a home of sorts at the Beacon, and a fine place to get lost.

We had been there three or four days, me and the wife of an acquaintance, shoving everything we had inside us, including, when we could manage it, each other. Those were good days, full of high vacant fervour and disregard. There was a sweet raw taste to time, and the room itself, according to our mood, became a vast cathedral, or a small velvet box. I remember the sheets had stars, hundreds of blue stars shattered all over. And I remember her breasts, how they buoyed, and the wet spikes of her nipples floured with coke. I jammed them up my nose and we floated off immense, above ourselves, empty and marvellous.

That couldn't last, of course. We wore out. The drugs evaporated. Our throats dried. Our skin grew tight and tender, and what air remained was from the desert, and had quills. We were dogs really, dragging around what was left of us like we'd been run over and didn't have the sense to stop yet. The room was just a room, and she had a husband to get back to.

Then one of us by miracle found some hash we'd trampled. It was heavy hash, import deluxe from Morocco. We did not have a pipe, so we knived it. The burn through our heads was hot and cool together, with a delicate edge of ambush. Straight away we brightened, and pretty soon we were feeling almost repaired. She began to look all right again, clean and filthy at once, which I like.

So I grew my arm across the room to where she was, stark there on the bed with a leg up, watching my hand enlarge and sniff about to find her. I took her hair, the spattery twists of her hair flashing in rivulets, and I twined it in my fist and wound, reeling her in until our foreheads banged. Then I said into her eyes that the room was on fire and we had twenty minutes to live. It wasn't much to give, but it struck her well somewhere and she clasped me down.

As we rocked I saw her face loosen and change. I watched it slide, dissolve, and then re-form into three. It was her in the middle, and the two others beside her rippling across, back and forth. They were emerging and blending so fast I couldn't make out if I knew them. It didn't matter. Their mouths were wide and lovely, they looked ready to sing, and everyone was smiling. We rowed and lolled. I swam on their tongues. And when I beckoned them they came and came and met me where I was, holding them there and waiting. When it was time the stars squeezed and blew apart. The force of it spasmed from my spine and bent me. It moaned me open and I gasped my love into their mouths, my full helpless love for all of us happy there together. Then the bed swallowed and we drowned.

We slept some, we must have. When I woke it was me alone that surfaced. She was one again, a fragile wreck smashed out still and far beyond. I checked to see if she was breathing. She was, so it seemed all right to leave her. I got my clothes and shook them on. In her purse I found a compact and broke the mirror off. I laid it between her legs and combed my hair. When I left she was just starting to stir. In my mind I blew her a kiss, and added one for Jonah. Then I was gone and out into the fresh shock of the air, and walking along on the lighted carcass of the city at night.

I was headed for a bar I knew in a hotel by the harbour. There was fog in the streets, and spangles of snow had shaken loose and were swirling around. I hurried because I knew we could sit, Chummy and I, sit there and drink, and be warm and easy, and listen to the horns muscle in.

He was there, of course, at a table where the bar ended. He was always there when I knew him, except when he was working, which he wasn't much then. He wasn't too drunk and waved me over. Before I asked he said, "Pretty fine. Pretty fine and the same, my man. Yourself?" I said I was fine too, the finest, and I sat, and we ordered Coronas and lime.

The arm he'd waved with stayed suspended. It was a while before it fell and I looked for the tattoo on the back of his

wrist that made him angry then and that he might get rid of.
It was true the trumpet was more a trombone and I thought
the cigar in the end too much myself, but the mantis was well
done. It looked stubborn and wise, and when he flexed it had
a jaunt to it. He had never shot through the mantis and I was
glad it wasn't gone.

The beer came and went and came again. Then Chummy
asked what was I going to do, if I was going to do anything,
about the wife. I said that was probably over.

"That's the way," he said. He'd had wives himself, and been
married twice. "It's always done and finished, and then it isn't."

"Sure. But it's finished sometimes. You can see the skid
marks." I liked talking left-handed like that, and trying to
guess where he was going.

"Yeah, it stops. But you can't know when it does. So what you
feel when you think it does is just yourself stringing yourself
along and hoping. That's the way it is, my man, all the freaking
way until you're dead. That's just the true smiling bitch of it."

This was a little beyond where I wanted to be at that time,
so I had to agree, and we let it drop. Before it dropped, though,
he said, "Sometimes I think you trust too much."

"So you do? And what does that mean?"

"I really do, and that's what it means."

"Well all right," I said. "I'll put a watch on that, and you
can show me the coin for the next round."

"Fair enough. I'm with you there, my man." Then he added,
"You realize I'm just slinging it, right?"

"Sure. Everything's good." And it was, even though I knew
he meant it then. I held up two fingers, a touch apart. "We're
like this."

"I see," he said. "Let it be tight like that then."

Chummy left for a bit to make a call for an arrangement. My mind wandered and I let it stretch. I thought of the wife – her name was Rebecca; Savannah, professionally – and how much she might tell her husband. He was a bit of a dealer and a bit of a thief – nothing serious, just what was easy – and a decent guy despite. Then I wondered why it was, although you couldn't be sure what even the decent were capable of, why it was really that I didn't care at all what she told. I didn't get far with that, so I forgot it and looked around the bar.

It wasn't crowded. The locals were drunks mostly – hawk-faced and devastated, hoarding their tables as though they were precious aeries of refuge – and the others were drop-ins, tourists from the cruise ships. I thought I heard some German but it was probably just Texans. They were blond and loud and what I could see of their faces bored me, so I waited for Chummy and twirled a bottle on the table. When it stopped it pointed at his chair, at the coat he'd draped over it. It was a huge coat, raccoon, and still in fair condition. For a time he kept a gun in the pocket over his heart. It wasn't for use, not directly. But it could solve a situation sometimes. Relax it, I mean, before it happened. But then, the guy who told me that hanged himself in a cell, so there you go. The gun had been pawned after a while, but Chummy kept the coat all the time I knew him. One summer, the whole summer, he wore it through the heat. He said he enjoyed it – the animal feel and breathing of the heat – of course, he was also timing every-one's conversations with a stopwatch then. I never saw him worse, and he couldn't play, but when he could he was some-thing rare.

When he was more or less fit for a time and playing regularly in a not-at-all bad quartet, I went to hear him in a club downtown. It was well after the hour and the rest of them were on the stand already. They tuned and waited, traded a few runs and waited some more, pretending without trying to be convincing that it was part of the show. But Chummy wouldn't come. He just stood at the back, in the raccoon coat against the wall as though nailed there, cradling his trumpet like a damaged child. He stared straight ahead, but what he saw wasn't anything there in the solid sense. In fact you'd have sworn he was completely blind. There was a clear chance of an incident, I suppose, but it didn't happen, and after a while a Korean girl I wasn't familiar with came and got him. She led him shuffling, testing each step like he was feeling for where the cliff was, up through the tables, through the smoke and the elbows and the noise. It was a long way, and he was slow, but he made it to the chair they had for him and gentled himself in. I didn't think he'd be able to haul back from wherever he was, but when they started he was right there, resurrected and sure.

The first notes were serene, with a lot of space between them. Then he played some half ones fast and stricken. He went on alternating like that, stacking them apart as though he were building two separate things. Toward the end he mixed them and soldered, and they held and made a kind of arch. For a moment we all passed naked through it into some place we did not belong, but was ours anyway until it ended. That's what I liked about music, and about Chummy too. Everything was as possible as nothing, and you weren't obliged to choose or be responsible.

So when Chummy came back at last and gave me the good word on the arrangement, we tossed around whether the foghorns should be thought horns, or a whole section of basses that the wind bowed. We decided on both and drank some more and considered the waitress. She was young and we admired her nylons, the soft brush when she walked, and her wrists' efficiency. She had china bones. Then we switched to scotch and talked of Clifford Brown and how rotten it was what happened. Chummy had a thing about Clifford. He used to say quite often that it was a source of wonderment that he, being what he was, had already lived nearly twice as long as someone like that, someone with so much jump and knowing in his horn, and so clean in his habits. That's the way, we said. Everything's yours, right in your hands the whole deal, then it's yanked and nothing.

And we talked of what impossible hurricane of luck might blow us clear to Guatemala or Belize, somewhere warm at least, and how we would live there rich for a long time like real human beings if we could, and enjoy the rain even, and be gracious toward everyone. Then we drank some more, and the horns welled and we were quiet.

It was probably about then I noticed the old people. They were some kind of couple and they were dancing, I guess. He was still tall and she never was, so he had to stoop to keep her his and gathered. They were both thin as pipes. The music was junk but they liked it enough. They picked up the pace, they swanked and juddered, and she held on her best.

Chummy by this time was blinking. He made a fist on the table, placed his head on it, and nodded out. I let him go and watched the old people again.

Jesus, they were ancient, and the strobes were merciless, badging them unearthly with reds and purples, and a very mean slash of yellow. But they were spry too, like they'd just been dug up and were hungry and they were meat to each other. They had the floor to themselves but were only using a foot of it. Then they kissed and kept at it. They were glued and feeding, working their jaws like pumps.

It was gruesome, I suppose, and it might have been disgusting. What made it amazing was, when they broke away for breath, there was a long loop of spit that drew out between them. It hung swaying from their chins and stayed with them as they danced, as they shut their eyes and danced, oblivious and serene inside their own scrap of forever. That's what knocked me out.

Chummy by that time had roused, and was humming or mumbling into his hand. "Chummy," I said, "you think you'll love me when we're old?"

He reared then. There was no blinking, and he seemed actually to focus, heaving his whole proud landscape of a face across the table into mine. "I don't even love you now, man."

PAUL HEADRICK

HIGHLIFE

Christopher, my husband, is angry – my husband is so angry – he is so profusely angry that he is dying that it is in everything, his anger is in everything. I can smell its sour smell and feel it burning, even in this shocking equatorial heat, and I can hear it buzzing in the air even as he sleeps beside me and the mosquito netting hardly moves in the lake breeze, which does not carry his hot, reeking anger away.

For three weeks after Christopher was diagnosed, his calm and confidence seemed as deep as ever, and then he sold his collection. I returned from a day at the institute just in time to see the last box loaded into the U-haul. It all made sense as Christopher, steady while I wept, explained what he had done. When he died I would not know how to deal with the records, or what was a fair price. He wanted them to go to someone who appreciated them. He had simply alerted his Internet discussion group to their availability, had announced his imminent death and his need to find a buyer promptly, and there had been no negotiation, only a thorough exchange among his followers and fellow doo-wop aficionados across the continent, a consensus on a fair price, and then a sale. He took my hand and we went down to the basement together, where we stood among the empty metal shelves and turned about in the frightening new spaciousness, and I think now that right then he began to shift and we began to separate. My throat tightened and something numbed and corrupted the contact of my feet with the floor, of my hand with his, and I knew, without realizing I did, that he was banishing me.

It's true that I would not have appreciated the records the way another collector would, true that I would have appreciated them differently, and the sale brought money enough to pay for this trip and more. We certainly had enough money to pay our way through airport immigration, but Christopher refused and continued to question and demand as the immigration agent continued to insist. Our papers were not in order, we needed different visas, something was wrong with our visas, we would simply have to turn around and reboard for the return flight to Heathrow. Behind us the whispering, coughing, grumbling grew louder, and yet I knew that I could not simply pay the bribe, that Christopher was already receding and I could not risk a setback. I would have to live with his new stubbornness, his useless anger, and try to find a way to slide by and reach him once more. "These visas are missing the second authority. They are not valid without the second authority," the agent said again. Christopher smiled.

We were at the passport office the first time I saw this smile, suggesting something like appreciation for a particularly cruel joke, one with a wit that Christopher could not deny despite being its victim. He had looked at the passport clerk and then leaned forward and reached forward with his short, strong arms to grasp the edge of the counter. He took his weight through his shoulders as his knees bent, and then he looked up, just over the clerk's head, to look at nothing and be distracted by nothing as he smiled appreciation for the witty twisting of his insides. There was no counter to lean on at the airport, and Christopher bent over, put his hands on his big thighs, and looked down. His chest heaved. He rose, closed his eyes for a moment, and dismissed his smile. He spoke again, in his "Mutual voice," which we named years ago after the lucrative national spots he recorded for an insurance firm, when he, in his words, "took all the black out," cooled his vowels and clipped his consonants to produce a flattened, actuarial authority. He said, "No, I am sure you will see that it is all in order; all is in order here. Look again." The immigration agent did not look again; he glanced at Christopher and then at the impatient lineup, shrugged, stamped our passports, and thus we continued. No look for me, no signal that relief or anything else from the experience was to be shared.

From the airport we took the *tro-tro* into the city. Twice as the little bus roared along the highway the power went out behind us, as though it had been on only for our passing, and I turned and saw the darkness where we had been. When we arrived I stood in the blue-tiled lobby, drained utterly, despairing and drained, while Christopher checked us in and asked the clerk about clubs in the city and the best highlife bands. Soon an eager circle of men materialized to share their enthusiasms for bars and bands, for brothers who sang, uncles who played guitar, and sisters who owned clubs, and they were inviting Christopher and me to dinners and parties, while he wrote down names, locations, and confusing directions. Only after one of these men interrupted to say, "Your lady looks so tired," which drew much sympathy and offers to carry bags, did Christopher put away his pen and with me follow a solicitous clerk to our room.

We have come for highlife. Christopher wants to hear it, not on record, not in a little Detroit club with an audience of the curious and the dutiful, but in its home, though he is emphatically not so naive as to believe he will be getting at something uninfluenced, some sound of an idealized, untouched continent, as he knows that the local musicians have been listening to the West for decades, playing guitars and horns, and that nothing pure exists now and never did. He hasn't had to tell me these things and we haven't talked about them; we've stopped talking in the old way. But I think he imagines that he will find something like the energy and meaning of doo-wop, of the original, not the anachronistic recreations. I know his position well; he's clear that it hasn't changed since he first wrote for *Zoom*. Christopher believes that the innocence, optimism, and beauty of doo-wop weren't a pose, but they weren't only what they appeared to be; they expressed defiance, insisted that these qualities could withstand the oppression, the humiliations, the decades of crimes against dignity, assaults on identity. In articles, at conferences, he has explained that doo-wop is as political, affirmative, and subversive as soul, hard bop, and gangsta rap. It is as connected as they to a tradition and history broken by slavery, and he hopes he will find something like it in the enduring exuberance of highlife and be uplifted before he dies.

In the morning, with no music to seek out yet and no energy to risk a walk in the city's sauna heat and confusion, we – Christopher – accepted a pitch from a share-taxi driver in front of the hotel to take us to the nearest fort outside the city. An hour's hot drive later, we moved from share-taxi directly to guide, but Christopher soon abandoned the tour. I was surprised he lasted as long as he did in the wet heat, listening to the guide's rote listing of the statistics – numbers of slaves caught per year, price paid per slave, numbers lost while being held waiting for ships to arrive, numbers loaded on board, numbers dying en route, hundreds of thousands upon thousands after tragic, unthinkable thousands. He headed off down the wide trail to the white beach. I followed. He went straight for the water, and he walked with such determination that I thought he might not stop till the waves came over his feet, or might not stop at all, and I asked myself could I watch him drown, but he halted at the water's edge, stood on the hard white sand, looked south over the water, stared south at the shimmering water and blinding sky while I stood beside him, wondering what he was thinking about: enslaved ancestors desperate on the middle passage; innocence, optimism, and beauty; onrushing death? He bent down finally, cupped up a palmful of Atlantic, splashed it on his face, looked blankly at me, and then walked back, me beside him this time but just as distant.

We never before let things separate us. I still remember our first months, when every day's set of odd glances and misunderstandings, every foot in a mouth here or unsuccessfully hidden bit of anger there, was every night's conversation before sleep. Once we entered a restaurant arm-in-arm, and the grinning hostess looked at me and said, "Table for one?" and that night we laughed hysterically together. Christopher always insisted that when people don't understand it isn't because they can't. It isn't because they're not white or not black or not men or not women. It's because they don't want to understand and change. When one of us didn't understand, then it was the other's task to explain, and to say that a black man and a white woman could not understand each other was to admit and accept stupidity. But now he is truly different, for he will die soon and I can't understand, Christopher believes that I can't understand, which he says every time his face tenses so as not to signal that his body is no longer his own.

In the early evening, after we both rested, Christopher arranged for a taxi driver to take us around the city. We visited a string of nightclubs along the central ring road, and when the music there proved unsatisfactory we moved farther out, to a makeshift metal shack with three tables, a guitarist, and a drummer; on to a passable small imitation of a seventies disco, complete with glitter ball and canned music; then a family home with a man rushing to get his guitar; then what seemed to be a wedding celebration with tables set up on the street and a full band that we heard for blocks as we approached, and where, as at every other place, we were warmly welcomed. I could not like the music, but only guess that I would have done so if I still had a right or a capacity to know whether I liked something. Christopher was not satisfied and we kept going, and it seemed to me that he had no true optimism, but was continuing just to make a point, a point to me; again he looked at me, waited, and then turned to the driver and asked him to continue, which we did till the city started to shut down and finally Christopher said no more, and we returned to the hotel. In their last conversation our driver told him that really one could not hear highlife in the city at all; it was necessary to get away, and he named the region and the town where the best, most authentic highlife bands were concentrated. The same collection of men who had given their advice the night before gathered again to assure Christopher that yes, everyone knew this town was the place to go for highlife, and it was a day's bus ride away.

In the night I was awakened by Christopher, who was beside me on his knees in the pose of the child, singing – trying quietly to sing but whispering, choking out the words, gasping, soaked in sweat despite the air conditioning, dripping sweat, his yellow night shirt soaked through and sticking to his broad back, and one of his outstretched hands shaking while he gasped the words, one at a time: "There's. A. Moon. Out. Tonight." He caught his breath and was silent, alerted to me, but I knew not to move, or speak, and to deepen my breathing in a successful enough imitation of sleep, successful enough, if not to fool him, then to allow him to pretend not to know and me to agree to pretend that I had not witnessed his agony and his urgent nostalgia.

His nostalgia. Christopher was fourteen when his nineteen-year-old cousin, Jerry, with his girlfriend, Andrea, drove all the way down from Halifax to visit him and his parents in Windsor for a week. In his family photo album there's a picture of Christopher, short but already taking on his adult stockiness; Jerry, tall and wiry, looking very hip in his stovepipes and pleased with himself; and Andrea, a more voluptuous Diana

Ross, on Jerry's arm. In the story Christopher tells, his voice had changed early that summer, became its impossible, deeply textured bass almost overnight, and when Jerry heard him he exclaimed, "We've got our bassman!" He and Andrea said they had been singing doo-wop the entire trip, with Andrea taking the falsettos in her soprano and Jerry the tenor leads, but were frustrated that they didn't have the bass. So Christopher was conscripted out of his book-reading loneliness and into the trio, and the family performance of The Capris's *There's a Moon Out Tonight* was, to hear Christopher tell it, the pinnacle of joy in an otherwise unrelievedly, archetypally wretched adolescence. When they were done Andrea leaned over, placed one hand lightly on Christopher's chest, cupped her other hand around his ear, and whispered to him, "Girls always go for the bassman." Jerry heightened the pleasure by hamming up some jealousy, exclaiming, "You stealing my girl? You making time with my girl?" Her lips brushing his ear, her fingertips on his chest – it was the erotic highlight of Christopher's life, he told me in our only conversation about respective romantic histories, easily overshadowing later conquests, when his confidence had caught up to his liquidy bass and drew lonely, dreaming girls to wait in the dark for the late-night FM deejay to finish his shift.

Christopher tells that story, the music part, not the sexy denouement, when he's asked to explain what began his obsession with doo-wop, but for him it's the unexplained that draws his attention, the puzzle about Jerry. "Why would he want to visit us for a week? God, my parents were the most uptight, the most dull, the most judgmental – why would he want to spend a week with us?" His theory is that Jerry planned to visit only a day or two before adventuring across the river to Detroit, but that he stayed for him, to rescue him, stayed to give his little cousin something to get him through the pain of the next few years. And Andrea seemed happy to join in and add her special bonus. He proposes the theory, then rejects it, because he cannot imagine anyone being that sacrificing, certainly not any nineteen-year-old guy with a world to explore and an Andrea to explore it with.

Before they left, Jerry and Andrea gave him the latest record by The Marcels, which became the first record in Christopher's collection. More importantly, they convinced his parents that they needed to buy Christopher a record player to play it on.

The highway out of the city was a badly paved, potholed strip that became a dusty, rutted dirt road, whose curves we followed into the countryside as the afternoon became evening, past small villages where we sometimes stopped for more passengers, past farmers herding goats, children playing soccer. Twice I got off and bought food from street vendors. Christopher ate little. I didn't ask how he was coping with the jarring ride. When we came to our destination, a town on the south shore of a long lake, Christopher began to rise from his seat and then fell back, and there was no smile then, no humour of even the most merciless kind to be found. He gasped loudly, and he started to cry for a moment before his anger and pride seized him. I was looking to see who might help me help him off the bus, but he stood then, and supporting himself with his arms on the backs of seats, made his way unassisted. I wanted so much to be able to help him but knew that I could not.

My idea for a way to reach the source of his anger and soften it, to reach Christopher and soften him and make it so both of us could achieve peace, or something, God, something – this idea came to me from no particular place but seemed so right. That night I reached for him and just rested my hand on his hip, and as usual he did not roll away or even tense but was still, still and so furiously tolerant. I started to sing, softly, "Are the stars out tonight? I don't know if it's cloudy or bright," and I knew that, as I continued, finally he would see that he was not alone after all, not so cut off and abandoned, and he would reach for me in the night when the pain came and not need me to pretend anymore. Even as I sang "cloudy or bright" I could hear the next line, "I only have eyes for you," and I knew he would turn to me then, without speaking, but he did speak – before I had completed my breath and sung that line. He said, "No. Don't do this," and of course I saw that I had been stupid, and sentimental, and that nothing so false could do anything or help anything, and I was stunned that I had been so stupid and disrespectful.

"I'm staying here till tonight. You go," Christopher said to me in the morning. He had not gotten out of bed.

"I'll bring you breakfast," I said.

"Please go."

I ate breakfast at a market stand near the hotel, lingering over my food forever, till finally, though no one showed the slightest displeasure with my occupying a table in the shade of the lean-to that sold the food, I felt too embarrassed to stay, and I set out into the town.

The heat was dryer, less heavy than on the coast, more fiery – shocking and hostile. Buildings – shacks – sharpened into focus and then shifted, their edges fuzzy, suddenly angling back, narrowing and rippling. I could see a large white structure down the dusty, rust-coloured road and made it my goal. It seemed near, perhaps a ten-minute walk. I looked at my wrists, half expecting to see my skin beginning to blister.

The white building retreated as I advanced through the blazing air, and time seemed to pulse and bend in the heat along with the small shacks I passed and the green trees in the distance behind them. Was I getting closer? I couldn't tell. No one was about – sane people hiding from the sun, I supposed.

A young couple I passed walking in the opposite direction, the first people I'd seen on my walk, smiled at me, their eyes widening. I could tell that they stopped after I went by, and I imagined them looking back at me.

In the yard before the white building, three men knelt on the ground, resting in the pose of the child, exactly like Christopher, and I pondered, amazed, the possibility of travelling all this way to find three afflicted as he was, suffering that way; perhaps this was a clinic, a rare medical outpost specializing in the treatment of his untreatable fate. Then they moved and I realized the absurdity of my heat-induced fantasy, remembered what I had read on the plane about the Muslim North and understood that these men were not practising yoga or coping with deathly pain: they were praying.

Beyond the white building I found another small market where I was able to sit again in the shade, drinking melon juice. My embarrassment at lingering was not as compelling as my pounding, pounding head and my exhaustion, and I spent the rest of the afternoon there, the girl who was the proprietor treating me like her fragile patient, commiserating about the heat, offering water, juice, and advice, joined sometimes by others passing by or stopping for something to drink or eat, all seriously concerned about me. I turned down several offers of escort back to the hotel.

Christopher was up when I returned, waiting, his eyes closed, hands folded in his lap, sitting in a chair under the ceiling fan in the small lobby. When I asked him what he had learned about music performances he told me that the desk clerk had said the town was empty of bands, that a festival was underway across the lake, and we would be taking the ferry in the morning, a twenty-four-hour ferry ride with several stops on the way till we reached the northern shore and the village where the highlife bands of the region had gathered.

If we had made this long overseas journey before, we would have talked about everything. Christopher is dark, the darkest black person I've met, till here, where everyone is darker than he is. He would have joked but also admired, speculated, and invited me to speculate. We would have talked about the music we heard in the city, and the heat, the slave fort, the food, the taxi driver and the hotel clerk, the city and the beauty, the beauty I noticed without noticing, and we certainly would have spoken of the potential symbolism of our trip up the lake to join the festival, about our pursuit of the music that seemed to retreat as we advanced.

In the evening, in our small room, like a sleeper on a train, boiling, with the rumble of the engines coming through the window and the vibrations humming through the hot floor, I said, "Christopher, please talk to me. Please let's talk." He was lying on the lower bunk, on his back, and he looked at me and said nothing.

"I know you're angry," I said. "I'm angry too. I'm angry that all my love for you can't do anything, and it seems so unimportant, our love seems so unimportant now, and I'd do anything, really, I'd do anything," and of course I started to cry as soon as I spoke, and I couldn't finish my sentence.

Christopher sat up and turned to me; he looked at me, incredulous, or disgusted. He was about to speak; he was going to say something to me about love, but then he grimaced, and he said only "Oh," and again "Oh," emitted each time as a gasp of pain and surprise, and he fell back on the bunk. He lay there, curled up, one hand gripping the edge of the mattress, and cursed through clenched teeth while I sobbed uselessly, uselessly, till finally his attack passed. Christopher rolled over to face the wall and covered his face with his hands. A breeze had come up and the ship had begun to roll gently.

What I said was true. Our love used to count for so much, enough for so much else not to matter; for twenty-six years all my life's problems, anything that threatened me, was disabled and finally dispelled by Christopher's love. Everyone could hear his voice everywhere, in commercials, voice-overs for coming attractions, in-flight audio, syndicated public radio, documentaries, but I heard him speak only for me; in a voice deeper and warmer than he ever used for anyone else, he would close his eyes and speak my name.

The village we have come to is a sprawling collection of circular grass huts. We have been told that the festival began two days ago, but we are in time for the last day. We are staying in someone's home; some family cheerfully gave up their home for us. Christopher could not disguise being sick, and his insistence that he would not see a doctor was met with a collective insistence that he must, till he said again that he would not see anyone and a woman spoke loudly in a native language, and the discussion among the impromptu welcoming group that formed when we left the ferry simply moved on to the topic of whose hut we would stay in. We were given dinner and then, respectfully, our privacy. Now Christopher lies on his back, asleep, fevered, sweating, his breath shallow and sour.

In the morning it becomes clear that the village has understood our purpose – Christopher's purpose – when a woman comes to us with food and explains that she will come again later, when the music is to start; she and some others will come to bring Christopher to the music. He must rest till then. Then she takes my hand and leads me away to give me a tour of the village. She takes advantage of shade cast by trees, huts, anything to avoid being in the sun for long. I carefully simulate interest till our last stop, the school, where the lesson is interrupted so the children can sing to me. My guide explains that the song thanks a visitor for travelling from very far to be with them, and when it's over and the children applaud, she tells me that they are applauding for me. She is looking in my eyes when she says this and then she takes my hand again, speaks to the children, and we walk away. "I told them how very much you liked their song," she says, and when our eyes meet I cannot tell whether she believes I did, or cares, or is hinting a criticism. She returns me to the hut where Christopher is sleeping. It's true that I liked the song, or that I would have liked the song if I could like anything, if I had a right to feel anything.

My guide returns later with two men who have a small wooden cart for Christopher, which he gets into with no complaint, and we go, the cart pulled by one man then another, me walking behind, out of Christopher's view to limit any challenge to his dignity. He holds the sides of the cart with his arms, to steady himself, but I can tell that his arms too have lost strength, and at intervals his head falls forward and bounces before he raises it again. We walk through the village and down to the lake, along the shore and then back, up through the trees, then the trees give way to a grassy plain, and there are cars, trucks – people have journeyed here from the north. A camp has been set up, and through the camp I follow Christopher in his cart to where a crowd has gathered, and then into the crowd, within view of a low stage, and now in my anxiety and anticipation I would take his hand, and he would look at me and smile, but I can't and he won't.

I can't describe music the way Christopher can. No band performs more than three or four songs. Members from one band reappear in another. Guitars, drums of all shapes, trumpets, even violins, marimbas or something like them, singers in groups and solo, dancers on stage and in the crowd. Someone brings large hats for Christopher and me, to protect us from the sun. Someone else brings us water. The crowd sings along with some songs, shouts to the musicians between songs, applauds and cheers after the songs. Christopher remains absolutely still in the cart, his face hidden by his hat, and I don't know whether he is transported and fulfilled, revivified, or as angry as ever, disappointed, defeated, in excruciating pain, or dead . . . or dead, and in an instant I imagine confronting all the difficulties of transporting his body through all the legs of our journey home. Then he takes a drink of water, and with the motion of his hand I'm staggered with relief and shame. I look around stupidly to see if anyone has noticed, and another song begins.

Something delays us, and after taxiing we wait a long time for takeoff. Christopher is limp beside me – limp and weak, as though his bones are becoming rubber. I have fastened his seat belt for him, as before I carried his baggage and pushed his wheelchair, helped heave him into a taxi. I review the series of struggles with his weight and his pain back to the moment at the end of the evening of highlife, when Christopher was not angry as far as I could tell, or revived, but only weak, confused, and saying in a hushed voice that he needed to pee. There was nothing satisfying in the apparent dissipation of his anger, and suddenly I was furious that we had arrived too late, that he had missed even the opportunity to be disappointed, and my fury made the world tilt and my vision blur. "Christopher," I said, trying to imagine a question that wasn't insulting and banal: "How was the music, was the music good enough, did the music help?" My legs failed and for a moment I had to sit on the ground.

Finally we take off. Christopher is perspiring and I reach up to aim the air nozzles in his direction. His eyes are closed and I hope he is sleeping.

I would like to sleep too; I am exhausted, but too many conversations intrude when I close my eyes.

I plug in the headphones, put them on, and Christopher is telling me, with such enthusiasm, belief and deep, warm authority, about how the Four Diamonds met in high school and got their start at a talent contest. And then the song begins. I take the headphones off and put them on Christopher. His mouth opens and closes, then his eyes open and he turns to look at me to share his surprise.

To share his surprise, not his anger, and surprise at the song, not at my having given him something. Nothing could be surprising in a gift from me and I cannot be doubting whether he ever was angry; nothing could be more certain. The seat belt sign turns off, a flick of hurt and then relief, like pulling out a sliver.

I take the headphones back, my timing right to hear Christopher introduce the next song, *True Darling, True*. The falsetto falters on the highest note, so vulnerable that he sounds achingly like a girl. At the chorus the harmonies drop away, the quartet sings in unison, and Christopher is right, there is something defiant in this a cappella innocence and beauty, something challenging and then enticing. It is as though the song leads me on, rushes me on and over the edge of a cliff, and if I look down I will see where I am and, like a cartoon character, plummet. But if I just listen I will be carried along by the song to its gorgeous end, and then I will hear Christopher again and the ground will be under me.

DAVE MARGOSHES

THE WISDOM OF SOLOMON

There he was in Cleveland. My father liked to use this expression for his life in those days: "I was still chasing the donkey, trying to pin the tail to it." The donkey had led him away from New York and now, at last, he had his first real job on a newspaper, though it wasn't quite what he had expected, and he was beginning what he hoped would be a glorious career. If not glorious, then at least exciting, interesting. He saw himself as Don Quixote, the hero of the famous novel he had recently read, tilting at windmills – righting wrongs – not with a lance but a pen. First, though, he had to learn to type.

And he held in his hands the hearts of thousands of readers. That was his chief concern.

"My husband beats me and the children. What should I do?"

A reader had posed this question in a letter and my father considered his answer with gravity. If he advised her to be a dutiful wife and bear what her husband meted out, he might be sentencing her to a life of drudgery, frustration, and pain, and possibly even worse for the children. On the other hand, what if he suggested she leave the man – what sort of life would she and her children face, without a roof over their heads and a source of food, clothing, and protection? Even the middle ground was fraught with danger, he could see: should he urge her to talk to her husband, to try to mollify him, she might instead provoke him into even more extreme acts of violence. Lives might well hang in the balance.

How to respond?

———

It was 1920, and my father was twenty-seven; as he liked to say, he was always a few years older than the century.

The *Cleveland Jewish World – Der Velt* – had a grand title, but the paper itself was somewhat less than grand. Its circulation was barely 50,000, just a fraction of that of the big Yiddish dailies of New York City, but it saw itself playing a role just as important in the lives of the Jews of Cleveland and other cities in Ohio, bringing them not just news but education, entertainment, and literature. It was that part that most interested my father, who had been writing a novel and poems, but he was assigned more mundane tasks at first, not the least of which were obituaries. He got a crash course in the history of Cleveland as he succinctly documented the lives of its Jewish residents as they died. "People are dying to get into our pages," my father's boss, Everett Heshberg, told him. "It's the last time most of them ever will. Some of them, the first time too. Treat them with respect."

My father's chief job, though, was as newswriter, another grand title that was somewhat less than it sounded. *The World* subscribed to the Associated Press newswire, which, of course, came in English. First thing in the morning, Heshberg, who as managing editor was the heart and soul of the paper, went through the overnight dispatches, selecting stories he thought would be of interest to his readers. These included local items of government, politics, human interest, and even crime – the same stories that on that day would appear (or already had the previous day) on the front pages of the Cleveland *Plain Dealer*, which had, in fact, originated most of the local and state AP items. He also selected many stories from Europe, which was still recovering and reorganizing from the ravages of the Great War. Cleveland's Jews came from many parts of Europe – Germany, Romania, Russia, Hungary, Latvia, Galicia, and elsewhere – and were hungry for news of home, even if they no longer really considered those distant countries their home.

My father and another young man, who was somewhat senior to him, shared the translation duties, which he enjoyed. The trick was not so much to literally translate as to read the story, absorb it, and write it fresh in Yiddish as if the story was his own. My father was ideally suited for such a task, as he was fluent in both English and Yiddish, and could write quickly, though his two-finger attack at the typewriter was the cause of much amusement in *The World* newsroom. When he had time to spare, he practised ten-finger typing but it seemed hopeless.

There was little spare time, though. *The World* was an afternoon paper, meaning it appeared on the street shortly after noon. My father reported for work at 6 a.m. and wrote news till the 9:30 deadline. Then he turned his attention to the death notices sent in by the Jewish funeral homes. As Heshberg had explained it to him, "Each death represents a life, and each life is a story." Again, my father's job was to translate, taking the bare essentials of those lives – the facts provided by the families for the mortuaries – and turn them into interesting stories, occasionally taking liberties.

"Do not fabricate," Heshberg counselled, "but bend."

This suited my father fine, for he was attempting, as he saw it, to tailor the soul of a poet into the mind of a journalist. Each obituary, in his hands, became a poem.

News and obituaries occupied almost all of my father's time – after that day's paper was put to bed, as the expression went, the process would immediately begin again for the next day's edition – but they took up only a small part of the paper, which was mostly filled with articles by real writers on all manner of subjects: essays on philosophical and theological subjects, usually written by learned rabbis; treatises on history, civics, and politics; and educational articles that helped the Jewish immigrant community of Ohio in establishing their lives in this new world: how to apply for citizenship, how to get a driver's licence, the rights of a tenant, and so on. Then there were poems, short stories, condensed novels, literary criticism. This is what my father aspired to write, but he knew he had to earn the right to it. So he was both thrilled and chagrined when Heshberg asked him to write the advice column.

The newspapers of New York were filled with such columns, which were wildly popular. Abe Cahan, the great editor at *The Forward*, the Socialist paper, had invented the form, which he called the *Bintel Brief*, but all the other Yiddish papers had followed, even the religious papers, which at first considered themselves too serious for such a seemingly trivial feature. But readers demanded it. Regardless of what paper they read, they had questions, often much the same ones. Even the English papers, like the *Sun* and the *Telegram* in New York, seeing all the fuss, were quick to follow.

Native-born readers and well-established immigrants, though, were less likely to pose the utilitarian questions of the recent arrivals, so the columns established by the English papers quickly narrowed their focus to the lovelorn. Heshberg made it clear to my father that his column would involve much more than just letters from unhappy lovers. This was just as well, since my father, who was still a bachelor then, was one of the least likely men on earth to give advice on affairs of the heart, as would soon be evident.

"There should be nothing to it for a smart fellow like you, Morgenstern," Heshberg said. My father recognized the flattery as a ploy, but he was flattered just the same. "You have the intelligence and sensitivity for the job," the editor continued. "Just as in the obituaries, every life is a story. Every letter is an opportunity for you to influence those lives. Think of yourself as having a conversation with the readers, a conversation about their deepest concerns, worries, fears. Think of yourself as a rabbi."

That was exactly what was frightening my father. The last thing he wanted to be was a rabbi, a calling that his eldest brother, Sam, had followed, but the notion of a conversation with the readers was appealing to him.

Heshberg had already determined that my father's own identity, and that of any subsequent writers assigned this task, would be concealed. To this end, he had concocted a fictitious advisor called Yentel Schmegge, a name which, he hoped, would convey a combination of humour and seriousness readers would find appealing. My father would assume the persona of Yentel as he composed replies to the letter-writers. When he tired of the assignment, "after six months or a year," Heshberg said, another writer would take his place and consistency would be maintained.

My father agreed to all this – he was relieved that he would not have to put his own name on his replies – and even agreed to Heshberg's plan to prime the pump during the first days that the column would run, although he objected at first.

"Make up letters?" He realized immediately that his aghast tone might be offensive to the editor. "What I mean is . . ."

"You're concerned about the ethics of the situation, Morgenstern?" Heshberg looked at him with a frank expression, but he didn't appear hostile.

"Well, yes."

"Ethics don't really enter into it, don't you see? This isn't news, it's what in the English papers they call 'features.' What if it were a short story or a novel you were writing?"

"That would be fiction," my father said.

"Lies, you mean?"

"No." My father hesitated. He recalled a definition of fiction he had heard from a well-known novelist during a heated discussion over coffee at a crowded table at the Café Royale in New York. "Made up, yes, but in the service of truth."

"Exactly," Heshberg said. "You see my point exactly."

"I see."

"Just make them believable," Heshberg said. "Don't worry, in a week's time your desk will be covered with letters. Real ones."

My father thought long and hard, taking long late-night walks on deserted streets near his rooming house, staring thoughtfully into his glass of beer at the nearby tavern. As it turned out, the first few questions and answers he wrote proved to be so sensational they immediately helped make the column a success, but one of them – the very first – also returned to cause my father some discomfort later on.

For his first column, he wrote this letter:

Esteemed editor –

Please help me!

I am a nineteen-year-old woman, in good health, well proportioned, attractive, or so men have told me. I come from a good, religious family. My blessed parents and my precious brothers and sisters love me. But now they have threatened to disown me!

I am in love with a Red Indian man, a member of one of the Ohio tribes. He is a good man, educated in a government school, and refined, not a wild savage. He claims that his people are one of the Lost Tribes of Israel, that he is a Jew! I have no reason to disbelieve him.

He knows little of Judaism but he seeks to learn. I love this man and want to marry him and together make a good, devout Jewish family. But my family say he is a charlatan and that I will be dead to them should I follow my heart.

I cannot give up this man, but I cannot bear the thought of losing my family. What should I do?

– A distraught reader

This was followed by a painstakingly careful reply, written with Heshberg's admonition in mind: "Avoid extremes. Take the middle ground whenever possible. Provoke but do not enrage":

Dear distraught reader –

Your dilemma is certainly a profound and unique one, though it points to a more universal problem, namely: how shall Jewry interact with the world? Shall we seek to preserve our unique identity, as the Chosen People of God? Or should we attempt to take our part among the larger Brotherhood of Man, in which all are equal?

This is a question for the *rebbinim* to ponder and debate, for philosophers, not politicians, and certainly not journalists. It is an old debate, and shows no sign of abating. As to your specific problem, we can only advise you to follow your heart, and wish you well.

As he'd been instructed, he finished the letter with the words, "With love, Yentel Schmegge."

My father stood nervously beside Heshberg's desk as the editor read his typewritten copy, filled with the inevitable xxxd-over typing mistakes. He raised his head, a broad smile on his usually placid face. He had a thin moustache that was several shades darker than his unruly salt and pepper hair, as if he had run the tip of a pencil back and forth against it a number of times.

"Brilliant, Morgenstern. Or should I call you Solomon? This is the stuff."

On the spot, Heshberg decided to change the title of the advice column from "With Love from Yentel" to "The Wisdom of Solomon," though the former would remain as the signature. My father went back to his typewriter with his heart soaring.

"The Wisdom of Solomon" was indeed what the column was titled when it appeared the following Monday and in days to come, always prominently displayed on the second page, above the obituaries, although within the offices of *The World* it continued to be referred to as "the Schmegge."

The letter from the woman in love with the Indian ran that Monday and others that my father had concocted in the days that followed, but the week was not even out before the first real letters began to arrive, by hand and then through the post, and, as Heshberg had predicted, by the following week a steady stream of letters was arriving and my father no longer had to concoct lives wracked with heartbreaking dilemmas. Instead, the time allotted to this task was more than taken up by reading through the letters, selecting a couple of good ones for each day, and writing the replies.

The replies, he found, were considerably easier to write than the concocted letters, but, though he had felt ambivalent about writing those letters, when they were no longer necessary, he missed them.

Many of the real letters were considerably more mundane, dealing with disputes with landlords, employers, and bureaucrats, like the man who wrote to complain about the barking of a dog in the night. My father's replies were instructive ("What is more important, the good will of a neighbour or a few extra minutes of sleep?" he inquired rhetorically), and thus played an important role, as Heshberg frequently reminded him, but they took no imagination or creative powers. To the question from a woman about the proper handling of garbage being put out for collection, for example, he merely telephoned the appropriate clerk at City Hall and quickly had the answer, just as the letter writer herself could have done, except that, perhaps, her command of English was not up to it.

"You are the reader's agent." Heshberg had instructed.

There were also questions relating to child-rearing, education, career choices, immigration, housing, and a variety of other issues as well as, always, those of a romantic nature. There was never any telling what the day's mail would bring, and my father was often hard pressed in producing answers that were both informative and entertaining, which was what his editor expected of him.

Despite the ordinariness of the majority of the letters the column received, there were always some letters, "gems," my father called them, that echoed those of his own creation during the first week.

"Most worthy editor," one man, who signed himself "Tormented and Torn," wrote, "I have been unfaithful to my beloved wife. Should I kill myself? Confess all and suffer the consequences? Or keep my own counsel and let God deal with me as He will?"

My father was delighted. "My dear Tormented, by all means, put thoughts of suicide far from your mind. But at the same time, mend your ways. Being unfaithful once does not give you licence to be unfaithful again," he replied in a column that quickly became known and was often quoted. "Bad enough the unfaithfulness to your wife. Do not compound the sin by being unfaithful to God."

He wrote more, jabbing furiously at the typewriter keys with the index fingers of both hands, but, on consideration, crossed the rest out. He was learning that the best answers should be brief. To matter-of-fact questions, factual answers were required, of course. But to questions of the heart, my father was realizing, it was best to be a bit enigmatic.

———

In matters of the heart, my father already had some experience of his own. He had been involved in a love affair or two, and his heart had been broken. He had observed envy and jealousies cause rifts within his own family. He himself had been the victim of betrayal by a friend. He was no Solomon, he knew, but he felt confident and stimulated. And he felt the first stirrings of what soon would become a new novel moving within him.

———

The envelope immediately announced itself as different from most of the others that crossed my father's desk. For one thing, it was neatly typed – whereas most he received were handwritten, often crudely so, and in a mixture of English and Yiddish – and addressed fully to Yentel Schmegge/The Wisdom of Solomon, *The Jewish World*, and the complete address. Of even more interest was the return address: Prof. M.E. Bell, Department of Sociology and Anthropology, University of Ohio, Columbus, Ohio. Columbus, my father knew, was some 150 miles away. He examined the envelope front and back and slit it open with interest.

The letter was addressed not to "esteemed editor" or "worthy Yentel Schmegge," but to "My dear Mrs. Schmegge (or is it Miss?)." Now my father really was interested.

> Allow me to introduce myself. My name is Madelaine Bell. I'm an assistant professor of anthropology here at the University of Ohio, in Columbus. Some of your columns have been forwarded to me by a friend in Cleveland, with rough English translations.
>
> I'm particularly interested in the letter from the woman who was in love with the Indian man. Do you recall it? I believe it was one of the early letters, and your reply was indeed Solomonic. I'd very much like to know what course this woman followed. Do you know how I can get in touch with her? I'd very much appreciate any help you can give me.

My father, flabbergasted, paused in his reading to rub his eyes. Then he continued:

> As it happens, I will be in Cleveland next week for several days. May I call you at *The World*? I realize "Schmegge" may be a pseudonym, but I will call and ask for you and hope for the best.
>
> Until then, my very best regards.

The signature intrigued my father. It was just the name, "Madelaine Bell," with no title, neither "Professor" nor "Miss" nor "Mrs." Bell, he knew, could be an English name, or it could be a shortened, Anglicized version of a Jewish name like

Belzburg or Belowitz. In New York, he knew a number of Jewish men who called themselves Bell. He looked closer at the signature. The hand was feminine, yet clear and somehow bold, he thought. He imagined it was the signature of a woman who was independent – a professor! – who would yield to no man on matters of principle yet might happily yield to the pressure of arms and lips. This was exactly the sort of woman he himself was seeking. He read the letter again and a third time, and studied the signature further. He imagined the author of this letter was an attractive woman – but not wildly attractive – with long brown hair and intelligent eyes that could hold and return a gaze. Assistant professor meant that she could not be too old, and he imagined she would be no more than thirty, perhaps younger.

Of course, what would such a woman see in a man who had dropped out of school after the fifth grade, whose education was mostly self-acquired? A man who fabricated letters for a newspaper column of dubious value? A man who she thought was a woman!

My father shook his head and chided himself for his vanity, laughed at himself. Then he took a look at the date on the letter: it had been written on a Thursday. His eyes flicked to the calendar on the wall above the city desk: it was Tuesday, next week already. He went to the front office and told them he might be receiving a call, and if so to put it through immediately. Should he be unavailable for any reason, ask the caller to come down to the paper and ask for him.

―――――

Madelaine Bell turned out to be very close to my father's ideal. She was attractive – but not wildly so – with long brown hair that was done up neatly in what my father thought was called a French roll. She had an aquiline nose and dark, intelligent eyes, but her thick eyeglasses masked the intent of her look. She was shorter than my father liked, but well built, and very well dressed in a brown tweed suit, something my father had never seen on a woman. She was, he guessed, about thirty-five, just a few years older than my father. She wore no make-up or jewellery, including no wedding or engagement ring, but her fingernails, he noticed, were long and well cared for, and covered with a purplish-red polish. She didn't look or sound even remotely Jewish.

They sat across from each other in a delicatessen a block away from *The World*'s offices, cups of tea in front of them.

"You really thought I was a woman," my father repeated, still amazed.

"You're very convincing," Professor Bell said.

"So convincing as to fool even someone as learned as you, a professor of anthropology! I'm pleased to know that."

The professor explained her interest in the correspondent in love with the Indian. She was involved in a study of the integration of immigrant Jews into American society. Inter-marriage between races and faiths of course played a large part. "This woman is exactly the sort of person I'm most interested in. I don't have to tell you the symbolic value of her predicament. In love with an Indian, an original inhabitant of this land. Then there's the lost tribe element, the possibility that, in terms of both faith and ethnicity, there is no actual intermarriage. This is invaluable. It could be emblematic for my entire study." After a moment, when my father didn't immediately reply, she added: "And the man's desire to study Judaism, to return to roots he didn't even know he had . . ."

My father had thought hard about what to tell this woman. Much as he hated to lie, it was unthinkable to admit the fabrication. "I'm sorry to say I can't really help you," he began reluctantly. "The woman wrote no more than what we printed. There was no name on the letter, no return address on the envelope."

"And she hasn't been in touch again?" Madelaine Bell asked hopefully.

"No." After a moment, my father added: "It's been almost four months now, so it's doubtful she will be. Who knows what may have become of her."

"Ah," Professor Bell said. "I would dearly love to interview her." She took off her eyeglasses and gently rubbed the bridge of her nose with her thumb and forefinger, a gesture my father found endearing. When she removed her hand, her eyes, a lighter shade of brown than he had first thought, were warm and inviting. "I wonder if I could impose upon you for a favour?"

"If I can be of service, of course."

"Perhaps you could insert a sentence or two in your column inquiring as to this woman's whereabouts, 'will the woman who wrote the letter on,' I'm sorry, I've forgotten the date, 'will the woman who wrote about her love affair with the Indian man please be in contact . . .' Something along those lines. Would that be possible?"

"Ah," my father said. Professor Bell had not yet put her glasses back on and he found himself gazing into those warm brown eyes. He felt a moment of panic, as if he were being drawn into those pools of liquid, chocolatey brown, where he would surely drown, but it quickly passed. What harm could such a subterfuge do – other than, of course, to compound the original fabrication? Heshberg, if he even noticed, would find it amusing.

————

In matters of the heart, my father found, each situation was different. His experience was useless for the situation he soon found himself in.

After some weeks had passed, he was able to imagine writing this letter:

Esteemed Yentel Schmegge –

I find myself unexpectedly in need of your sage advice. I'm enmeshed in an impossible love affair. In fact, I have inextricably entangled myself in a web of deception for which I have less and less stomach every day. The Americans have a phrase for it: "painting oneself into a corner."

I am a young man from a good Jewish home. Our family was not religious – I would characterize myself as an agnostic – but Jewishness, if not Judaism, is important to me. Yet I am involved with a Gentile woman, a *shiksa*, for whom ethnicity and faith are merely subjects of interest, to be examined and studied rather than adhered to.

She is a professional woman, a woman of learning, for whom education is of the highest importance. I have very little formal education, though I have done much to improve myself. She is part of a profession that follows a strict code of ethical conduct, that draws a sharp distinction between theory and data. I follow a trade that has high ideals but is essentially amoral.

I love this woman and we are involved in a passionate affair that has gone beyond my wildest dreams. But, in order to advance this affair, I resorted to a number of falsehoods; now, to preserve the affair, I must pile falsehood upon falsehood. There is, I fear, a void at the centre. It is only a matter of time, I'm certain, until this woman, who is no fool, will see through the facade I've erected.

So, I implore and beseech you, tell me, dear, wise Yentel Schmegge, what am I to do?

My father had not really written the letter, but the situation and the question were real enough.

He considered the question, and the one contained in a letter that had come that day, a real question, in a real letter, from a real reader: "My husband beats me and the children. What should I do?"

He had been sitting at his desk in *The World* newsroom for an hour or more thinking of how to answer this question. It was late, and the newsroom was deserted. There was a bottle of whisky in the bottom drawer of his desk. He opened the drawer, took out the bottle and a small glass, and poured himself a drink.

The only answer my father could think of for either dilemma – his own and that of his distressed correspondent – was the one he had written so often in the newspaper: "Follow your heart." In the dim light of the empty newsroom, the inadequacy of the answer – and its falsity – loomed enormous.

ALEXANDER MacLEOD

MIRACLE MILE

This was the day after Mike Tyson bit off Evander Holyfield's ear. You remember that. It was a moment in history – not like Kennedy or the planes flying into the World Trade Center – not up at that level. This was something lower, more like Ben Johnson, back when his eyes were that thick, yellow colour and he tested positive in Seoul after breaking the world record in the hundred. You might not know exactly where you were standing or exactly what you were doing when you first heard about Tyson or about Ben, but when the news came down, I bet it stuck with you. When Tyson bit off Holyfield's ear, that cut right through the everyday clutter. All the papers and the television news shows ran the exact same pictures of Tyson standing there in his black trunks with the blood in his mouth. It seemed like everything else that happened that day had to be related back to this moment, back to Mike and what he had done. You have to remember, this was before Tyson got the tattoo on his face, and the rematch with Holyfield was supposed to be his big comeback, a chance to go straight and be legitimate again. Nobody thinks about that now. Now, the only thing you see when you look back is Mike moving in for the kill, the way his cheek brushes up almost intimately against Evander's face just before he breaks all the way through and gives in to his rawest impulse. Then the tendons in his neck bulge out and his eyes pop wide open and his teeth come grinding down.

Burner and I were stuck in another hotel room, watching the sports highlights churn it around and around, the same thirty-second clip of the fight. It was like watching the dryer roll clothes. Cameras showed it from different angles and at different speeds and there were lots of close-ups of Evander's mangled head and the chunk of flesh lying there in the middle of the ring. Commentators took turns explaining what was happening and what it all meant.

The cleaning lady had already come and gone and now we had two perfectly made double beds, a fresh set of towels, and seven empty hours before it would be time for us to go. We just sat there, side by side, beds three feet apart, perched on top of our tight blankets like a pair of castaways on matching rafts drifting in the same current. Mike kept coming at us through the screen. You know how it gets. If you look at the same pictures long enough even the worst things start to feel too familiar, even boring. I turned the TV off but the leftover buzz hanging in the air still hurt my eyes.

"Enough?" I asked, though I knew there'd be no response.

Burner didn't say anything. His eyes were kind of glossed over and he just sat there staring straight into the same dark place where the picture used to be. He'd been fading in and out for the last few hours.

If I have learned one thing through all this, it's that you have to let people do what they're going to do. Everybody gets ready in his own way. Some guys play their music loud, some say their prayers, and some can't keep anything down and they're always running to the toilet. Burner wasn't like that. He liked to keep it quiet in the morning, to just sit around and watch mindless TV so he could wander off in his mind and come back any time he liked. One minute, he could be sitting there, running his mouth off about nothing, and then for no reason he'd zone out and go way down into himself and stay there perfectly silent for long stretches, staring off to the side like he was trying to remember the name of someone he should really know.

It didn't bother me. Over the years, Burner and I had been in plenty of hotel rooms together, and by now we had our act down. I didn't mind the way he folded his clothes into perfect squares and put them into the hotel dresser drawers even when we were staying a single night, and I don't think he cared about the way I dumped my bag into a pile in the corner and pulled out the things I needed. You have to let people do what they do. When you get right down to it, even the craziest ritual and the wildest superstition are based on somebody's version of real solid logic.

After fifteen minutes of nothing, Burner said, "I'm not going to wear underwear."

He was all bright and edgy now, and his eyes started jumping around the room. He licked his top lip every few seconds with just the tip of his tongue darting out.

"No, not going to wear underwear."

He nodded his head this second time, as if, at last, some big decision had finally been made and he was satisfied with the result.

I didn't say anything. When he was this far down, Burner didn't need anybody to keep up the other end of the conversation.

"You feel faster without underwear, you know. But I only do it once or twice a year. Only for the big ones."

That was it. A second later he was gone again, back below the surface, off to the side.

I turned away from him and punched a slightly bigger dent into my pillow so there'd be more room for my head. I knew there was no chance, but I still closed my eyes and tried to sleep. The alarm on the table said it was 12:17 and no matter what you do you can't trick those early afternoon numbers. Every red minute was going to leak out of that clock like water coming through the ceiling, building up nice and slow before releasing even one heavy drop. I waited, and I am sure I counted to sixty-five, but when I looked back 12:18 still hadn't come down. I flopped over onto my back and looked at the little stalagmites in the stucco. I thought about those little silver star-shaped things that are supposed to go off if there's a fire.

I'll tell you what I was wearing: my lucky Pogues T-shirt for the warm-up, a ratty Detroit Tigers baseball cap, the same pair of unwashed shorts that had worked okay for me last week, and a pair of black track pants that weren't made of cotton, but some kind of space-age, breathable, moisture-wicking material. On my left foot, I had one expensive running shoe that Adidas had given me for free. Its partner was on the floor beside the bed and I had about a dozen other pairs still wrapped in tissue paper and sitting in their boxes at home. My right foot was bare because I had just finished icing it for the third time this morning. The wet zip-lock bag of shrunken hotel ice cubes was slumped at the end of my bed, melting, and my messed-up Achilles was still bright red from the cold. I could just start to feel the throb coming back into it.

I meshed my fingers together on my chest and tried to make them go up and down as slowly as possible. It was coming and we were waiting for it. The goal now was to do absolutely nothing and let time flow right over us. It would have been impossible to do less and still be alive. I felt like one of the bodies laid out in a funeral home, waiting for the guests to arrive. You couldn't put these things off forever. Eventually it had to end. In a couple of hours, some guy dressed all in white would say "Take your marks." Then, one second later, there'd be the gun.

I don't know how much time passed before Burner hopped off his bed like he was in some big rush. He went around our room cranking open all the taps until we had all five of them running full-blast. There were two in the outside sink, the one by the big mirror with all the lights around it, two in the bathroom sink, and one big one for the tub. Burner had them all going at once. Water running down the drain was supposed to be a very soothing sound that helped you focus and visualize everything more clearly. This was all part of thinking like a champion. At least that's what the sports psychology guys said, and Burner thought they were right on.

At first there was a lot of steam and we had our own little cloud forming up around the ceiling, but after a while, after we'd used up all the hot water for the entire hotel, the mist cleared and there was only the *shhhhhh* sound of the water draining away. It was actually kind of nice. You could just try and put yourself inside that sound and it would carry you some place else, maybe all the way to the ocean.

When Burner surfaced for the last time, when he came back for good, he looked over at me and said, "Do you know what your problem is?"

I took a breath and waited for it.

"You can't see," he said. "You don't have vision. If you want to do this right, you need to be able to see how it's going to happen before it actually happens. You have to be in there, in the race, a hundred times in your head before you really do it."

I nodded because I had to. This season, unlike all the others, Burner was in the position to give advice and I was in the position to have to take it. For the last three years I had beat him from Vancouver to Halifax and back a hundred times and in all that time I had never said a thing about it. He'd never even been close. But this year – the year of the trials, the year when they picked the team for the World Championships and they were finally going to fund all the spots – this was the year when Burner finally had it all put together at the right time and I couldn't get anything going. For the last eight weeks, in eight different races in eight different cities, he'd come flying by me in the last one-fifty and there was nothing I could do about it.

I don't know where it came from or how he did it, but Burner had it all figured out. For the last year, he'd been on

this crazy diet where it seemed like he only ate green vegetables – just broccoli and spinach and Brussels sprouts all the
time. And he hadn't had a drop of alcohol or a cup of coffee in
months. He said he had gone all the way over to the straight
edge and that he would never allow another bad substance to
get into his body again. He broke up with his girlfriend and
quit going out, even to see a movie. He drank this special
decaffeinated green tea and he shaved his head right down to
the bare nut. I think he weighed something down around 130.
He practised some watered-down version of Buddhist mysti-
cism, and he was interested in yoga and always reading these
books with titles like *Going for Gold!: Success the Kenyan Way*,
or *Unlocking Your Inner Champion*. Whatever he was doing, it
was working. Out of all that mess, he had found some little
kernel of truth and now he was putting it into action.

"The secret is to think about nothing," he said. "Just let it
all hang out. Mind blank and balls to the wall. That's all there
is. Keep it simple, stupid. Be dumb. Just run."

It's hard to tell anybody what it's really like. Most people
have seen too many of those CBC profiles that run during the
Olympics, the ones with the special theme music and the
torch and all those fuzzy, soft camera shots that make everyone look so young and radiantly healthy. I used to think –
everybody used to think – they were going to make one of
those little movies about me, but I know now it's never going
to happen. It's timing. Everything is timing. I was down when
I needed to be up. If we were both at our best, if Burner and
I were both going at it at the top of our games, he would lose.
We both knew this. My best times were ahead of his, but I was

far from my best now. There were even high-school kids coming up from behind now, and they were charging hard. I don't really know what I was waiting for in that room. I might cut the top five, maybe, but I knew I wouldn't be close enough to be in the photograph when the first guy crossed the line. It wasn't really competition anymore. For me, this was straight autopilot stuff, going through the motions and following my own ritual right through to the end.

"What about Bourque?" I said.

This was the last part for Burner. I'd say the name of a guy who was going to be there with us and he would describe the guy's weaknesses. Burner needed to do this, needed to know exactly why the others could not win. There were maybe ten people like us in the whole country, and no more than five or six who had a real shot at making the team, but Burner needed to hate all of them. That was how he worked. I couldn't care less, but I did my part. I kept my eyes on the sprinklers and didn't even look at him. I just released the words into the air. I let Bourque's name float away.

"Bourque? What is Bourque? A 3:39, 3:40 guy at the top end of his dreams. We won't even see him. Too slow. Period. We won't even see him."

"Dawson is supposed to be here," I said. He was the next guy on the list. "He ran 3:37.5 at NC's last month."

"Got no guts," Burner sort of snorted it. "Dawson needs everything to be perfect. He needs a rabbit and a perfectly even pace and he needs there to be sunshine and no wind. He can run, no doubt, but he can't race. If you shake him up and throw any kind of hurt into him, he'll just fold. Guy's got tons of talent, but he's a coward. You know that, Mikey. Everybody knows that about Dawson. Even Dawson knows it, deep down. If somebody puts in a 57 second 400 in the middle of it, Dawson will be out the back end and he'll cry when it's over. He will actually cry. You will see the tears running down his face."

"Marcotte will take it out hard right from the gun," I said. "He'll open in 56 and then just try and hold on. He's crazy and he will never quit. There's no limit to how much that guy can hurt."

"But he can't hold it. You know how it'll be. Just like last week and the week before. It'll be exactly the same. Marcotte will blow his load too soon and we'll come sailing by with 300 to go. If we close in 42, he'll have nothing in the tank. He'll collapse and fall over at the finish line and somebody will have to carry him away."

That's how we talked most of the time. The numbers meant more than the words and the smaller numbers meant more than the bigger ones. It was like we belonged to our own little country and we had this secret language that almost nobody else understood. Almost nobody can tell you the real difference between 3:36 and 3:39. Almost nobody understands that there's something in there, something important and significant, just waiting to be released out of that space between the six and the nine. Put it this way: if you ever wanted to cross over that gap, if you ever wanted to see what it was like on the other side, you would need to change your entire life and get rid of almost everything else. You have to make choices: you can't run and be an astronaut. Can't run and have a full-time job. Can't run and have a girlfriend who doesn't run. When I stopped going to church or coming home for holidays, my mother used to worry that I was losing my balance, but I never met a balanced guy who ever got anything done. There's nothing new about this stuff. You have to sign the same deal if you want to be good – I mean truly good – at anything. Burner and I, and all those other guys, we understood this. We knew all about it. Every pure specialist is the same way so either you know what I am talking about or you do not.

"In the end, it's going to come back to Graham," I said. I'd been saving his name for last.

"Graham," Burner repeated it back to me. "Graham, Graham, Graham, Graham."

It sounded almost like a spell or a voodoo curse, but what else could you say? We both knew there was no easy answer for Graham.

When we were kids in high school, back when we first joined the club and started training together, Burner and I used to race the freight trains through the old Michigan central railway tunnel. It was one of those impossible, dangerous things that only invincible high-school kids even try: running in the dark, all the way from Detroit to Windsor, underneath the river. When I think back to it now, I still get kind of quaky and I can't believe we got away untouched. It didn't work out like that for everyone. Just a few years ago, a kid in the tunnel got sucked under one of those big red CP freighters, and when they found him his left arm and his left leg had been cut right off. Somehow he lived, and everybody thought there must have been some kind of divine intervention. The doctors managed to reattach his arm and I think he got a state-of-the-art prosthetic leg paid for by the War-amps. The papers tried to turn it into a feel-good piece, but all I could think about was how hard it must have been for that kid to go through the rest of his life with that story stuck to him and with the consequences of it so clear to everybody else.

Burner and I used to race the trains at night from the American side, under the river, and up through the other opening into the CP railyard, over by Wellington Avenue, where all the tracks bundle up and braid together. At that time, before the planes flew into the World Trade Center, there weren't any real border guards or customs officers or police posted on the rail tunnel. They just had fences. On the American side you had to climb over and on the Canadian side someone had already snipped a hole through the links and you could just walk. The train tunnel is twice as long as the one they use for the cars, and I think we had it paced out at around two and a half miles or about fifteen minutes of hard blasting through the dark, trying not to trip over the switches or the broken ties or the ten thousand rats that live down there.

We'd drive Burner's car over to the American side, we'd hop the fence, and then we'd just watch and wait for about fifteen minutes, trying to estimate how long it would be before the next train set out. We always went one guy at a time because there wasn't enough space between the side of the track and the wall of the tunnel and you couldn't risk getting tangled up. It was pitch black in there so we took these little flashlights that we wouldn't turn on until we were inside and even then you could only get a quick look at where you were and where you were headed. Once, I remember that Burner tried to tape one of those lights to his head so he could be like a miner and see everything more clearly, but he said that the light wouldn't stay where he needed it and that he had to rip it off after only a few steps.

When you think about what could have happened but didn't, it makes you wonder why we weren't more strategic or careful. We should have timed everything right down to the second, but back then it seemed so easy. We'd crouch down in the shadows beside the tunnel and then if everything looked OK, we'd shake hands and say something like "See you on the other side." Then the guy going second, the guy left behind, would count it down – three, two, one, go – and that would be it. The first guy would just take off.

We were always good runners, but 90 per cent of racing the trains is just learning to deal with straight fear and the sensation you get from that hot surge of adrenaline flowing through you. It was all about going forward and just trying to stay up on your feet. If you did go down and you felt your leg brush against that damp fur of a rat or caught your arm on some chunk of metal or got scraped up against the exposed wall of the tunnel, there was no time to even think about it. You just got up as quickly as you could, and even though you could feel your pulse beating through an open cut and you might have wrenched your ankle pretty bad, you still had to go on as if everything was working perfectly according to plan.

It wasn't really racing at all. There's no way to actually win in a contest like that and you could never go head-to-head with the trains. This was more about just trying to stay ahead and that's something completely different. When they set off and they're just chugging out of the gate, those trains look slow and heavy and it seems like it should be easy to stay out front, especially when you're working with such a big head start. It doesn't work like that though. The trains pick up their momentum on the way down into the tunnel. They used to say that once you were in there running, if you ever heard the train coming up from behind, or if you even just caught the sound of that first echo, then that meant you had something like three minutes before it caught up and pulled you under. The other thing they always talked about was the light. They said that if the light ever touched you, if that big glare of the freighter ever landed right on you, then that was supposed to be the end. By that time the rig would be going too fast and even if he saw you the engineer wouldn't have time to shut everything down and stop. That's what happened to the kid who lost his arm and leg. By the time they radioed and got the paramedics and the stretchers all the way down there, the kid nearly bled to death in the dark. Then they had to go searching for his missing limbs and I guess they found one on the track and the other one, I think it was the leg, caught up underneath the train. Even after all that, he somehow pulled through.

Nothing ever happened to me. I must have run the tunnel half a dozen times, but I never heard or saw the train, and the only thing that ever pushed me along was the need to get out. It just kept you going faster than you thought you could go and it kept you rolling right up until you felt the ground leaning up again, climbing out. In the dark, just that little shift in the angle of the earth under your feet would be enough to tell you that you were getting closer and you'd probably make it.

The worst time was the last time. It was my turn to go first and when I came through I was so messed up I knew I would never do it again. As soon as I made it out, I kind of collapsed off to the side, just one step beyond the tunnel. I must have fallen two or three times in there and I had a bad, pretty nasty gash oozing down the front of my shin. I don't know why, but when I got out, I started throwing up and I couldn't make it stop. I thought I might pass out because I couldn't get a clean breath and my stomach was kind of convulsing and dry-heaving. My vision went all blurry and I couldn't see anything.

I was lying there in the scrub grass beside the tunnel, kind of curled up in the fetal position when I heard it – that long slow regular blast of the train. Usually Burner and I left a five-minute gap between the first guy and the next guy and I was sure that much time had already passed. When I heard the horn again, I knew I'd been waiting too long. There was nothing I could do so I just pulled myself up and tried to peek around the corner of the concrete as best I could. I kept staring down into the dark and I was shaking and shivering now because I was so scared and the sweat was turning cold on my skin. I wasn't sure if I should try and find some official person and tell them to radio in and watch for Burner, but there was no one around. I was actually hoping that he'd been caught on the other side, or that he'd chickened out, or come to his senses. I didn't want to think about the other possibility but it still came flashing into my head. For one second I imagined how even at top speed, there would still have to be this one moment, just before the full impact, when Burner would feel only the beginning of it, just that slight little nudge of cold metal pressing up against his skin.

When I heard the sound of his feet banging on the gravel, coming closer, I thought I must have been making it up. I couldn't see anything, but I stood in the opening and waved my light around anyway, shouting his name. For a second I thought I could just make him out in the distance, maybe a hundred yards away, but then the sound of the train blast rose up again and the whole rig came rolling around the last corner of the tunnel. I saw the big round light and it touched me and filled up the whole space, illuminating everything. I put my hand up like you do when you're trying to block out the sun and I saw him. Burner was there, charging toward me, the only dark space in front of the light. He had this long line of spit hanging out of his mouth like a dog and the look on his face wasn't fear, but something more like rage. The gap kept closing and it seemed to me like the big light was almost pushing him out. I emptied out my lungs yelling up against that bigger noise. I said, "Come on, come on," and I waved my whole arm in a big circle, as if I could scoop out the space between us and reel him in.

In the end, it wasn't as close as it seemed. Burner came up and around the corner and he kind of ran me over as I tried to catch him. We had about ten or fifteen seconds to spare before the train came roaring through and that was enough time for us to take off and scramble through the hole in the fence. We knew they'd be making their calls and trying to track us down, so we spent the next half hour running and hiding behind a few dumpsters and trying to make our way back to my car. We never had any time to talk about it until later that night when it became, like everything else in our pasts, a kind of joke. We called it "The night when Burner pulled a train out of his ass."

But that's the image I keep of him – Burner running in the light and getting away. That's the one I keep. For those few seconds, he was like one of those fugitives trying to break out of prison and they just couldn't catch him. The train kept coming down on him like some massive predator and he shouldn't have had a chance, but he was like that one stupid gazelle on the nature show, the one who somehow gets away even though the cheetahs or lions or hyenas should already be feasting. Burner was one of those fine-limbed lucky bastards, but he was still here and his life, like mine, kept rolling along, filling in all this extra time.

We got our stuff together and left the hotel at around four o'clock with our bags slung over our shoulders. We took a shuttle bus, one of those big coaches with dark tinted windows that ferried the athletes back and forth. On the day of any big race, those buses are tough places, crowded with all kinds of people who just want to be alone. The big-shouldered sprinters are the worst. You don't want to be anywhere near them in the last hours. For them it's going to be over in ten seconds, good or bad, so they don't have room to negotiate. You've seen them – some of those hundred-metre guys are built up like superheroes, or like those stone statues that are supposed to represent the perfect human form, but when the race gets close, everyone of them is scared. As Burner and I squeezed our way down the aisle, we passed this big black guy sitting by himself, completely cut off from everything else. He had the dark glasses on and the big headphones so that nothing could get in or out and he just kept rocking back and forth, slow and silent and always on the beat so you could almost see the music he was listening to. He looked like one of those ori-ental monks, swaying and praying and perfectly out of it.

Burner was at the jumpy stage now and he was nearly shaking because we were on our way and it seemed like things had already started. We dumped ourselves into an unoccupied row and right away he started drumming his hands on the seat in front of us.

"I am feeling it, feeling it," he said, almost singing, and he had this big goofy grin on his face. It was impossible for him to be still even for a second and he kept drumming along on the seat, hands blurring.

"It's the big one today, boys," he shouted, revving it up.

"Got to bring everything you got." Again, way too loud.

"No tomorrow."

The clichés dribbled out of him, but this wasn't the place for it. There were too many other people around and they all had their own things to take care of. After about a minute, the tall, long-haired javelin guy who'd been sitting in front of us got up and turned around like an angry bear up on his hind legs.

"You touch this chair again," he said, and he put his finger directly on the spot where Burner had been banging away on the back of the headrest. "You touch this chair again, and I swear to God, I will twist that skinny piece of shit neck right off your skinny piece of shit body."

You could tell this guy wasn't one of those macho body-builder, roid-raging throwers. He just wanted his quiet and needed his time like everybody else. You wouldn't know it by looking at them, but most of the throwers are like that, quiet and turned in. They try to make it look easy and some of them can spin a discus on their pinky finger like it's as light as a basketball, but if you watch you see they never let it go. Some of the others just sit there, rolling the shot from hand to hand, getting the feel for its heaviness as it thuds down into their chalky palms. Those guys are faster and smarter than you think. I heard someone say that all the best throwing performances come from guys with good feet and good heads. I bet the bear in front was one of the good ones. Burner couldn't retreat fast enough.

"I didn't think, man," he sort of stammered. "I didn't know you were there. Sorry. Sorry."

I looked the bear right in the eye, just like you're supposed to, and I tried to show him that I sympathized and understood. I said "Nerves" as if that single word could explain everything about Burner.

The guy nodded and he said he knew all about that but, come on. He wasn't happy, but eventually he settled back down, sort of deflating back into his seat.

When it was over, Burner gave me this wide-eyed look of relief and pretended to wipe the sweat off his forehead and fling it off to the side. Then he rested his head against the window and just watched the traffic going by.

I looked over at him and thought about all the buses we'd been on together. Almost since the early days as juniors, he'd been on every trip I had ever taken. At first, it was only short hops up to London and back or maybe Toronto, but after a while, as we kept at it and got better and better, we eventually hit the bigger circuits. Now we were only home four or five weekends a year and the rest of the time we were exactly like this, squished up against each other on a bus or on a plane, trying to sleep sitting up or trying to read our books under those little circular lights in the ceiling and always waiting for the next fast-food stop or bathroom break.

I used to think that a bus full of track people on their way to a meet was like one of those old fashioned circus trains, the kind that used to roll into a small town carrying the big top tent and pulling a bunch of different crazy looking cars, each one painted with curly red and gold swirls. You know the one I mean? In the Fisher Price version of that train, every animal gets his own car and the necks of the giraffes stick out through a hole in the roof. All the freak show people live in that train: the strongman with his curly moustache and Tarzan outfit; the little girl contortionist who can roll herself into a perfect circle; the guy who can take anybody's punch and never get hurt. I used to think that's what we were like, the track people. Each of us had one of those strange bodies designed to do only one thing. The lunatic high jumpers who talked to themselves could leap over their own heads, and if you gave the pole vaulters a good, strong stick, they could put themselves through a third-storey window. The long jumpers could leap over a mid-sized station wagon and the shot putters could bench press it. Even the fragile-looking, super-thin girls with their hair tied back in harmless looking pony tails. Those distance girls might be iron deficient and anorexic and maybe none of them have had a regular period in years, but they could all run a hundred and twenty miles in a week, almost a marathon a day. Those girls had pain thresholds that hadn't been discovered yet, and if they tried they could slow their heart rates down so far you'd actually have to wait between the beats. We all had our special skills, our fascinating powers, and we just barnstormed from city to city, performing them again and again in front of different people. Back when Burner and I started with this, every trip seemed like it was part of the tour, part of this bigger adventure, but I wasn't sure anymore. Sometimes I thought it might be better to be able to eat fire, or swallow a sword, or hang upside down on the trapeze and catch my cousin as he flung himself through the air.

The hydraulic door hissed open when we got to the stadium and everybody bounced off and split up into their natural groups. Burner and I blended in with a bunch of distance people we knew from other clubs and we checked the schedule to see if everything was running on time. The air was perfectly still and the temperature was right where we wanted it, just inching its way over toward cool. Burner breathed it in deeply through his nose and I caught the way he smiled his small, secret smile.

"You're going to have a good one today," I told him. Sometimes you can just recognize it in other people.

"Wait and see," he said. "I guess we'll find out soon enough."

That's what it's like when you taper down your training in the right way. There's just this weird feeling you get when you're finally ready to race. It's like you can barely keep your own body under control. In the beginning, when you're pounding through those early weeks of the training and building up your base, you can never get away from the ache of being so deep-down tired and you feel like you're slowly breaking down, right to the core of your last, smashed cell. Eventually though, time passes and you get used to it. Everything balances out and you can kind of reset yourself on this new, higher level. Then, when you get close to the competition, you cut your mileage right back almost to nothing and start sharpening up and taking lots of rest. It's the trickiest thing to do correctly, but if you can lighten up at exactly the right time then it all kind of reverses and the hurt you put in earlier comes back out as strength. All of a sudden you feel like you have more energy than you need and everything seems easier than it should be. That's where Burner was now. I could see it. You maybe get that feeling three or four times in your life, if you're lucky.

If I ever have kids, I think I'll let them participate in the grade school track meets when they're little, but that's it. Before it gets too serious, I'll move them over to something else like soccer, or basketball, or table tennis. Something with a team or something where you can put the blame on your equipment if it all goes wrong. But when my child is still little, I'm definitely going to push for the grade school track meet because it never gets better than that. In the grade school track meet, you give the kids one of those lumpy polyester uniforms and they turn all excited. They get the day off school and they get to cheer for their friends and maybe they get picked to be one of the four that runs the shiny baton all the way around the circle without dropping it. At the grade school track meet, they give out ribbons that go all the way down to the "participant" level, and if you do well, they read your name over the announcements at school so everybody will know about it. You get to pull on a borrowed pair of spikes and go pounding down that long runway before you jump into the sand. It's always hot and sunny and maybe your parents let you buy a drumstick or one of those overpriced red-white-and-blue popsicles from the acne-scarred high-school kid who has to ride around on a solid steel bicycle with a big yellow cooler stuck on the front. Maybe the girl with the red hair is there, the girl from the other school, the girl who wins all the longer races like you do. Maybe the newspaper takes a picture, you and the red-haired girl, standing on the top step of a plywood podium, holding all your first-place ribbons in the middle of a weedy field while all the dandelions are blowing their fuzzy heads off.

That's how it should always be. The stands should always be full of parents who don't know anything – people who can't tell the difference between what is really good and what is really bad – but they're there anyway, clapping and shouting their children's names, telling them to "go" and "go." You see why it's so nice. The lanes are crowded with kids clunking their way home to the finish line and trying so hard. They go sailing way over the high jump bar – it looks so easy and they come down on the other side, rolling softly into those big, blue, fluffy mats. It's sunny and everybody's laughing and everything is still new.

All that disappears when you get serious. At the very top end – and, when you come down to it, Burner and I were still far from the *real* top end – it's completely different. Everything starts to matter too much and too many things can go wrong and everybody knows the difference between what is really good and what is really bad. It comes back to the numbers. At the top end, we count it all up and measure it out and then we print the results so everybody can see. The guys I raced against were the mathematical totals of what they had done so far. That was it. Nobody cared about your goal or about what you planned to do in the future. It might take two full years of training to drop a single second or just a couple tenths off your personal best but you couldn't complain. We were all in the same boat. For us, every little bit less was a little bit more.

Really, it's the opposite of healthy. People will do anything to make those numbers go down. Some of them gobble big spoonfuls of straight baking soda before a race, even though they know it gives you this brutal, bloody diarrhea an hour later. That's nothing. It's even legal. They can't ban you for baking soda, but I know guys who cross over, guys juiced up on EPO and guys who just disappear for a year and then come back like superstars. They say they've been training at altitude on some mountain in Utah, but everybody knows they've been through the lab, getting their transfusions and playing around with their red blood cell count. Burner and I never did that, but we used to go to this vet, a guy who worked on the racehorses out at the track. If you came at night and brought him straight cash, he'd give you a bottle of DMSO and a couple of these giant horse pills that you were supposed to chop up into little chunks. It sounds bad, but this was all perfectly legal too. His stuff was nothing more than super-powerful aspirin delivered in massive doses. We'd go see him and he'd say, "Now you're going to have a big dinner and a full stomach before you touch this stuff, right?" and we'd lie and he'd give us what we wanted. As if he couldn't tell that none of us ever ate a full meal. I used to pop anti-inflammatories like they were candy love hearts, going through a handful of naproxen every day.

Even the dangerous cortisone injections in those big needles, the ones they fire right into that band of tough connective tissue at the bottom of your foot, I've had those. They say you're only supposed to take three of those in your whole life – that's all a regular person can handle – but the year before the trials, I got six in five months. I just kept going to different doctors, in different crowded clinics, guys who didn't know where I'd been two weeks earlier. It was the same thing every time. They'd go through their whole spiel again, and I'd pretend to pay close attention as they explained it all out.

"You can only get three of these," they'd say, "just three, you understand?"

I'd look and nod my head seriously and sometimes I'd even write the number down for them, a big loopy three on one of their little pads and I'd underline it. Then I'd hop right up onto their tissue-covered table, rip off my sock, stick out my fucked-up foot, and brace myself for number 4 or number 5 or whatever came next.

It always got bad before the biggest competitions like this one, or before the Olympic trials or if there was a big trip to China on the line or carding money. You'd get stuck with this feeling like when you're blowing up a balloon and you know you're almost at the limit and you're not sure if you should give it that little extra puff because there might still be room for a last bit of air, or it all might just explode in your face.

Burner and I started our warm-up jog about an hour before the race was scheduled to go. It took me a while to get started, and for those first few minutes I hobbled along doing the old-man shuffle until my body came back to me and my Achilles remembered what it was supposed to do. Burner was smooth right from the beginning. While I jerked up and down, fighting against the parts of myself that didn't want to do this anymore, he kind of hovered beside me flat and easy. We were like two people at the airport. He floated and seemed to move along without any effort – like one of those well-pressed, put-together guys who zooms past on the moving sidewalk – and I was like the slob with too many carry-on bags, huffing and puffing and dropping things, hauling all this extra stuff and just hoping to find the right gate. Even my breathing was heavier than it should have been.

We made a big loop out and around the stadium, winding our way up and down the quiet little side streets, past houses full of people who couldn't care less about what was happening just down the road. Burner and I had probably run thousands of miles together, but I was pretty sure these would be the last ones. I'd been thinking about it for a while, but I decided it there, during that last little warm-up jog. I think all those houses where nobody cared kind of forced themselves into my head.

"This is going to be it for me," I told him, after about fifteen minutes.

"What do you mean 'it'?"

"This is it. The last real ball-buster race for me. I think it's over. Time to get on with everything else."

It was easier than I thought it would be. All you had to do was say it. As soon as the words came out of my mouth, I felt better and calmer, but Burner didn't take it the same way.

"What?" he said, and he looked at me with this kind of confused sneer.

"Come on, Mikey. What else is there for you to do? You can't be finished. You've got lots more in the tank. You can't be one of those guys who gives it up and sits on the couch for a year eating chips and dip. You'll never be the guy in the fun run, the guy with a walkman, the loser who wants to win his age group. You can't just turn it off like that."

I felt bad for springing this on him at such a bad time. It hadn't been part of my big plan, but it's hard to hide it when something that used to be important suddenly isn't important anymore. I felt like I was kind of abandoning him, dumping him out there in the middle of those empty houses, and it was difficult and sad and correct all at the same time. Like when my mother and father finally broke up: difficult and sad, yes, but correct too, the right thing to do. Burner should have seen this coming from me. He could read the results sheets as well as I could, and he knew where my name fitted in.

"I've gone as far as I can," I told him. "You know you can't do this if you don't have the feel for it."

"Come on," he said, "you're kidding me."

He reached over without breaking stride and gave me a little shot in the arm like he was trying to wake me up and bring me back to the real world.

"Give your head a shake," he said. "Think about next year. You'll heal up and be back good as new."

We turned the corner and I could see the stadium coming back to us, getting bigger all the time. The stiffness was gone from my legs and I was rolling now, back to my old self, purring along. I felt fine, better than I had in months. The taper was giving something back to me too. But I was sure about this.

"Sorry, buddy," I kidded him. "You're going to have to find somebody else to kick down in the last hundred."

"Stop it," Burner said. He was looking at me hard. His lips pressed together and his mouth made a tight straight line across the middle of his face.

"Seriously. Stop it. You can't quit now. You and I do this together. That's our deal."

"No," I said, "it's not." I thought he already knew about this part of it. "We have never done this together. It's one of those things that can't be done together. In the end we have to be by ourselves."

I didn't want it to sound as bad as it did.

"Think about it," I was smiling now, trying to show him that everything would be fine. "Think about it. When you come around that turn today, you'll be alone, and when you head down the stretch by yourself you are going to surprise a lot of people."

"Fuck you, Mikey," he said. "I don't need a cheerleader."

His face was a little flushed and he turned on me quickly.

"You're just covering your own ass. In about twenty minutes, I'm going to rip you apart and you can't stand it. You can't stand to lose to me and now you're making excuses. Fuck you and your retirement party."

I wanted to laugh it off and make it slide away, but before I could even get to him, before I could say anything, he took off. Burner put his head down and shifted gears. In ten seconds, he had pulled away and opened up a gap that couldn't be closed. I had to save everything I had left and I couldn't go chasing after him so I let him go. It was just jitters, just nerves. That's what I told myself. After it was over, everything would be fine again.

When we got back to the field we split for good. He grabbed his spikes and his bag and went under the bleachers by himself. The last fifteen minutes are the most important. You want everything to feel easy. I put him out of my mind and lay on my back for a while, feeling the air coming in and going out of my body. I pulled my knees up close to my chest and wrapped my arms around my legs. I held it all in like that for about fifteen seconds before letting everything go as slowly as possible. I rolled over on my stomach and did a few easy push-ups, and when I got back on my feet, I put my hands flat against the wall and tried to get my calves and my goddamn Achilles to go out as far as they could. I didn't want to push it because you can only take as much as your body can give you on the day. I took off my socks and put on the ugly fluorescent spikes I'd been wearing all season. They were another Adidas freebie and I was expected to wear them, but I didn't like them much. It had taken months to break them in, and the red blood stains were still there around the toe and heel from all the broken blisters I had to go through before my feet finally hardened up in the right places.

When the announcer's voice called us out, I took off my sweats and did a couple of short sprints down the back stretch, trying to keep it all quick and smooth and under control. All the rest of the guys were there too, and we did our usual nervous hellos and our cautious smiles as we passed one another. When they called us to the line, I came up behind Burner and put my hand on his back, just kind of gently, so he'd know I was there.

"Have a good one, buddy, you little psycho," I said, and I smiled at him. The officials made us stand there, side by side, each of us in our pre-selected spot along the curved white start line while the announcer read out our names and listed all our best times and our biggest wins. He said this was shaping up to be one of the best 1500 metre finals of the last decade. When the voice got to my name, he said I had the fastest personal best in this group and he named all the different times I'd made the national team. He said Burner was always dangerous and that he had put together a great season and was rounding into top form at the right time. Then the rest of them each got their turns and their compliments, Marcotte and Graham and Bourque and the others.

Burner stood still through all of this and didn't even acknowledge his own name. Instead, he closed his eyes and made this big production out of rolling his head all the way around in a big circle. He went very slowly – first down, with his chin touching his chest, and then way over to the side and then straight up and back again. I could hear the bones in his neck crackling as he made the loop. He kept his mouth wide open, and when he looked up it seemed almost like he was waiting to catch a snowflake or a raindrop on his tongue. They called us to our marks and we crouched down, bending our knees just a bit and holding our arms away from our bodies. When they fired the gun, you could see the smoke before you heard the bang.

The announcer's voice took over after that and he described everything that happened to us. We were bunched up around the first turn so I made a little move and went into second place, just trying to stay out of trouble. Even as it was happening, the voice said, "There goes Michael Campbell, moving into second place, staying out of trouble." It was like being inside and outside of yourself at the same time. I kept bumping back and forth with Marcotte and Bourque, trying to settle myself down and find a clear place on the outside of lane one. All the time the big voice kept going, describing how we looked and calling out the splits and telling the crowd what kind of pace we were on and our projected finishing times. I couldn't see Burner, but I knew he was close by because I heard the voice say something like "Jamie Burns is safely tucked in at fifth or sixth place." I remember this only because the announcer used Burner's real name and it sounded so strange to me.

The pace was fine, not too fast, not too slow, and after a lap and a half there were still lots of people close enough to the lead and feeling good. The problem with feeling good in a 1500 is that you know it can't last and that eventually, sometime in the next ninety seconds, everything you have left has got to come draining out of you, either in a great explosive rush at the end or some painful slow trickle. The kickers would've been happy to let it go slow and leave it all to some blazing last one-fifty, but the rest of us didn't want that to happen. As we went through 800, most of the serious guys were looking around, waiting and watching to see who would make the first move. After about thirty seconds, Dawson decided it would have to be him. He threw in this big surge coming off the turn and broke the whole thing open, dividing the race up between those who could go with him and those who could not.

The voice said, "Eric Dawson is heading for home early."

Graham and Bourque and I hooked up a couple steps back and it felt like we were breaking free of the others. I never turn around when I race and everybody knows it's not a good idea to look back, but I was sure Burner must have been close by. Even then it was clear that Dawson didn't have a chance. He'd given it a pretty fierce try and the rest of us probably owed him something for being brave enough to go, but he didn't have enough left and I could see he was starting to break down.

People in the crowd always wonder why the guy with the lead heading into the last lap almost never wins. They wonder why he can't hold on and why he can't look as good as he did just a minute earlier when he came flying by. Some people believe that myth about Roger Bannister and John Landy back when they ran the Miracle Mile in Vancouver in 1954. That was probably the only time in history when the whole world actually cared about two guys who could run a mile in under four minutes. Bannister was the first to do it, everybody knows that, but by the time they met in Vancouver, Landy had gone even faster. He was the new world record holder and most people were betting on him to win. You can look it up if you want. The Miracle Mile was pure craziness, like the Tyson/ Holyfield of its time. Every country sent their reporters to cover the story and more than a hundred million people listened to the call on the radio. It was the first time CBC Television ever broadcasted live from the west coast. If you go to Vancouver today, the famous statue is still there, the one where Landy is looking over his left shoulder as Bannister comes by him on the right. The press and people who don't know anything always say that if Landy had looked the other way – if only he'd looked to the right – he would have seen Bannister coming and he never would have let him go by. They call it the phantom pass, as if Landy was just a victim of bad luck and bad timing. As if Bannister was like some ghost, slipping past unseen.

That's the story they tell, but it's not true. If you ever watch a tape of that race you'll see that poor Landy is dead before he even starts the last lap. It's one of those things you recognize if you've been through it yourself. When a guy is done, he's just done and no amount of fighting can save him. The exercise physiology people will explain that it's all about lactic acid fermentation and how when you push beyond your limit your legs run out of oxygen and the tissue starts to fill up with this burning liquid waste. We called it "rigging," short for rigor mortis. When your body started to constrict, to tighten up involuntarily, first in your arms and your calves and then your quads and your hamstrings and your brain – when parts of you gave out like that, dying right underneath you at exactly the moment you needed something more – we called that rigging. At the end of a mile, everybody is rigging, everybody is dying, just at different speeds. Dawson was dying in front of us that day and we could see it in every broken down step he took. Just like Landy was dying in front of Bannister fifty years before and he knew it too. Look back at the grainy black and white video of the Miracle Mile. You'll see it. Landy wasn't taken by surprise. He knew exactly where Bannister was coming from – he just couldn't do anything to stop it. For that whole last lap Bannister is right behind, tall and gangly and awkward and just waiting, deciding when to go. When Landy looked to his left – in that moment they made into a statue – he wasn't trying to hold on for the win. That possibility was gone and he knew it. No, Landy was looking out for the next guy; he was trying to hold on to second and not to fall even farther back. People forget that Richard Ferguson, a Canadian, finished third in the Miracle Mile. He's the important missing character, the one who didn't make it into the statue. Ferguson was the threat coming up from behind; he was the guy Landy feared. It's always like that. The most interesting stories in most races don't have anything to do with winning.

Dawson was almost shaking when we came by him. The last lap was going to be a death march for him. Graham and Bourque and I went past in a single step and there was nothing left in Dawson to go with us.

The voice said, "Graham, Bourque, Campbell. It will be decided by these three."

I couldn't believe I was still in it and feeling OK. Graham looked like he was getting ready to drop the hammer and put an end to this, but as we headed down the final back stretch Bourque seemed a little wobbly, and for about five seconds I thought I had a real shot at bringing him down and getting myself in there for second and a spot on the team. I was just about to release my own kick, trying to gauge how much I had left and deciding how I could fit it into that last 250 metres. I got up on my toes and I was getting ready to charge when I felt this hand reach out and touch the middle of my back, kind of gently, just a tap so I'd know he was there. I looked to my right and Burner came roaring by with his tongue hanging out and that enraged look in his eyes.

The voice said, "Look at that. Burns is making a very strong move."

I understand that sometimes people get their priorities mixed up. And I know that when you give yourself over completely to just one thing, you can lose perspective on the rest of the world. That's a feeling I know. I think it's what happens to those old ladies who donate their life savings to corrupt televangelists or to those pilgrims in the Philippines who compete for the honour of being nailed, actually hammered, to a cross for their Easter celebrations. We have to scrounge for meaning wherever we can find it and there's no way to separate our faith from our desperation. You see it everywhere. Football hooligans, scholars of Renaissance poetry, fans of heavy metal music, car buffs, sexual perverts, collectors of all kinds, extreme bungee jumpers, lonely physicists, long distance runners, and tightly wound suburban housewives who want to make sure they entertain in just the right way. All of us. We can only value what we yearn for and it really does not matter what others think.

This is why I cannot expect you to understand that when Jamie Burns came past me and started up that now infamous kick which won him the national title in the 1500 metres – his wild, chased-by-the-train sprint that carried him around me, past Bourque and all the way up to Graham – I cannot expect you to understand that when this happened, I was caught up, caught up for the first and only time in my life, in one of those pure ecstatic surges that I believed only religious people ever experienced. Even as it unfolded in front of me and I watched Graham hopelessly trying to hold him off, I knew I had never wanted anything more than this, just to see Burner come up even and then edge his way forward in those last few steps and come sailing across the line with both his hands in the air. I did not care that this was such a small thing or that it could be shared with so few. I knew only that this event, this little victory mattered to me in some serious way that was probably impossible to communicate. I didn't pray for it to happen, because there would be nobody to receive a prayer like that. But I did wish for it and even the wish told me something I had never known about myself before. We are what we want most and there are no miracles without desire. That's why a mom can lift a car off her child after the accident and a guy can survive a plane crash and live in the woods for a week drinking only the sweat wrung from his socks. That's how Burner won that race, by miraculous desperation.

If you are not the person who wins, then the finish line of a 1500 can be a crowded place. There are bodies collapsing and legs giving out and people wandering around with dazed and exhausted looks on their faces. Burner's kick caught everybody by surprise. Even the announcer lost control of the story. For the last fifty metres he just kept shouting, "Will you look at that. Look. It's Burns at the end. Look."

I'd been so busy watching that nothing changed for me. I ended up exactly where I was before and never got past Bourque. I finished fourth, the worst place to be, but it was still more than I expected. People from the paper were taking pictures as I walked over to Burner. When he turned around we both just started laughing and shaking our heads.

"You bastard," I said, and I pounded both my fists against his shoulders. "Where did that come from? How in the hell . . ."

"No idea," he said. "I thought I was out of it, but I decided to go in the end and everything else just happened."

Other people, strangers I had never seen before, were coming around slapping him on the back and giving their congratulations. The whole place was still kind of quivering because no one had ever seen a guy come back from being that far down. Every eye was on Burner and everyone was talking about that last stretch and trying to find a place for it in their own personal histories.

One of the drug officials came over and took Burner away to go pee in his cup and prove that everything was natural. As he was being led off, he turned back and told me to wait for him.

"You're going to be busy," I said. "Forget it."

"Just wait," he said.

For those next fifteen minutes, I was kind of stuck between two different versions of myself. I wandered back over to my bag and started to get dressed again. I looked around the track and it seemed like this big chunk of my past was kind of crystallizing behind me and freezing into permanence. Whatever the next thing would be was still way ahead, indistinct and foggy, and I had no idea what it would look like. I pulled off those ugly spikes and in a mock-dramatic moment I tossed them into a garbage can.

"Good riddance," I said, and I just stood there for a while feeling the cool grass on my bare feet.

Burner came jogging back from his test soon after that, but every step he took there was somebody else there shaking his hand and patting the top of his bald head. All around him people were smiling and a couple of younger kids asked for his autograph and wanted to get their pictures taken with him. Burner drank it in like one of those actors standing on the red carpet before the Oscars begin, and even though it took him a while to make it across the track, he kept looking up at me every couple of seconds, letting me know that I was still the final destination and our planned warm-down was still going to take place.

When he finally made it over he had this ridiculously huge grin on his face and he kind of shrugged his shoulders.

"What can you do?" he said. "It's all crazy."

"Did they get your pee?" I asked. "Everything okay in that department?"

"No problem," he said.

He pulled on a dry T-shirt and his own pair of high-tech sweatpants and said he was ready to go.

When we made it out of the stadium everything quieted down very quickly. The announcer's voice had moved on to the final of the women's 100 hurdles and we could just barely hear him as we turned away and went backwards along the same streets we had run earlier. Whenever you do that – go back along the same course, but in the opposite direction – it's strange how some scenes are so familiar while others look so completely different you wonder how you missed them the first time around. It's just the change in perspective, but sometimes, especially when you're in a foreign city, you can get yourself pretty disoriented and lost. Then you have to slow down and look around and try to locate a recognizable landmark before you can be sure you're on the right track.

Burner and I fell into a nice rhythm right away and our feet clipped along almost in unison. We went back past all those houses where nobody cared and it felt fine and comfortable. Our breathing was the only conversation and it said that we were both relaxed and taking it easy. Some of the neighbourhood kids were still out shooting baskets in their driveways and practising tricks with their skateboards.

We just floated down those anonymous sidewalks and carved our way though the maze of minivans and garbage cans. We made a turn and were just about to head back to the stadium when a bunch of kids came streaking past us on their bikes.

There were four or five of them, a couple of boys and a couple of girls, probably between the ages of seven and nine. Real kids, not yet teenagers. One of the boys almost hit us as he went by and another one kept trying to jump his BMX up and down over the driveway cut-outs of the curb. There was a girl on a *My Little Pony* bike. She had multicoloured beads on all her spokes and red and white streamers trailing back from her handlebars. Her hair was wispy and blond. As she came by, she turned around and yelled, "I'm faster than you are." She sort of sang it in a mean, bratty way, using the same up-and-down teasing music that accompanies every "nah, nah, nah, nah, nah."

"You can't catch me," she said, and she stuck her tongue out and pedalled harder. Her pink shoes swivelled around in circles.

One of the boys, a kid wearing a tough-looking camouflage T-shirt, zipped around us and swerved in tight to cut me off. As he pulled away, he shot us the finger and said, "Nice tights, loser."

I glanced over at Burner and said "Let it go," but it was too late. His face was tightening up and that angry stare was coming back into his eyes. He wasn't looking at me.

"Hey," he yelled, and you could feel the edges hardening around that one little syllable. He pulled ahead of me and started tracking them down. I was caught unprepared and a step behind and I couldn't figure out how we had managed to arrive at this point. Burner was charging again and the kids were running. They didn't know. There was no way on earth they could have known. The little girl was pedalling as fast as she could and there was this strange, high-pitched, wheezing sound coming out of her, but there was nothing she could do. Burner had already closed the gap and his hand was already there, reaching out for the thin strands of her hair. It all disintegrated after that. He must have been a foot taller than the oldest one.

YASUKO THANH

FLOATING LIKE THE DEAD

Cleaning his ear with a long stalk of grass, Ah Sing filled his wood stove with kindling. Alder leaves were fluttering in the trees, displaying their yellow undersides, which meant rain. Ah Sing shivered but did not light the fire; instead, he put a rough wool jacket over his cotton shirt. His room had no hooks but all his clothing was tidily folded and stacked on the wooden stool in the corner by the door. On top of the clothes he laid a few bone-white sticks. Sun-bleached, lighter than the pine branches he had originally whittled down for his kite, the driftwood would make a good frame. He sneezed and shivered again. He had lost his upper incisor yesterday.

The nerves of Ah Sing's arms and legs had grown hard as jade; he was turning into a mountain, solidifying. Even his face was like a palace statue. Smooth. Hairless. Varnished-looking. He had lost his eyelashes and three-quarters of his eyebrows; and lately, his ulcerated feet left tracks of blood on the wood floor. But he refused to wear the government-issue overshoes. His extremities felt no heat, no cold, no pain, anyway. In the next life he would be a mountain, the mountain he was now turning into, eternal and hard.

He had wept at the official diagnosis of leprosy.

"They sick but I not," Ah Sing would say in English to the doctors who accompanied the steamer *Alert* to the island and took flakes of skin from the backs of his hands. (Speaking English was masonry work, the words like bricks laid by hands; he spoke Cantonese with the other men on the colony, and the words flowed easily then, even when they had nothing to say.) His lost fingers, he explained to the doctors, "Coal mine in Nanaimo. Frostbite." He had difficulty pronouncing the word and it came out sounding like "flossed bite." Grunting once or twice, he would pry an oyster off a stone with his remaining fingers and hold it up.

"You send away Ah Sing," he always said to the visiting doctors, "back to China."

Today Ah Sing had fallen asleep on the beach next to his half-eaten lunch of sea urchins. Awoken by the sound of birds near his head, he had opened his eyes and was startled to see four black cormorants flying away. They reminded him of something: the cormorants he had felt sorry for when he was six years old and had laughed at by the age of nine, black birds circling the ancient uplifted seabeds in Chongwu Bay, catching fish they could taste but never swallow because of the white choke collars around their necks.

Three men left on D'Arcy Island now. They lived in the main building. Four cubicles side by side, each with its own door that opened onto a verandah facing Cordova Bay. Ge Shou hadn't been right in the head since a tree fell on him, and he spent his nights in the woods singing. Gold Tooth, who had never told Ah Sing his real name, cried all day and then sat at the edge of the forest, dulled and deadened, refusing to move. He had a cough that possessed him like a malevolent spirit, wracking his body until he spat blood. He was the newest resident.

Gold Tooth had arrived at the colony three years ago with his bowler hat and a Swiss pocket watch on a chain. Slipping on patches of seagrass in leather shoes, over barnacle-covered stones still wet from the tide, refusing any attempts at help from the government official from Victoria. Ah Sing had laughed at his vanity, but the watch – the watch – was as round as an eye. He stared at it until he felt like he was staring into a thousand tiny suns.

When they had the energy, Ah Sing and Ge Shou said they would murder the filthy thief while he slept. But the daily chores sapped their passion, the harvesting of clams and mussels, the chopping of firewood, the collection of rainwater from below the eaves or in the summer from the bog. Most days, when Ah Sing had finished, he would sit on the boulders that ringed the bay and watch the waves, pondering Buddha's question: *How does one stop a drop of water from ever drying out?*

Now, in his room, Ah Sing picked up his Buck knife and eyed the driftwood. He was searching for the most evenly balanced of sticks. He would carve the exact spaces needed to neatly wedge two smaller sticks into either side. He would wrap the joints with sewing thread. He would cut a tail to look like phoenix wings, or find some cormorant feathers on the beach to stand in their place.

As curly shavings collected around his feet, he remembered how, as a child, he had believed the most ornate kites could talk to the spirits. His thoughts were interrupted by the sound of something heavy being dragged across a wooden floor. A sob. Another. He dropped his knife.

Gold Tooth was on the verandah, dappled light sifting through the fir trees and falling in shadows across his back. It was hard to tell which were shadows and which were stains, for Ah Sing could not remember when Gold Tooth had last taken off the silk suit he wore. Gold Tooth's face was flushed with terror and his eyes darted like birds in the trees, afraid of being caught.

"Take it easy. What are you doing with your bed?"

Gold Tooth shook off Ah Sing's hand like a dog shakes off water. He heaved the cot against the doorframe, where it got stuck. "I can't breathe," he said. "I can't breathe in there. The walls. They'll try to crush me if, if I go to sleep." He yanked. He stumbled backward.

"Do you want me to hold up the walls while you pull your bed outside?"

Gold Tooth stopped.

Ah Sing squeezed over the straw mattress and into the room. Half-eaten plates of food had been scattered from one side to the other by raccoons. The air smelled like yeast.

Ah Sing, his legs shoulder-width apart, spread his arms wide against the two walls and held them with his clawed hands so they wouldn't crush Gold Tooth, who unhinged the bed from the doorway and wrestled it outside.

On the verandah, Gold Tooth nodded toward the forest. He motioned to Ah Sing. "Pick up that end," he said.

The two men carried the wooden bed with the straw mattress past roaming chickens and beyond the storage shed with the rice, sugar, flour, meal, gardening tools, and coffins. They carried the bed beyond the vegetable garden. Past three graves, each marked with a pile of stones – the resting places of the men who had arrived with Ah Sing when the provincial government had left them on this island four years ago with a load of construction supplies. They carried it past the bog and into the forest. Ge Shou followed them, chattering.

"Do you have any pigs' feet for me?" Ge Shou asked. Ah Sing shook his head.

"Can we fly your kite?"

"When it's ready, I promise."

"Washing Matilda, washing Matilda," Ge Shou sang, "who'll come a-washing Matilda with me?" He stopped and stretched his arms above his head. "Are you going swimming tonight, Sing, you going swimming in the ocean?"

"No, not tonight."

"Swimming, swimming." Ge Shou made breaststroke motions. "Swimming in the ocean. I feel happy. Washing Matilda, you'll come a-washing Matilda with me?"

Ah Sing and Gold Tooth set the bed down in a clearing among the ferns and salal, where the ground was soft with pine needles. Through the trees they could see the ditch system that ran from the bog to the garden, where they grew lettuce, potatoes, carrots, and onions; Ge Shou playing among the vegetables. Gold Tooth shuddered onto his bed and immediately rolled onto his side as if in a deep sleep.

Ah Sing shook his shoulder.

"Go away."

———

After sitting near Gold Tooth for a time, Ah Sing came to a decision. He shuffled past the crops, spoiled before men with waning appetites had been able to eat them, and the pigs rooting in the waste. He nodded to Ge Shou, who sat among the pigs. He passed the site where they would soon start an orchard.

Back in his cabin, Ah Sing filled his shoulder basket with a Hudson's Bay blanket, a cast-iron kettle, a wok, a dead grouse, a handful of onions, some mint leaves, a cupful of cooking oil in a canning jar, and some government-issue opium. Returning to Gold Tooth, he touched his shoulder again. Gold Tooth grunted.

Ah Sing opened the blanket over him; then he placed stones in a circle on the ground around some kindling and lit a fire with the wooden matches in his pocket. He emptied his shoulder basket, picked up the kettle, and went to the wood shed, filling his shoulder basket again. The load weighed him down. He trod to the bog, sinking deep into the mud. He dipped his kettle, filling it with brown water. When he came back, neither of the men spoke, but Ah Sing didn't mind. He added more branches to the fire and set the kettle upon it.

A few minutes later, Gold Tooth said, "Why do you talk to me?"

Ah Sing shrugged. Before the disease had made his threats to beat up the other men laughable, Gold Tooth had hoarded the best rations, stashing second barrels of salt pork in his cubicle while the others looked on with mask-like eyes. But Ah Sing, at fifty-two, had himself hit a woman; had fondled the flesh of his brother's wife; had ignored the unemployed after the smelters closed; had beaten a man when he was drunk while onlookers cheered. He sat cross-legged by the fire, poking the embers with a stick. He felt feverish, strange. Far away through the trees, he could hear Ge Shou singing.

Ah Sing poured the oil into the wok and dried the canning jar with the hem of his shirt. He put two stalks of mint inside it and some of the opium. The mint grew wild near the bog. Ah Sing usually hung it from his cabin's ceiling. He poured the boiling water into the canning jar. He wrapped a green maple leaf around it and passed the jar to Gold Tooth, but Gold Tooth pushed it away.

Ah Sing put the jar on the ground. The steam rose and scented the air with mint. He fussed over the flames, moving the kettle to make room for the wok. He busied himself with the onions and the grouse he had killed just that morning with his shotgun until the aroma rose into the air, overpowering the mint.

"I used to be a cook, you know," Ah Sing said. "I worked for Mr. and Mrs. Edward Price in Victoria."

"Shit work."

Ah Sing moved coals and added more kindling to adjust the heat. He rotated the wok and stirred its contents with a stick, testing the mixture frequently and inhaling its scent with his eyes closed.

Gold Tooth turned to him and snorted. "Look down. Your hand."

"Oh," Ah Sing said. "I've burned myself."

A patch of flesh two inches wide was stuck to the outside of the wok.

"No one will notice. Look at your face. Have you looked in a mirror lately?"

When the food was ready, Ah Sing placed the wok down between them. Gold Tooth eyed the food with a strange appetite Ah Sing had not seen in weeks. Ah Sing chewed in silence, watching Gold Tooth eat; his clawed fingers, scooping the mixture into his mouth, were like fingers made of tree bark or elephant's hooves – strange but beautiful.

"It gets easier," Ah Sing said.

"I'm not a leper."

"No one wants to believe they are. I'll tell you something. I'm going to escape. I've got to go back to China. To my son and wife."

Gold Tooth gave a disgusted grunt. "Has anyone escaped before?"

Ah Sing didn't answer. He told Gold Tooth he'd heard that two lepers had been shipped in a crate by the CPR as far west as Saskatchewan, and he thought they'd been deported. "My son," Ah Sing said, changing the subject, "my son would be eighteen years old now. He was five the last time I saw him. It would be good if he could come to Gold Mountain. He would find work."

They sat looking at each other while dusk fell. Neither one said a word. Ah Sing cracked open grouse bones and sucked out the marrow. Gold Tooth lay on his back and smoked tobacco from the supply ship. The fire had turned to coals and the coals had turned ashy before Gold Tooth spoke.

"I used to get all the girls. Best one's name was Zao. I called her 'Zao,' *chirp*, because of the sound she made when we had sex. On hot nights she ran ice cubes up and down my spine, and on cold nights she tickled me with cotton balls. When I couldn't sleep, she massaged my feet while humming Strauss.

She polished my shoes and every morning brought me my gambling spreadsheets. The way she pencilled in her eyebrows. I'm going to give you a piece of advice. Only hit a woman when she needs it, and only with an open hand. You got to keep them in their place because they want it. You have to answer their questions for them, that's love."

"Did she turn you in?" Ah Sing asked.

"No!" Then after a moment he said, "They raided the Kwong Wo & Company Store; we were in the back, gambling."

It was pitch-black now. Ah Sing drew a stick through the ashes. The bark caught an ember and he blew at the small flame. He threw on more kindling until the wood crackled. The only light came from the small campfire; its shadows highlighted the heavy ridges of Gold Tooth's overgrown brow.

"When I was a kid I found this bottle with a note inside," Gold Tooth continued. "It'd washed up from Taiwan," he said. "Funny thing is, I don't remember what the letter said. It was a wide, fat bottle, like a medicine bottle. It was dull, scratched up by the rocks. I remember grabbing it and trying to open it while the older boys were gambling by the fishboats, and then it started to rain and I ran under an overturned dory. I tried to untwist the lid but it was rusted closed. Then I tried to get it off with a broken clam. I ended up smashing the neck off. I remember the bottle, but not the message. Strange, huh?"

Ah Sing drew his knees up to his chest. "Memory is a funny thing."

"I wonder what it said. Was it a love letter from some guy? Who knows? I don't remember."

Ah Sing didn't answer.

"I remember lots of other things. Swimming in the Zhu Jiang

River. Ducks and geese. I ate lily roots. I loved water chestnuts and dates. Have you been to the hills of Guangxi? Limestone towers. I would visit my uncle and play in the fish ponds."

Gold Tooth turned on his side, away from Ah Sing, and curled up in the fetal position. Ah Sing's mother had turned on her side and died facing the wall. She had first lain in bed talking about her childhood, but when the sun rose, she had turned inward and fallen silent.

"In Canton the laundry waved like flags. We threw cats into the fetid canals. I had no parents. Stole food from the seething mass living on boats along the waterfront. Ran through the alleys making cutthroat signs at people and they feared me. I grew up to be a Tong, never did any grunt work. Laundry, houseboy, gardener. Never did any of that. I'm in extortion."

An hour or so later, Gold Tooth started to cry, softly, under his breath. He mumbled something inaudible.

"What?"

"Will you send my bones back to China?"

Ah Sing sat up.

"You know the worst thing about it?"

"What?"

"I never knew her real name."

"Who?"

"First it was the cotton balls, I couldn't feel them. Then I couldn't feel the suit against my skin. This is my best suit. My best suit."

"I called her Zao," he said. He started sobbing.

Ah Sing dozed in the forest to the sound of Gold Tooth's laboured breathing. The stretches between his exhalations grew longer, as if each breath was becoming too precious to release. Another and another. He clutched the life within him and refused to unleash it, greedily holding the air for ten seconds at a time, fifteen, twenty.

Ah Sing dreamed a man with a roomful of rice was trying to make him swallow it all, and awoke choking. Gold Tooth's eyes appeared fixed on an immature bald eagle circling overhead, and in the dawn light he almost looked alive. Ah Sing rubbed his clawed hands vigorously over his own cheeks. He closed Gold Tooth's eyelids and touched the man's chest. He felt along the body, found the Swiss pocket watch and slipped it into his own pocket. An object valuable enough to buy passage off the island, maybe even to pay the deportation costs back to China. Ah Sing couldn't see clearly and stumbled toward the ocean, moving branches away from his face through the brush.

He ran to the beach, to the emergency flag on the hill.

The Victoria Tug Company steamer *Alert* delivered quarterly supplies: tea, dried fish, axes, razors, handkerchiefs, and, in the last load, a looking glass. It was surprising to see the tug so soon; often they would raise the flag and no one would show up for weeks.

Ah Sing had fought to bury Gold Tooth in his silk suit, but Ge Shou had slipped away with the jacket. So when the boat came, Ah Sing was digging alone, near the bog, past the vegetable garden where the ground was soft, and far enough away from Ah Sing's cabin that even a spirit as restless as Gold Tooth's couldn't haunt him.

As the steamer cut through the chop, Ah Sing flung a last shovel of soil onto the coffin. Then, brushing his hands

together, he scrambled down the gravelled slope to the shore,
pebbles tumbling away from the edges of his footsteps. He
watched as a dory was lowered from the boat, loaded with
supplies, and rowed toward the shore.

Ah Sing grabbed hold of the wooden dory with two men
aboard, helping to pull it onto the beach. A man with a red
moustache that hid his upper lip got out of it with the doctor.

The doctor straightened his back.

"Good, sir. Still strong, see?" Ah Sing said, lifting a barrel
from the bottom of the boat.

Ah Sing recounted what had happened the night before. The
doctor pulled a bag from the dory and withdrew a ledger of
dates, names, and other notes. He looked down his spectacles.

"The one you call . . . Go Chou?"

"No, sir."

"Fong Wah Yuen."

Ah Sing nodded.

The doctor wrote something on his ledger and turned
toward the main building. When he was halfway up the slope,
Ah Sing tilted his head toward a termite-filigreed log to indi-
cate he wished a word with the other man, whom the doctor
had introduced as a reporter. The man's pants were cinched
high upon his waist. He took two steps toward the log and
stood, smoothing his hands over his thighs.

Ah Sing stepped over to the log and sat down. His mouth
was dry. The man was smiling, but his gaze jumped from Ah
Sing to a spot beyond his head, then back to Ah Sing, then to
the doctor stumbling up the gravel slope. The man did not sit.

Ah Sing cleared his throat. "I favour you . . . no, me . . . no,
you favour me." The disease in his larynx made his voice no

more than a loud whisper. "I, I have something." He stood up and pulled the Swiss watch from his pocket, where he had been clutching it so tightly that it was slick with sweat. He wiped it against the leg of his pants. He dangled it between them, letting it catch the sun.

"This is for you," Ah Sing said.

"Look at that." The man scratched his head and smiled.

"Nice, yes?"

The man nodded. "This is a nice island," he said, rubbing the back of his neck. He looked from the boulders that ringed one side of the bay to the mud flats on the other. He glanced at the doctor, who was talking to Ge Shou at the main building. "I hear you men hunt, and fish, too."

"You take."

"No." The man's moustache brushed his bottom lip when he smiled. "I don't think I should."

"No," Ah Sing nodded his head. "For you."

The man looked down at the watch.

"But is gift."

The man fingered his eyebrows.

"Gift," Ah Sing repeated. "A gift for you. Your wife?"

On the verandah of the cabin, Ge Shou danced, circling the doctor, his long black ponytail bouncing on his back.

A sudden gust of wind blew the reporter's hat off his head. It rolled a few feet, snagged on a log, then rolled again with the next gust. The man chased it but Ah Sing bounded ahead, stopping the hat with his bare foot. Ah Sing dusted off the sand and shards of clamshell. He held the hat toward the man.

"Oh. Well, then." The man inched his fingertips forward. "Thank you."

The man took his hat between his thumb and forefinger and walked to the dory. Leaning into the boat, he dropped the hat onto one of its wooden benches. He grabbed a heavy sack. Ah Sing did the same. Sack after sack, barrel after barrel, crate after crate, the two men, Ah Sing and the reporter, worked in this way until they were done unloading. When the man began rolling a barrel up the beach toward the slope, his shoes slapping on the gravel, Ah Sing rushed after him.

"Gift, you help me. Gift," he said, his throat tightening so he could not swallow. "Please, please, you take." He pushed out a laugh. It felt like choking on a ball of rice. "You remember Ah Sing to the CPR."

The man stopped, his eyes focused on Ah Sing for the first time, clear blue eyes the colour of frozen ponds in the spring when the ice cracks. Ah Sing was sure he heard the man sigh. The man shifted his weight from one foot to the other and rubbed his wiry eyebrows that shot straight up. Ah Sing held the watch in his open palm.

He imagined slapping it into the man's hand. The man would laugh and throw it over his shoulder; it would shatter into a thousand golden pieces.

"It *is* a beautiful timepiece," the man said.

"Yes, beautiful," Ah Sing answered. His throat was a bird's throat, filled with small stones.

"A gift, you take."

The man smiled. "Right, then. Thank you." The man dropped it almost without touching it into his jacket pocket.

Then he said, "Look, man, look what I have here." He undid the buttons of his tweed jacket and fished around in the breast pocket of his blue shirt, the same colour as his eyes.

"Here, look at this. This is a Kruger coin. It's all the way from the South African Republic."

Ah Sing raised what was left of his eyebrows.

"I've got some others at home, a pocketful, in fact. But they're rare, quite rare, in spite of that. You'd have to go all the way to the South African Republic; I came back with them after the Boer War." The man stopped and buffed the coin against his chest. "If you would take this to show my appreciation."

Ah Sing stared at it. He felt an ache in the bottom of his stomach. It grew worse. He would vomit. He knew it. His legs tensed, waiting for it. He imagined running. Running. The man would start chasing him. Would throw handfuls of Kruger coins. They would hit him on the back, handful after handful. Stinging, like golden hail. What a silly, infuriating man. Ah Sing could decorate his cabin. He could use them as sinkers when he fished.

Ah Sing held the coin between his thumb and forefinger. He spat on its tarnished surface.

The man widened his eyes.

"Superstition. It bring more money when spit. Bring good luck."

"Oh," the man said. He clapped his hands together. "Well, then."

Far from shore, the steamer bobbed in the chop. A crow cawed. The waves tumbled.

The man walked to the dory and Ah Sing followed. Reaching in, the man picked up his hat from where it lay. It was a green plaid cheese cutter, wool, with yellow and orange stripes. Under the leather strap at the back he had tucked some heron feathers, and for an instant Ah Sing was reminded of the ladies of Victoria who had worn hats adorned with enough feathers to drive certain birds to extinction. These wealthy of Victoria who had called men like Ah Sing their "Celestials." Romanticizing their roast duck, their porcelain figurines for sale in every Chinatown store, their opium pipes.

The man held his hat out to Ah Sing. "Do you like this hat?"

"It's fine hat."

"Take it."

Ah Sing walked with the coin in his pocket where the watch had been and the hat on his head, counting his footsteps as he rolled the barrel up the slope. He fought against quick breaths, trying not to hyperventilate. He stacked the barrel in the storage shed next to the coffins and the axes.

He was walking toward the cabin, looking at the ground, when something hit his shoulder. He looked up. A heron in the fir tree. He looked at the ground. Frog bones. And he noticed a drop of red blood that had fallen onto a green alder leaf.

In his cabin, he packed an empty burlap bag, his driftwood pieces, his Buck knife, his cast-iron kettle, and his tin cup. He looked around the cabin, at the clothes folded on the stool by the door, the walls papered with the *Daily Colonist* and Chinese New Year's decorations, their glossy black characters jumping off the red background. Then he went back to the beach.

He sat in the loose shale by the boulders. He dug for his Buck knife in his bag. Waiting, he whittled eight sticks and two larger ones. He carved grooves into the two big sticks and then he fitted in the small ones, trying them each in turn. If he finished in time, he could leave the kite for Ge Shou.

Leaning against a boulder, watching the ocean, Ah Sing was reminded of his thirty-ninth year. With his back against the rock wall of Kwangtung and the South China Sea spread out wide before him – trapped by famines in Anhui across the border, and by the dirt and drought of Jing Gang on the eastern border with Hunan – he had paid a CPR labour broker and hopped a freighter bound for Canada. He smiled now, remembering. As the journey progressed, his excitement had been replaced by tense muscles. He had felt trapped, with no breath, no arms to fight; the mountains of black waves spanned for miles in any direction. How he had trembled on the deck! How he had been convinced the waves would swallow him, the same way Gold Tooth had trembled on the verandah as he heaved his bed outside, convinced the walls would crush him – solid walls that Ah Sing himself had built. And how, on the freighter, another man from Fujien had touched Ah Sing on the shoulder. The man had said, "There's nothing to be afraid of."

The sun shifted; the boulders cooled. In the distance, he saw the reporter and the doctor. They were taking off their shoes and wading out to the dory.

"Hallo! Hallo!" Ah Sing yelled.

They nodded to him and waved.

He stood up. He threw his bag around his shoulder.

They plunged their oars into the water. They were rowing back to the *Alert* that pitched offshore. Ah Sing narrowed his eyes at the doctor and reporter and could feel the hot sun falling onto his back.

He bent down and dropped his knife back into his bag. He could hear the waves, and Ge Shou singing in the background. He touched the coin in his pocket. His jaw tightened. He undressed so quickly his shirt got caught on his ears. He pulled down his pants and dropped his wool shirt onto the rock next to his bag.

"Hallo! Hallo!"

He dove. His breath froze inside his lungs, and his limbs froze, too: he was a stone, armless and legless. He began to sink, watching the bubbles rising past his face.

Fear made a body heavy; fear made a person sink and drown. Dead bodies floated because all the fear was gone. Once, a leper had swum toward the lights of Cordova Bay. His body had floated with the grace of a lotus flower back to the gravel slope. Then Ah Sing and Ge Shou had buried him, silently, beyond the goldenrods. If only he had let the water flow through him as if he were made of it, he could have floated to freedom. Another leper had once escaped D'Arcy Island by swallowing a vial of poison. He swallowed it on board the steamer, had died before even arriving at the colony.

Ah Sing thought he would never stop sinking, but then his arms and legs sprang to life. He kicked as fast as he could while whitecaps crashed around his ears. The doctor and the reporter were not stopping. He slapped the water. He cried into the wind, his eyes open against the salt and the horrifying green.

The seagulls laughed. Ah Sing sputtered, yet the two men ignored him and boarded the steamer. His breath felt scant and thread-like in his lungs. His ears rang, his head thudded.

He plunged his head under. When he surfaced, he squinted at Ge Shou standing on the rocky outcrop of beach, who had picked up his clothes and was waving them, flag-like. Then Ge Shou reached for the kite but stopped short of picking it up.

Ah Sing swam back to shore and clung to a rock. Ge Shou looked down in silence. Ah Sing breathed deeply, filling his nostrils with salt air and water droplets that burned. He wiped his eyes with the back of his hand. Water remained on his lashless lids and formed prisms, through which he looked at the setting sun. Oystercatchers circled and screeched.

Ge Shou lowered his hand to help Ah Sing onto the boulder. Ah Sing shook his head. He spat over his shoulder and then heaved his body out, panting as he clambered up. There he hunched forward and held himself.

After a while, he stood up and took the hat from the rock; he spun it around on his hand a few times. Holding it aloft, he pulled out the heron feathers. Then he tossed the hat into the ocean.

He reached for the coin. He put it in his mouth. It tasted like oak. His tongue moved it from one side of his mouth to the other and warmed the metal. He spat the coin back out, into his hand. He hurled it toward the ocean. It glinted in the air. When it hit the water, it skimmed like a cormorant before sinking into the grey-green waves.

A breeze dimpled the ocean. Ah Sing picked up the kite frame and offered it to Ge Shou. Ge Shou rubbed his forehead.

"Don't be scared, Ge Shou."

Ge Shou hopped from foot to foot, holding the kite.

"Don't cry, Ge Shou."

Ah Sing put his arm around Ge Shou's shoulder. He stroked him up and down. He could feel the warmth of his flesh through the damp cotton of his shirt. Ah Sing's arm was covered in goose pimples. Ge Shou's black braid tickled his armpit.

"There's nothing to be afraid of," he said to Ge Shou. "Do you want to help me fly the kite?"

When he was a boy, Ah Sing's bed had been a strong rush mat, and he had slept on it with his four brothers and sisters, his parents, and their parents, by the great mouth of the Yangtze River where it emptied into the East China Sea.

The sea touched everything with lapping hands, probing fingers, reaching across countries and exploring fjords with whales, bays of volcanic rock, and ancient crevasses. A single drop could circumnavigate the globe in five thousand years.

As a boy, he would float in the warm waters of Chongwu Bay until he felt his body liquefying, his loose limbs pulled by small currents and pushed by gentle swells. He would float as if dead while the sun burned his back. He grew and fished with the older boys. He went to work in the tin mines of Malaysia. He went to the plantations of Borneo. He forgot how to turn into the sea.

The water dripping from his body had formed a puddle at his feet. Ah Sing shook the remaining drops from his limbs and stood on one leg to dry the bottom of his feet with his shirt. Then he used his shirt to towel the top of his head. He stepped into his pants. He pulled his shirt over his neck and the hair that was still wet dripped down his back. The fabric of the shirt stuck to his skin.

The warmth was returning to his body, but the back of his head still ached with cold. He looked out over the water.

"Hey Ge Shou, here's a riddle for you: *How does one stop a drop of water from ever drying out?*"

"A riddle." Ge Shou clapped. "I love riddles."

SARAH L. TAGGART

DEAF

The mother believes in making healthy dinners for the whole family. She will not be like their babysitter across the street who makes herself steak but gives the kids plastic bowls of Kraft Dinner. Sometimes the orange kind, sometimes the white kind. The son is smart enough not to ask for junk like that at home but the child always looks disappointed with supper after a day spent across the street.

The mother watches her from behind. The child doesn't speak. The clack of plastic and marbles from the one-girl game of Hungry Hungry Hippos becomes such a din it starts to fade. She would close the spare-room door to cut the noise. Keep things manageable until dinner. But if the husband comes home and finds that she shut the child in a room alone, he will yell.

The last time the babysitter watched the kids was Friday. The mother returned from dropping them off to find the husband pulling his Audi into the driveway. He didn't shut off the engine. She tapped the driver's side window.

"We should take the Firefly. It looks better," she said. They were going to an appointment with the loan manager at the bank. She checked her reflection in his aviators.

"Sheryl, get in."

The husband wanted to start a new business, wanted to be part of the housing boom he said was coming to Calgary. He had started using words like *capital*. He used to say things like, "You're being eccentric on purpose." She liked that better.

"I need to get back to work A-sap." He wrapped and rewrapped his fingers around the steering wheel.

"Is that the Hugo Boss suit?"

"What? Yes. For God's sake," he said and put the car in reverse.

Things went shrill. "You paid nearly a grand for that suit –"

Then he said shut up, said get in.

At the bank, he sat stone-faced while the loan manager went over numbers that didn't add up in their favour. The answer was no. Afterward, she stepped out of the Audi in low heels chosen specifically for the meeting. The husband scraped the undercarriage when he left their driveway.

Back across the street, Wendy the babysitter opened her door, all smiles and sweatpants. The son scooted around the woman's ample backside, skipped down the stairs and trotted home. He had always been quick like that.

"Jenny's sure slow with the talking, eh?" said Wendy. The mother had once corrected Wendy, had told her not to call the child Jenny because that wasn't her name. But it didn't stick. Wendy sometimes said inappropriate things like this. The mother swallowed words. Free babysitting was worth something.

"Yes. She's very shy." Beyond Wendy, the mother could see the white-blond back of the child's head. She sat on the carpet – unvacuumed from the looks of things – watching the fish tank. The mother squeezed past Wendy, walked into the house. It smelled like cat.

"Come," she said to the child. Nothing. The mother stepped closer and put a hand solidly around the child's arm. "Come!"

The girl's head popped up. She pointed to the fish tank.

Wendy said, "Jenny, you can come back whenever you like and look at the fishies."

The mother and the child left the house. The mother called back to Wendy – "Thanks!" – and Wendy waved.

That night, the mother said to the husband, "I'm not letting Wendy take care of the kids anymore."

"Why not?"

"They have a new cat."

"She's free."

"Price over quality, John?"

"We can't afford daycare, you know that."

"Then you can take our son to the doctor when he gets asthma."

"You don't get asthma that way. You're overreacting."

"Better than underreacting."

While the child slaps around in the spare room at the bottom of the stairs, the mother will make homemade Caesar salad, meatloaf, and open a can of whole tomatoes. The husband went to a naturopath who said his liver wasn't well, said no red meat. Now they only eat beef once every two weeks. He doesn't drink milk anymore either but he understands the children need it. They used to drink two per cent but now they're down to one. She likes the creamy taste of milk, sometimes sneaks a small carton of homo at work, but she's getting used to the lower fat. As soon as the child hits four, she knows the husband will demand they only drink skim.

Nobody in this neighbourhood knows how to make Caesar salad. All croutons and dressing, they think. When the mother, the father, and the son first moved here, the mother was intent on becoming part of the community. But the potlucks were full of women who talked about their husbands and brought their kids too. She wanted the company of women, but not women like that. What was the point of female company if you only talked about your husband and your kids?

The husband is late. The mother knows she said seven and so, at seven, she puts out dishes for the child, the son, and the husband. She serves the Caesar salad, something she's proud of.

"Where's Dad?" asks the son.

The mother hasn't even had a chance to give him his glass dish of canned tomatoes.

"He's probably late," she says. But there's no probably about it.

She gives the child a bowl of tomatoes. The child is staring at the wall. Not at the calendar or the phone that hang there, but at some point above the kitchen table. Nothing. The mother grabs a damp cloth from the sink, moves behind the child and wipes the wall. Maybe a food splatter. The child looks away and down at her tomatoes.

They make the child's mouth itch. She likes the taste on the tongue but the corners of the mouth sting after. She doesn't

like canned tomatoes. Meatloaf. Full of onions. She reaches for
the ketchup, a tomato paste she can handle, but her brother
grabs it first. He is slow about screwing off the cap, slow about
the ooze and then the plop plop of the ketchup onto his plate,
slow about returning its cap, slow about putting the bottle on
the far side of his plate, away from her.

She reaches with her palm out, flaps the fingers in a sideways wave. Gimme. The brother ignores her, goes into his
meatloaf. The mother is at the stove. She turns, walks toward
the kitchen entrance, is met by the father. They speak. The
mother opens her mouth to say more, then shakes her head
and returns to the stove. Spoons out the father's meatloaf, puts
it on the table, dishes up her own, sits down. The father sits.
The family, at the table. She reaches again toward the ketchup.
Intent. Pointing. Stretching over her brother. Looking at the
mother. The mother goes for the ketchup, but the father
raises a hand and speaks. She pulls back her arm, puts her
hands in her lap. Looks into the father's face. Waits.

"Use your words," he says, again.

"Chup, chup," she says and reaches. Her brother sighs.
She feels the outing of air on her arm. She hopes he doesn't
hit her.

The mother looks at the father. He turns to her and shakes
his head, speaks. She speaks back and rolls her eyes, reaching
for the ketchup. She takes off the top, pours a disc of ketchup
onto the child's plate, beside meatloaf overflowing onions. A
red moon of ketchup on her plate. Its edges round, then stop.
She will leave the meatloaf until last. It will take the burn off
her mouth from the canned tomatoes.

"We could ask your mom," the husband says.

"I don't want to ask Mom."

She reads one of the books she borrowed from the library. Often the second child speaks later. This is because the older child talks enough for two.

"It's a good time."

"I don't want to ask my mother." Puts the book on her lap, watches her feet make a point in the covers.

"We fucked up."

"I didn't fuck up, John." She says his name to the reflection of him in the mirrored closet doors across from the bed. "You're not going to get me on your side by saying this is our problem."

"Goddamnit Sheryl, do you have any better suggestions? We need the money."

"Do we?"

Back to the book. If there is a problem, know that you and your child are not alone. There are resources in place in your community to assist you through this potentially challenging time. His hand on the spine. He presses it down. For the first time all evening, she looks at him.

He says, "This is serious."

It is, dear John, yes it is.

"We could lose the house."

Yes we could. She says, "It's just a house."

The booth man speaks. The child watches his face, watches his mouth. He tells her, "The sound is like this." A boop, like the TV going funny, echoes through the booth. She nods. She understands. "When you hear that, press the button." He holds a black plastic stick with a red button at the top. Hold it like this. He mimes with his hand, fingers wrapped around the plastic, the thumb ready to push the button. It's powerful. The man waves his other hand in her face, gets her attention. She watches. He says, "The sound might be loud or quiet. When you hear it, press the button. It might be soft like this." She waits. Somewhere, there's a sound. Maybe she hears it. She waits for his reaction. It doesn't come. She nods. He smiles. She doesn't want to disappoint. "I'm going to shut these so you aren't distracted." He pulls the navy drapes across the window. She is surrounded by felt and carpet, dark blue. "If you need me, just speak. I will hear you." He stands and takes the headphones from the hook on the booth wall. Here. "You wear these headphones. I'm going to close the door. Your mom and me are right outside." He fits the headphones over her ears. The silence is complete. He smiles, waiting. Yes. She nods. The door shuts without a sound, like it's surrounded by pillows.

The warm room closes in on all sides. The headphones make her feel like a pilot. In control. She holds the stick in her hand, the stick that drives the plane. Push it forward to fly and pull it back to put the nose in the air. Press the button and shoot the guns. The chair is comfy. The chair her father would take in a room, because he always wants the best. The largest. The warmest. Take it. The headphones click. The booth man, on the other side of the window, in his own plane. She can't see him but she knows. He locks into his cockpit. He puts on his headset. In her ears she hears his voice: "We're starting now." The headphones make everything clear. She nods. Of course.

They start easy. Boop. Button. Boop. Button. Boop boop boop. Button-button-button. He's trying to challenge her. Boop. Softer, in the distance. She gets that one too. She waits. Boop. Behind her, off to the side. Button. She watches the closed door. Her co-pilot fiddles with his instrument panel. He swoops behind her, where she can't see him. She concentrates. Harder. She's on her own. Wait, was that a boop? She's not sure. Maybe she imagined it. Button. Maybe she's wrong. Another two almost-imaginary boops come from somewhere. Maybe they're not even in the headphones. She buttons once, not sure either way. Silence. More silence. Trying to slip her up. Her thumb poised. Button. Shoot. A clear mistake. Relax. Boop. Loud. Obvious. He's giving her a break. She takes it, sits straighter, ready. She can almost find the pattern in the boops, but holds off because she's afraid she'll miss it when it breaks. Boop-boop combos are nothing for her button button thumb. She dismisses her earlier imaginings and every time she thinks she hears a boop, she hits the button. And then she waits, her eyes on the twists of carpeting on the back of the door. Booth man must be reloading his guns. She got him good that time. Silence. The silence warms her again. The boops have gone. She appreciates the calm her co-pilot gives her. She hopes she passed the test. She wants to fly again.

A few days later, the husband's at the stove.

The mother forgot to turn on the oven. The meatloaf's been sitting in there raw for two hours. She noticed it about a half hour ago. Let it continue cold as she sat at the kitchen table. When the son came in for dinner she told him to get himself some cereal. He went right for the sugar stuff. She had forgotten they still had some. Maybe from his birthday, or the child's. He knew she wouldn't protest. Everyone just another person to take advantage of. The woman at the bank didn't give them the loan because she saw that they had nothing left to take.

It was difficult to explain to the husband.

"She's deaf."

"What?"

"Funny."

He doesn't take off his overcoat. He wants to hear this.

"The doctor said she's deaf."

He shakes his head.

"The ear infections," she says.

"She hasn't had an ear infection in over a year."

"Eleven months."

"She's not deaf."

"She's deaf."

"Qualify it. How?"

"They need to do more tests, but at this point he says it could be as much as a seventy-five per cent deficit in the right ear."

"So she's not deaf. She can hear."

"Can you do math? Seventy-five per cent means she only hears twenty-five per cent of noises that every other child hears."

"But that's the right ear. The left ear. Fine, right?"

"No. Probably half."

"Half deaf, then."

"Goddamn you."

"Swearing at me because you know our daughter can't hear you?"

"Goddamn you."

The husband puts his hands on the sink and stares through the window. It looks onto the brown, blank stare of the neighbour's wood-panelled house. Better than looking through one of their windows, he'd said when she had complained about the view, years ago. It wasn't so bad, after all. In between the houses was a deck, instead of a yard or a cement walkway. The kids from both families charged down it in the summer. A sandbox lay hidden under removable boards, off to one side of this kitchen window. If the mother stood on tiptoes, she could watch her children play.

"I don't want to lose the house," she says. "I just think you need to consider this first, that you've got your priorities mixed up here."

"I'm tired of hearing 'I just think' come out of your mouth."

"You didn't marry me because I was an airhead, John," she says, though at that moment she's not sure why he did marry her. Beauty, a girl who laughed at his jokes, circumstance. Good things are so easy to forget late on a weekday evening. The house is cold with good memories past remembering.

He seems about to say more but perhaps he too feels the chill of a home turning back into a house. He shrugs off his overcoat and escapes downstairs to his leather armchair, to a movie, to two hours of no thinking whatsoever.

The father is angry when she says "Hawpital." "Hosssspital," he says through the rearview mirror. She tries not to shrink into the car seat because he'll be more mad. "Hopstill," she tries again. She knows her words don't sound the way he wants them to. Since the booth, the father does this more. Makes her speak for food. No pointing. The mother sometimes looks into her face and asks with her own if she's okay. But today the mother leans against the car window. She looks for the mother's face in the side mirror but the reflection's wrong. "Hosssssspital," he says, even louder. They go again to the Children's for a second set of booth tests. She must have done something wrong the first time. Looks down from his face in the mirror.

"Gen–!" the beginning of a shout but the mother's hand goes out and onto his hand on the gear stick.

The child sees him flick off the hand and yank on the stick and under her the car pulses forward into the exit and her neck bends and the father's mouth in the rearview, thankfully closed, and the mother's head tucked tight against the seat. The little red car holds onto the off-ramp, the white *H* of the Children's coming into view. The car stutters underneath her. She feels the car speed up and the mother's head leaves the headrest in surprise. The child watches the mirror but she can't see the mother's mouth.

"John, for Christ's sake."

She drops her head. Hands in her lap. Wishes she couldn't hear anything at all.

The mother's parents had come. Her mother ran around with the son all day and in the evenings rubbed her feet with lemons. The child took her time. The due date came. Went. They waited.

The night before the child's afternoon birth, she couldn't sleep. Her father was still alive then. Every ten, sometimes fifteen minutes the contractions. She took the couch downstairs. Each time she woke, she found him looking at her with tears in his eyes.

They broke her water in the delivery room. No epidural this time, she felt it all. And they didn't know then, people didn't know. She had hoped for a girl and out the child came, a girl so perfect, her heart rate right. The child came out perfect. The husband took the first photo and in it, the child's smiling. Rolling to the right, gums wide at her mother, the doctor smiling at them both.

But eighteen days later, a scare. She came home from her first evening out to find the husband pacing and the child screaming.

"She's been crying all night. And she has these bumps." His fear so quiet and intense she could barely hear him. At the child's crib they watched her squirm, her ovaries sticking out of the tiny groin. In emergency, the chart read "abdominal mass." As if hernias could be called such a thing. The mother cried. And when the child came out fine, the almond-sized organs pushed back in and the abdominal wall stitched by a surgeon with hands as big as the child herself, the mother cried more. The husband cradled his three-week-old as if she were new, his face etched with a terrible relief.

"Nothing so small should bear so much pain," he had said. The mother had seen tears for the first time in his blue eyes. She had cried herself out, wondered if there would be enough fluid in her body to breastfeed.

"She's not hurting anymore," she said to him then. But a family is designed to bear a continued series of hurts. The ear infections of months ago had abated, but they left damaging traces behind. Now, myringotomy. A scary name for something simple. A minor surgical procedure in which a small slit is made in the eardrum, allowing fluid to drain from the middle ear. All of it was very minor, yet the word minor meant nothing to the mother of an almost-four-year-old girl she had long suspected was going through life in a daze of half-heard sounds, the angry mouths of her parents moving in patterns of loathing.

The mother wondered what was worse: hearing yelling or seeing it? She wondered if it looked like the melodrama of a silent film and if the child played a tiny piano in her head to accompany the action on screen. If the surgery was successful, what would happen to the child when she woke up? Would the world crash and bang into her head, alienating her? Would she cover her ears and demand back her silent world? The child had never complained, had not asked to hear.

The group of sick kids sit in a circle and the nurse shows them on a bear what the needle will do. She is not scared. She hopes the other kids aren't scared either. The nurse gives them a colouring book and inside it is a bear like the needle bear. He is going to the hospital too and he's worried, but the hospital is a good place and he smiles in other pictures. No crayons though. She will colour in it when she goes home. She likes the hospital. The group of children breaks up. She says goodbye to her new friends. She waves at them. She is happy, she will see them soon. Another nurse leads her to the room she started in, this morning. The mother stands and holds out a coat. She puts her arms in. She is confused. Why isn't she staying? The other children are staying overnight. She imagined a slumber party. They would all put on hospital pyjamas and sit on their beds, separated by curtains. She doesn't want them to be too scared.

They will be okay.

The mother takes her hand to leave. As they walk through the corridors ribboned with yellow and blue and red, she looks for the faces of the boys and girls in her group. She is the only one leaving. The mother pulls harder on her hand. They go down stairs, out a door, into a parkade. Their little red car waits for them. "No," she says, pulling her hand free. The mother continues. She stops walking. The mother stops, turns around. "Let's go," she says. Loudly. "No!" I don't wanna go home. I don't wanna go! She screams, high-pitched like a baby. And the mother grabs her hand and pulls. The child wants to stay. The mother doesn't understand. She doesn't understand. She wants to stay. She doesn't understand.

Family dinner.

The mother has made pork chops. The child likes the apple sauce. Caesar salad on the side, not too much lemon in the dressing. She serves the child first, pausing at her seat to cut the chop into bites. And then the son. And then the husband. She considers telling him, "Get your own goddamn pork chop," which would be an expression of the mood that made her put an expensive steak in the cart at Food for Less. Stay positive. Put back the steak. Got the good pork chops, on sale.

Took absolute care with the oven, adjusting the temperature on a whim, seeking for once not to make the bloody things dry as pemmican.

She sits down. The son watches her and then the husband. The child picks a leaf from her salad and puts it in her mouth. Then she puts a finger in the apple sauce and puts the finger in her mouth.

"Eat," the mother says to the son. He pauses, not convinced. She smiles. Smiles again, real. He picks up his utensils, begins to saw. The meat oozes some moisture, but it might be, once again, too dry.

She speaks to the son, and looks between him and the child. "Tomorrow your sister will go into the hospital for surgery. When she comes out, she'll be able to hear much better than she can now."

"How deaf is she?" asks the son, voice laced with scorn. Does he get this attitude from the father?

"Deaf enough that she probably can't hear what we're saying right now," she says. The child chews and watches the wall.

"Oh." The son looks at the child. Puts his fork down. The light reflects off his forearm scar. Last year's compound fracture a perfectly reasonable injury for a young boy, a passing worry for her, a cast he waved with pride. He studies the child. He squints, opens his mouth as if to speak.

The child looks up. "Eat," says the father.

The mother sighs. Fuck it.

"Honey, your sister is going to be fine. Don't worry."

The husband grabs his glass of water and slurps. She hears the liquid wash around the bits of pork chop in his mouth. The son returns to his duty. The husband claps the glass back on the table. The child pushes a bite of pork chop through apple sauce. The family returns to silence.

The room is bright with people and lights. The nurses are very nice. There are two, a man and a woman. When they speak to her, they curl over the bed and look right in her face and talk. She is not scared. She is the bear at the end of the colouring book. She is surrounded by yellow curtains. She knows sick kids are in beds like hers on both sides and beyond the curtain at the foot of her bed. It is a room of boys and girls like the boys and girls from her group. She wasn't allowed to play with them today.

The man has dark curly hair and glasses. He leans close on the good side. Smiles and says, "Sweetheart, we're going to put a mask on you and there is air in it that will put you to sleep. The gas tastes funny."

"Like what?"

"They tell me it tastes like pop."

Her father doesn't like pop. She nods.

"We're good to go then," he says and clamps his lips together like he's a monkey. He's making fun. She looks to the curtain.

"So we just put this –"

And the mask descends over her face like a black toilet plunger and it's chocolate that hits her throat.

"I don't know why they gave her so much. I told them she's sensitive. Maybe they're used to all these fat kids or something."

The mother stands with her head against the wall beside the pay phone. The hospital has a high ceiling and the midday sounds echo. She could be in an atrium or the Devonian Gardens downtown. She listens for bird calls.

"But she'll come home today?" asks the husband. This morning he asked her to call him as soon as she could.

"Oh yeah. Yeah, I'm just waiting though. They said she'll sleep the rest of the day."

Silence. She can't hear his office, either. He must have shut the door and turned off the speaker phone. She can't remember the last time she spoke to him in the middle of the day.

"Did it work?" His voice is a weight holding down his end of the phone. He is exhausted.

"Doctor says she'll hear as soon as she wakes up."

"Easy."

"Not really, John."

"I know."

"I feel –" She stops. Sighs into the phone. Rolls her head against the wall. The brick cools her forehead like a cloth for a fever. The buzz of voices in the hallways surrounding her and over the PA system remind her of the many lives she is not living right now.

"It's not your fault," says the husband.

"I never said it was. Even now you still can't say the right thing." She says it with nothing but the matter-of-fact tone it deserves. She coils the heavy phone cord around her wrist, pulling it tight, palming the brick wall.

"Oh Sheryl," he says. And then, "Sorry."

For the first time in months, she cries. She drops her hand and it pulls the receiver down with it, yanking her head. She cries into her chest, tears dripping onto the black phone receiver and then to the floor. And the mothers and the fathers who walk by the row of phones on their way to the wards where their children are much sicker probably think she's losing a child but she hasn't lost a child at all.

On the ward, the child wakes. She blinks, fills her eyes with light. A nurse shuffles near the bed. She turns her head, watches. Licks the inside of her mouth. Dry. She clears her throat.

The nurse comes over. She wears bright pink lipstick. When she smiles, her lips leave pink on her teeth. The child laughs.

"You're awake, sweetie," she says. "How do you feel?"

The child nods. Fine.

From somewhere the nurse has a pen. She holds it in her hand like the booth button and a light blares into the child's face. She blinks and turns her head.

"Okay. Sorry, bun!" The nurse smacks her lips like they're bubble gum. "Just checkin'. Dear, can you tell me where you are?"

"The hawpital."

"And what's your name, sweetie?"

"Genevieve," she says.

The mother enters the room. Her eyes are red, but her face is as stiff as ever. She pauses at the end of the bed, her mouth half open. Nothing comes out.

The child speaks again. "Genevieve."

SARAH KEEVIL

PYRO

At a bar in Soho, the walls bathed in electric blue light, I met Leo Olm for the first time. He had cappuccino eyes and scour-pad hair, and cast pink and yellow shadows on the floor. The salamander tattoo on his arm writhed among licks of flame, more lively than the light from the potted tea candles on the tables. He said he felt hemmed in by the lab colours that divided the environment into cold, clean spaces. So we went outside, where the heat of London smog was strong enough to turn white moths black and curl the corners of scattered flyers.

I wasn't as comfortable as he was walking down the tight alleyways of Soho. My fear of hypodermic needles set in. There were too many sunken doorways and smoky sulphur corners. But Leo rushed along the streets with his hands in his pockets, walking razor-straight.

When the streets finally opened out onto a square packed with jugglers and firespinners, I was gasping for air. We walked by a dancer who liquefied his limbs like a puppet and slowly pieced himself back together in strobing jolts, a body fluttering and fighting against unseen strings. An old man in plaid and acid-washed jeans was fanning gusts of lime-green smoke into the air. We reached the centre of the square and Leo began to pull things out of the pockets of his cargo pants: a Scotch bottle, an old dishtowel, a tube of Vaseline, a lighter, a pack of cigarettes.

First he coated his hands with Vaseline, then with kerosene from the Scotch bottle. He brought the lighter to his right hand, tapped his hands together briefly so his left would catch fire, then spread and clenched his fingers, creating wisps of firelight that expanded into rolling, turbulent balls. A gawking crowd formed a circle around him. A few reached into their pockets, paused, unsure whether it was polite to throw coins to a man for lighting himself on fire. Leo used the last lick of flame to light a cigarette, sat down on his heels, gathered up the few coins he got for the display and dropped them into his topmost pocket.

"Wanna try?" he asked.

I shook my head, bending down to examine his hands. They were still greased with Vaseline and covered with black soot. He wiped them on the towel and showed them to me again – they were soft and smooth, with a slightly pink tinge.

Like the slow withering away of a log, Leo's hands must have been changed. But the change was invisible to the eye. Contained fire turned twists of newspaper into black dust, roused a slow chemical blue from cereal boxes, electrified nails with pops and sparks, melted marshmallows into lava-like goo, and turned leaves into dark skeletons before they flashed away. Leo's fire was ethereal, not of this world, brilliantly shivering for a moment before spinning out in unfelt bursts. Timeless in another dimension, a ghost of light that had no power in ours.

"Does it hurt?" I asked.

But Leo just flexed and released his fingers, staring off into the city, where small areas of black seeped between the buildings.

When I got home that night, Eddie was sitting cross-legged in front of his aquarium, watching his fish as intently as a cat stares into a shadowy crevice. I walked across the tile floor to the fridge, my heels making that clicking sound that always makes me feel overdressed. Eddie had been shopping and had filled the fridge's shelves with loaves of pumpernickel and rye, halved papayas and pineapples, smoked salmon and fresh-caught sole, capers, Saran-Wrapped plates of sushi and spring rolls, blue cheese, havarti, pimentos, three bottles of Cabernet Sauvignon lying sideways on the metal wires, and a mango. I closed the fridge without choosing anything; instead, I filled a glass with tap water.

Eddie's chin dropped away from the aquarium and he let his gaze travel over to me. "There's apple cider in the fridge."

"I know. I saw."

He turned back to the aquarium and began wiping the glass with the end of his sleeve. His toes popped out from underneath his calves, clenching and spreading, then he dropped his hands into his lap and turned back to me. The corner of his mouth turned up in a smile. I could tell he was about to enter into one of his half-hour monologues.

I said, "I'm going to bed."

"Wait." He leapt up, landing squarely on his large feet, and came over to hug me, pressing his chin down onto the top of my head. "I remembered you didn't like Merlot after I'd already bought a couple of bottles so I went to the park and shared one with a wino, then split another bottle with a teenage boy who was pierced all over with kilt pins." He pulled back so he could look into my eyes. "Then I came home wanting to get high and go to the planetarium, but you weren't here."

I shrugged and peeled myself away from his chest, heading down the cream-coloured hallway. He followed, dragging his palm against the wall as he walked.

"Then I went and broke a beautiful ex-con out of jail, we went on a murderous rampage, ate three calves worth of milk-fed veal, and had sex on a Ferris wheel."

"Why a Ferris wheel?" I asked, entering the bedroom and kicking my shoes into a corner.

Eddie stopped me before I reached the closet. "You're listening."

He generously helped me take my shirt off and flung it toward the laundry hamper, where it hung like a Dali clock.

"You know, when the Ferris wheel was first invented it was considered quite exciting – only the most daring people would ride at those speeds." He planted a kiss on my belly button and slipped my skirt down around my heels. "Same with the auto-mobile," he continued, stripping off my nylons. "Twenty kilo-metres an hour was absolutely dizzying, and if you brought the machine to thirty, you were considered a homicidal maniac." He lowered me to the bed, squeezing me between his body and the mattress while he unhooked my bra, and I decided it was only fair to help him take off his own shirt. "Nowadays, of course, we can go up to speeds of 150 without noticing much difference in the landscape. Some say this is evidence," his voice was muffled briefly as he shifted his body weight, pressing his lips against my breasts as he successfully removed my underpants, "of evolution in the human brain." Eddie raised himself on his knees to allow me to slide his pants down. "Which means evolution itself occurs at rapid speeds, and in two hundred years we could all very well have gills. Which means," he added, tracing his finger along my lips, "we would no longer have any use for these."

I raised an eyebrow at him. "Are you sure?"

He sketched a figure eight over my breasts and another one over my thighs, then slid his hand up and secured it alongside my neck.

"Where were you tonight? Out being naughty? With the girls?"

"With a boy," I whispered.

He rocked onto my body so that his weight spread evenly along the length of my torso. "Horribly disfigured, I hope."

"Terribly," I agreed. "A real charity case."

I imagined his hands leaving charcoal prints as they slid up over my chin and into my hair. I arched my head back and gasped as he fit himself into my body, felt his lips tugging at my ears, and saw the yellow walls recede into a deep ochre. The two dimensional leaves on the Henri Rousseau painting above my head began to sway in and out, the lion rippling and curling as though it wanted to break free of the painting and prowl around the room. I reached up over my head and pressed my wrist backward on the wall, trying to steady its surface. Eddie pulled my hand away but it was too late. I was sinking away from him, into the mattress, into a dark void where humans still roll with the waves that rock them, absent and unaware.

Leo and I met again at Camden Market, fusing with the crowd and racks of second-hand clothes. Leo winced as he looked around, unused to the harsh daylight that flooded the wharf. He scratched his fingers against a pair of polyester pants, smiling at the crackling sound. We pushed our way past tall glass bottles full of infused oils and hash pipes carved with the rotund faces of gnomes. Leaving the main square, we entered rows of unplanned streets lined with peeling warehouses that echoed the city noise through their open doors. One of these old buildings was stacked high with cobwebs and second-hand furniture. A man in a grey golfer's hat sat in the middle of the room beside an antique cash register.

"Have any old horsehair couches?" Leo asked.

The man eyed Leo's army-green tank top and studded wrist band. "You want an old Victorian settee? I've got one of those. Fifty pounds."

Dry, brittle horsehair, eroded into dusty clumps, peeped out between rips in cornflower-blue fabric. Split, faded wood emerged from the head and foot of the settee, giving Leo an excuse to lower the price twenty pounds. He brought his van around and we rocked through the London streets, tossed about on bad shocks. Through the back windows a polluted sunset dripped crimson. I was half asleep when the night turned sapphire and Leo stopped the van.

We were at a schoolyard. A tube slide protruded from the sides of a jungle gym like a tongue. Some giant metal studs, holding the wood together, gleamed in the sinking twilight.

We placed the couch in the middle of a chalk-lined field and sat, smoking a little, stuffing our hands inside the couch to feel the grainy, crumbling horsehair. I was reclining, watching the stars develop in the filmy sky. Laughter filled my rib cage as I slipped my feet up Leo's shirt. Gentle shocks. Spontaneous and everlasting, converting soil-sprung minerals into airy gusts. We waited until cars stopped travelling by and the bite of city noise was thinned out by a spreading void. I savoured the expectant air, imagined prowling beasts winking at us, licking their front teeth, fang to fang. Leo had chosen a place that lacked streetlights. He seemed to stare into a ripped darkness distorted by the sawtooth edges of trees. I closed my eyes until I felt him tense beneath my feet, and then slowly rose, straightening my hair and my shirt and shifting to a space on the edge of an imaginary ring that circled the couch.

Leo opened the back of the van and brought out a container of gasoline. The liquid inside rang out with a ritual gong as he placed the container by my feet, bending to one knee to twist off the thick black cap. After he had fitted the yellow nozzle in place, he closed his eyes and placed his lips against his hands, taking a long, slow breath as the salty fumes leaked into the night. He rose without looking at me, one hand firmly around the handle, the other at the base as he tipped the gas, first up and along the field's centre line, then over the couch in swirling figure eights. The dark patterns he made slowly bled into one another, saturating the couch. He retraced his steps over the chalk and back to me. We stood shoulder to shoulder, leaning into one another as our legs threatened to crash out from under us. Leo took some matches from his pocket and offered them to me.

"I can't," I said.

"Yes you can. Just drop the match and watch it burn."

"I can't."

"You're going to miss the opportunity." He held a match in one hand, the book in the other. I grabbed them, struck the flint, and dropped.

Fire appeared with a whoosh, leaping into our dimension with sparkling clarity. Heat crackled around us and into the space between us. Horsehair rose from the settee like brilliant butterflies. The wood carvings were engulfed by lavender flame and edges gleamed gold where the settee's skin peeled away from its frame. I let my hand drop as the firelight pressed against its own boundaries, heaving and swelling, stopping just before it touched our faces.

I was worried that Eddie would be able to smell it on me that night. Lemon sourness that hits the back of the throat and turns sweet on the tongue. Grainy remnants of smoke resting in almost invisible waves on my skin. I felt that the flavour of fire would rise to overwhelm the faint tendrils of jasmine incense and the mossy soil of houseplants, that the smell of gasoline would take shape in front of Eddie's searching eyes.

He was reclining on the couch, his feet up on green silk pillows, a copy of *Discover* lying open on his chest – which he read for the pictures, not the articles. I leaned against the doorframe, slipping off my shoes. "It's hot out tonight." I pushed my bangs back from my forehead. "I need a shower."

"Wait." He came over to me, pressed his face into my hair. When he pulled away, my hair stuck to his day-old beard. "You smell like soda."

"I'll have a shower."

"No wait." He held me by my arms. "I came home early to tell you about these tree frogs I found. They're illegal, but fuck it, they have these great pod toes that look like they're about to explode. I got them from this guy who wore a silk robe like some sort of geisha. He's got a flat overlooking Camden Market – I thought I saw you through the window. Were you there?"

He still gripped me with his hands, and I saw that his pupils were dilated. "Have you been licking tree frogs again?" I asked.

"You know me, always communing with nature. But no. It was this bag the old guy gave me. The bag was full of brown things, small and wrinkled. I thought it must be shrooms. But I don't think so. He told me how to make a tea out of it, and he gave me the frogs, and the bag, for forty pounds, which is like one hundred Canadian, I know."

He showed me the bag. The stuff inside looked like decomposing thumbs surrounded by dust and dead skin. "I made the tea, I was waiting, and it got stronger and stronger." He pulled me over to the kitchen counter and showed me the liquid, which was as thick as blood. I dipped my finger in and tasted a bit – sour and bitter, like coffee grains. I spat into the sink. "There are little particles on the bottom that you're not supposed to drink," Eddie warned. "But try it." Eddie lifted the cup to my lips. I looked into his saltwater-blue eyes, their thin irises like the rim around a well. "Please try it."

I drank. The tea poisoned my blood. I began to lose my clarity, felt the experience of the night fall away, shedding it in translucent waves, like snake skin. My hands broke my fall as I tumbled onto the couch. Eddie fell behind me and pointed at his fish. They were leaving trails of deformed fetuses with bubbly fingers and many limbs. As the strange shapes began to fade, others appeared in their place – creatures with exo-skeletal spines, or ridges along their skulls, tails wound around their necks and eyes, wing-like webs between their arms and torsos. Finally someone unfolded in the fish tank, a human shape, like a water sprite, pointing at me, her silver hair swirling up and stroking the belly of the angelfish. She traced a word on the glass. "Fire," it said. I told her she couldn't bring it in there with her. I told her she was doomed. "Fire," she mouthed, banging on the glass with open palms. "No," I whis-pered. It would go *tstz*. Even a candle. *Tstz*. "Climb out," I whispered. She folded her legs and sank into the gravel. Eddie placed his arm around my waist, pinning me in place. "Climb out," I repeated. But she wasn't listening – she was rubbing her hands together, back and forth, faster and faster, trying to strike a flint, to create a spark among the algae.

After my shower, mist saturated the bathroom. I wiped the mirror with my palm, expecting the film to coat my hand with a larval white glaze. The crinkled skin was barely moist. I wiped again, trying to open the hole long enough to see my face.

Eddie was snoring when I went into the bedroom to pick up my wallet. If he had been awake, I would have told him I was going out. Then I would have padded to the door, pulled it closed behind me, turned the doorknob to avoid a click, and locked him in, just as I did the night I left to go to the woods outside of London.

The busy roads degraded into highway as Leo drove us toward midnight, then they transformed into inky trails that sought a horizon line I could barely make out in the dark. Trees rose around us in spiky lines as we entered the forest, our headlights finding the smooth metal curves of a makeshift parking lot. Leo parked beside the other cars and led me through the dark, guided only by a pulsing glow that signalled to us like a bodiless Pied Piper.

Leo's friends lit a bonfire and used it as the centre of a circle around which beer and cigarettes were passed freely. A group of drummers lit a smaller fire and played their rhythms while light flickered against their brows. A violinist played something skittish at a fire of her own, the bow not matching her rhythm because her fingers were doing all the work. Her back arched on the high notes then snapped back like a rubber band. All the fires were well contained within their stone circles.

After hollering hellos, Leo unlooped his firespinners from his belt and dipped them into the jar of fuel he had carried over in his knapsack. The twin globes cut shafts of light into the air, leaving patterned trails like roller coaster paths around the shadowy statue of his torso. The kerosene's slow burn turned the flames a deep vermillion. Sparks rained down from between the stars, down around the violinist, who continued playing, her music pulsing like an adrenaline-pumped heart.

Leo's fire spinners burned off all their kerosene and faded. Someone shouted for him to come over, so I sat down alone, a jag of rock poking into my back. I was in the cold shade, watching the firelight meet in folds over the cleared ground. If I took in the shapes, only the shapes, I would lose the need to make sense of what I saw and would hear only the flickering of a film reel.

The violinist slowed her fingering down, drawing out notes with a shiver of her hands, staring with unfocused eyes into the fire, her jaw pressed shut by the violin. Then I saw the violin fall into the fire. A blue tongue licked over its surface, peeling away the rich mahogany coating, exposing the original wood. The wood creaked and split into fine lines, the fire slipping inside and bursting back out into the open air. The strings screamed, pitched higher and higher, until the violin released its final song in four ear-shattering pops.

A tree caught fire behind Leo, flames bursting from the leaves. The fire spiralled down the branches, leapt to another treetop, seeped slowly down the trunk, growled as gravity yanked it home. Leo ran past the violinist and grabbed me from the rock – I could see his dilating pupils absorb the light.

Everyone in the clearing scattered, weaving paths of escape like ant trails.

Soon a siren's wail was just audible over the fire, descending on the clearing from the ash-filled sky. Helicopter blades chopped through the air, beating like drums. The mosquito-shaped machine washed spotlights over the clearing. The blades showered us with sparks as the helicopter pulled away and slipped back into the night. I turned and saw Leo backing away from me. When I caught up, he turned and picked up his pace, heading for the forest.

The forest was so dark I could only see the shape of Leo's shoulders and a few trees that shook with the wind of the fire. We ran until the forest closed around us, the only sound our footsteps crunching on pine needles. Leo slowed. I could hear him breathing.

I stopped and collapsed against a tree, my back against the ridged bark, my hands clasped to the jagged edges. "Why did she do that?"

Leo came over to me and pressed his hands against my waist, slid them up until the sides of my rib cage were supported by those two centres of liquid warmth. "Everybody's a pyro," he said.

I slipped away, gazing toward the lines of trees that drifted in the smoke. My legs began to propel me forward, away, toward the highway. Leo grabbed my arm.

"Before you head back to your nice warm flat and watch TV, ask yourself, where do you think we would be now if that first person hadn't lit that spark and said, holy shit, I wanna do that again?"

I shook my head. "But it could destroy the entire forest. How are they going to put it out?"

Leo released me. "With a plane, I guess."

I listened until I heard the seashell hum of the highway, then began heading downhill. Behind us, the trees shook their flames free. Centuries of growth unravelled in black folds against the sky, but I could only smell the edges of the fire now. I was growing more distant from it, immersed in the swamp of night. I shivered. I'd never seen fire spread so fast before – even the settee had burned slowly, fighting against flame retardant chemicals.

Then I thought of the warehouse where we had bought the couch. Thick metal walls, special insulation, and no oxygen allowed through the windows if we closed them up first. I wondered how much heat the glass would withstand. Probably enough.

I turned and located Leo's dusky grey form floating in and out of the dark slashes of tree trunks. He was coming toward me at a steady pace, pressing back the branches that I had crashed through. His hair was painting the sky, his hands were tempering space. When he was almost there, I reached out and cupped the collar of his jacket in my palms, then shifted my weight toward the blanket of needles. But he held me up, his hands skimming across my back, his eyelashes fluttering away from my face. "We have to get back to the car before they find the parking lot," he said.

"Okay," I said. But I held him for a minute longer, thinking, the tragedy of a forest fire was that trees could not be insured.

The TV was on to the local station – news of the fire. Eddie was passed out on the couch, arm over his face, snoring. The room smelled foul, and looking down I saw fish pooled on the carpet. I shook Eddie awake.

"There was a tidal wave in Japan," he said in a hoarse voice. He grabbed the back of my head in his palm.

"You were dreaming."

He rubbed his eyes and brought his knees up for me to rest on. "I dreamt you were a sorceress who controlled the waves, and you made dolphins jump out of the water, and they had hands, and they started running after me." He yawned. "And then I was drowning. I couldn't move. But you were there to save me. I don't remember how, but I knew you would."

I didn't know what to say. I had never dreamt of Eddie, not even once. I dreamt constructions. I would find myself reclining on an elephant's back as though it was a bed, walking along a carpet of crushed potato chips, cycling down the road on two spinning mandalas and a canoe paddle. I would step on paper clips as though they were stairs or bathe in ash within a scooped-out television. Then, as I woke, these things would separate and arrange themselves around my room, become the patterns on a poster, perch themselves between the candles on my dresser. The objects and animals would fade as the painted drywall became clear.

I pushed a strand of hair behind his ear. "Eddie, what have you done?"

Eddie dropped his hand over the edge of the couch, felt the wet carpet with his bare hand. "I meant to clean that up."

I stood up, still wearing my shoes to keep from stepping on glass. I walked over to the window and opened the curtains. Eddie squinted against the light.

Now the damage glowed. The pool of water, the colourful bellies of fish. Shards of tempered glass, jagged and glinting. Only the tree frogs remained alive in their planted aquarium, perched on their branches, breathing in gulps.

"That was a forty-dollar angelfish," Eddie said, looking at the big white one with the yellow stripes, fins now closed tight. He tried to sit up.

"Don't move," I said. I went over to the door to retrieve his shoes, returned and slipped them over his bare feet.

Eddie pointed at the fridge. There was an orange paste running down the front, mango skin and a hairy pit drying on the floor. "It had gone bad, Serena. It burst in my hands."

"How did you shatter three aquariums?"

"With a fossil." He corrected himself. "With two fossils and a lamp stand. I think I'm slightly electrocuted." He put his arm around my shoulder as I pulled him up. Leaning over my neck, Eddie whispered, "They arrested your friend."

I stayed still. I knew if I let Eddie go, he would drop back down to the couch. Maybe he would even fall asleep again.

"It's true. They caught Camden Market guy for arson." He motioned toward the TV. "His name is Leo Olm." He drew the sound out in his cheeks. "They said he did it alone."

I turned to the TV, saw the warehouse fire burning, the light too dim because the camera couldn't pick up its full force. Water from the fire hoses was turning the vibrant sparks into insipid ashes. They disintegrated in the dawn light.

When we'd arrived at the warehouse, Leo had smashed the window, then spread the ignition fluid around. I had lit a match. The tiny flame had burned slowly, cupped in my palm.

When I looked into the flame, I saw her. She was a Neanderthal, hairy, jaw protruding from her dented forehead, eyes heavy and sunken beneath her peaked brow. The inventor of fire.

Leo had grinned. "Lost your nerve?"

The fire would be swallowed by the warehouse walls, snuff itself out. I had looked around at the shadowy furniture.

"I'll give you one more chance," Leo had said.

The match shed ash as I clenched my hand over it. When I reached the warehouse door, I squeezed the matchbook between my palms. Leo was still standing behind me in the dark.

In the centre of the living room, Eddie reached down and picked a piece of glass up off the floor. It had once been part of an opalescent window into another world, fashioned in a kiln at a temperature of 1,500 degrees Celsius. Now it was a possible weapon, or trash.

I went to the fridge, ignored the mango plastered to the front, and took the cheese out. I began to make grilled cheese sandwiches.

"Dinner?" Eddie came up beside me, looked into the frying pan. "I'll set the table."

"It's morning."

Eddie stepped away. "I had expected you home, and when you didn't come, I had to drink all the wine myself."

"And then the whisky?" I asked.

Eddie's hands trembled as he spread the placemats on the table. "I was having a wake," he said. "For the fish."

The sandwiches sizzled as they hit the pan. I turned to Eddie. He was lining the cutlery up on the placemats, trying to get them straight. Peering at his work, he ran his fingers along the edge of a knife, and it shifted off-kilter. He tried to shift it again, and it went in the other direction. He brought both his hands to it and carved out the space on either side of the knife, leaving it straight. He put a spoon beside the knife, knocking the knife off-kilter again. He held the bottoms of their long handles and brought them parallel to one another, abutting the bases with the bottom of the placemats.

"Eddie," I said. "They're sandwiches."

He looked up at me, then back at the silverware. "Then we don't need these," he muttered, and began to put the utensils away.

SHAWN SYMS

ON THE LINE

I won't go out with another man who works on the kill
floor. I can't handle the smell of them, or their attitudes.
Forget about men from the plant altogether, that's what I
should do. It would drastically cut down on my chances for a
date though. Maybe a better solution would be to get out of
town altogether.

I take a deep breath, inhaling the eucalyptus scent, then
immerse my head in hot, soapy bathwater. My knees rise above
the waterline, the tips of my breasts poke out above water,
still covered in suds. Underwater, I rub my temples with both
thumbs. I stay submerged as long as I can, until I come up
gasping for breath again. Work ended at three-thirty. It's
almost ten now, and I'm finally beginning to feel human.

Turning up the tap to add more hot water, I pour silvery
conditioner into my hand and lather up my scalp. Run my
fingers through the full length of my dark hair, starting at
my forehead and tracing behind my shoulders. Touching my

scalp, I feel a phantom fingertip – as if the last half-inch of my right baby finger were still there.

The accident was over two years ago. Can't complain much; I got $2,700 in insurance money and seven days off work. I don't even think about it anymore. Except the occasional Friday night – like tonight – when I drag myself to the Ox for cheap beers. Even then I only think about it for a second, reminding myself it's one less nail to paint. A lot worse coulda happened.

In the grit of a dive or between sweaty sheets, most guys don't notice. Some men I've dated took weeks to mention the finger. Then again, roughnecks aren't much for holding hands or paying close attention to you. Some don't even kiss.

I ease my head back under to rinse out my hair. I'll be in this town till Dad dies. Don't know how long that'll be, he's taken to falling, though. He needs me; living right downstairs has come in handy more than once. Valerie got to escape to Vancouver once she got married. I'll get there too someday.

What'll I even do in B.C.? I've been cutting meat so long I don't know what else I'm fit for. Maybe lick my wounds and go on pogey for a while? That's hard to imagine. I've always had a job. Val stays at home raising three boys, and I don't envy her. I like to work.

You get used to the plant. You cope. I wield a sharp knife all day long. It's ridiculous, I know, but sometimes I pretend I'm slitting fabric to make little girls' dresses, instead of carving carcasses into steaks. Agnes, who works next to me, sings Sudanese songs to help get through the day. She taught me one, called "Shen-Shen." I asked her once what that song is about. "Life is unfair, Wanda. That is what it is about," she said, and went back to singing. Agnes sends money to her mother and father in Juba every month via Western Union. Can't complain about the wage. Fifteen dollars an hour is nothing to sneeze at. The men you meet though. Christ.

Last guy I dated from Slaughter was Karl Willson – a blond behemoth, prairie farming stock. He was twenty-four, six-three, and very strong – so he was quickly recruited for the harshest job on the kill floor. He's a stunner and sticker: he kills live cattle and drains their blood. I don't think less of guys in Slaughter because their jobs are dirtier than mine. The rest of us can't feel holier-than-thou about chopping steaks, filling sausage links, or grinding burger meat. The reason I don't like Karl is he's a prick.

He came to Alberta a few months ago from Saskatchewan with his younger brother, who got hired to dress carcasses. Karl was well suited to a job as a cutthroat. He didn't mind killing, he liked it. He was fast. Speedy workers are the company's wet dream.

We only dated a few weeks. Karl was brooding and edgy. That made for rough, satisfying sex – but I knew something bad would spring from his constant, simmering anger. One night at the drive-in, I teased him about something – I think it was a cowlick that made his hair look funny – and he punched me hard in the face. I don't put up with bullshit – that was the end. We haven't spoken since.

He got moved to B shift. That means I work days and he works nights. When I go to the Ox on a Friday, he's usually not there because he can only make last call by coming right from the plant. He sometimes does, the need to drink out-weighing the duty to clean himself up first. The smell of

Processing wasn't as bad as Slaughter, but I never went to the bar without taking a long bath.

Standing up to dry myself off, I close my eyes a sec. Hope I don't run into Karl tonight. I shouldn't be going out – it's the height of summer so we're on a six-day week at the plant. I need to be there tomorrow morning at seven, even though it's a Saturday. But I need something to make me forget for a while.

Pulling a towel off the rack, I dry my breasts, my belly, the insides of my legs, the bottoms of my feet, and then scrub at my wet hair with the efforts of nine determined fingertips.

———

The harsh blare of the alarm clock seeps into my consciousness through the hot haze of slumber. I stretch across Makok's broad, dark shoulders to finger the snooze button. Unable to stifle a belch that reeks like last night's whisky sours, I slump back for nine more minutes of rest, draping my arm across the width of his back. He stops snoring, but doesn't stir.

Morning's light streams through the bedroom window, and I squint. Makok works on Karl's floor but I don't think they're friends. His wife does dayshift on the line. She's not in my section, but I can see her from where I stand at the boning table. I've seen the two of them at the IGA together; they've both worked at the plant for a few months now.

I think back to last night, and don't recall much. Makok smiling at me as he leaned over the pool table, cue in hand. Asking him to buy me a drink though I could afford my own liquor. Flattering compliments in halting English. More drinks. His brown eyes locked with my own, an unspoken decision to go ahead.

He faces away, hugging a pillow. I scan his smooth back, visually tracing its one blemish: a three-inch, curved white scar across his right shoulder. Must have been a meat hook; that's common. Or something that happened back home – like many at the plant, he's from Sudan. I'm not going to ask.

The alarm buzzes again. Makok shakes awake; both of our hands reach for the noisemaker this time. He smacks the top of the clock and then grabs my fingers.

He turns and our eyes meet. I lean toward him, we kiss. He pulls his bulky frame onto mine and I welcome the pressure. We fuck one more time; fiercely and quickly. Before the alarm sounds again, we're done. Makok eases out of me, strokes my cheek, then abruptly pulls himself to his feet and stands naked above me, a drizzle of semen still hanging off the tip of his foreskin.

"Mende is pregnant." He walks to the bathroom.

I sit on the toilet and piss while Makok showers; I put out a clean towel. He doesn't offer me a ride to work – he leaves while I'm in the shower. I tie my hair into a loose braid and throw a sweater into my knapsack. Hot as it is outside, my part of the plant is refrigerated.

I pop four ibuprofens on my way out the door. Hop into my Civic and head for the plant. I crack the window. It's too hot not to, but you don't open it very far. The closer you get to the plant, the more the air smells like shit. Bosses call it "the smell of money." No matter which way the wind blows, you can't escape it.

The locker room smells like wet sawdust and it's crowded. The air's humid with steam emanating from the shower stalls at the end of the room. On a bench between two rows of lockers, I'm surrounded by women. I recognize some but have never talked to them. You can't know everybody in a plant of two thousand people. Once we're suited up, recognizing anyone is hard.

Lockers are assigned in numerical order based on hire date and then reassigned because of turnover – not everyone can handle this job. All around me, women chatter, yell, laugh – none of it in English. You get used to that.

I put on my gear in the same order every morning. First the yellow rubber boots. Next I pull on my steel mesh apron. It runs from my shoulders to my knees. I reach around to tie it in the back, drawing my head to my chest. There, I catch my first whiff. Though I scrubbed it at the end of yesterday's shift, my apron still hosts the faint but dizzying scent of bull's blood.

I hear a rumble from the shop floor; they're turning on the grinders and getting ready for the shift to start. I check my pockets for earplugs. Rubber sleeves that run from my wrists to my elbows. A hairnet, then my bump cap – a yellow construction helmet. Plastic safety goggles that hang from my neck by a nylon cord; I'll put them on once I'm on the line. I grab my long, thin knife and stuff it into the waist pocket of the apron. Thank God I sharpened it yesterday. With this hangover, I'd cut myself if I tried today.

Last, thick rubber gloves, with a crumpled paper ball jammed into one fingertip to keep it from flopping, or getting caught in anything. All around me, women who've arrived late crowd in and clamber into the same uniform. We have to be on the line when it starts up.

Wading through the crowd and the roaring machines, I

arrive at the boning table to find my co-workers already in position. With a smirk, Kwadwo calls out in his West African–accented baritone.

"Wanda, you look like you were up late," he says in a chastising tone.

My shoulders slump. Then I puff out my chest and beat him at his own game. "I was with your dad last night, Kwadwo. I hope you have as much energy in bed as him!"

Kwadwo giggles like a tickled schoolboy. "My father is fifty-six – and he still lives in Ghana. No wonder you are tired . . ."

"I went out to the Ox for a few – but not much was going on," I confess.

"As long as you weren't with Kwadwo's father – or any other fathers – then it is good," Agnes pipes in, arching an eyebrow as she adjusts her hairnet over a short-cropped Afro.

Agnes is a generation older than me, but the Sudanese community is close-knit. Could she be friends with Makok and his pregnant wife?

She smiles and gives me a friendly elbow. "Use protection, or you will make someone a father!" I grin, relieved.

Next to me, Kwadwo, Agnes, and three girls from Newfoundland work at our compact boning table. We're short one man, a French-Canadian, the nephew of Mr. Leger, the floor supervisor. Funny that our table is mostly whites – we're a minority on the floor. That's another thing you get used to.

With another clickety-clack rumble, the line kicks into gear. Meat moves into the room from the kill floor downstairs. Along the west wall, enormous whole cattle emerge from the trap door, suspended from above by hooks that pierce one of their back limbs. The men at the front of the room take them down one by one and begin to cut.

First, off with their heads. Then, out with their guts. Next, off with their hides. The carcasses hit three other cutting tables before reaching ours. We get manageable, medium-sized slabs ready to be reduced to supermarket-grade cuts. The first will reach our table in just under ten minutes. Several hours of slicing and dicing later, we get lunch at eleven o'clock. I'm so used to separating meat from bones I could do it in my sleep.

Mid-morning, I glance at the bone-shiners table further down the line.

There, a group of women wield electric knives to remove excess meat from bones before they're sent to Rendering. It's hard to tell anyone apart between the mouth protectors, goggles, hairnets, and helmets, but I think I recognize Makok's wife, Mende, among the dozen African women at the table. Most chat and smile while they work – with one tall, rigid exception.

At lunch I sit with Agnes, Kwadwo, and Kathy, one of the girls from our group. The cafeteria fare is bearable today: lasagna and fruit salad. We keep it light – no sex, religion, or politics at the lunch table. My aching, dehydrated brain is glad for that. Normally, I love to listen to Agnes talk – she is passionate about current affairs in her homeland – but I couldn't cope right now.

Taking my tray to the garbage bin, I feel an object thunk onto my back. Turning around, I look at the floor and see a leftover grape from someone's fruit salad. A loud guffaw, and then a big, blond dickwad is in my face – Karl's brother, Kevin

Willson. He has a V-shaped scar on his cheek and the smile of a carved pumpkin with one front tooth missing.

"Oh sorry, Wanda. I was aiming for the trash. Guess I missed."

I offer a fake smile.

"Hey, heard you had a busy night. Up late, weren't you?" He sneers. "You like the dark though, don't you?"

That fucking piece of shit. I didn't see him at the bar last night. I shove him out of my way, and head back onto the floor.

Leger approaches our table as we ready to go back to work, a young girl in tow. She looks nineteen. Vietnamese probably, with a very pretty face. She won't last long – she'd be better off in another section. This girl is too short. She'll have to reach upward to make all her cuts. The boning table is designed for people of average height; she'll end up with very sore shoulders.

"Kids, this is Anh. Show her the ropes." With that, he walks away. From behind, it looks like he's picking his nose.

Agnes and I exchange a knowing look. But she smiles when she turns to Anh.

"Where are you from, girl?"

Her voice is a whisper but I manage to hear because she's right next to me. "Cambodia."

"Pull your face mask over your mouth, Anh. I'll show you what to do."

Anh exhales visibly. Agnes has a way of making people comfortable. We all pull our face masks on and get to work. Because of staggered lunch breaks, meat has begun to pile up.

I pick up the first piece and carve, glancing from time to time to watch Agnes and Anh. The girl's cuts are tentative, which is to be expected at the start. Given the jostling from the other tables when things get busy, she'll likely cut herself today. Might as well get her first self-slice out of the way. In contrast to boisterous Agnes singing and carving next to her, Anh looks fragile. I fear one slit from a sharp knife might cause her to completely disassemble.

Just as Anh gets the hang of things, a loud male scream erupts from a table ten feet away. A tall white guy grasps at the red gush of blood coming out of his right biceps. His still-buzzing hock cutter, a hand-held version of a small buzz saw used to slice the limbs off cattle, bounces onto the table in front of him. The electric saw falls onto the concrete floor, glancing off the woman next to him. Shit. Continuing to cut my meat, I watch Leger rush over with a nurse, face riddled with anxiety. I know the bastard's worried about keeping up the speed of the line, not some poor sucker's hacked limb. It wasn't fully severed anyway. I put my slices into a grey plastic tub, put them back on the belt, and grab my next piece of meat.

Anh has dropped her knife on the ground. She watches with widened eyes as the tall man, now hunched over with a white towel pressed against his red and sopping shirt sleeve, is led away by the nurse, sobbing. Meat continues to pile up on the belt in front of us.

Agnes reaches down to grab Anh's knife up off the wet floor and holds it lightly by the blade, pointing its handle back at the young woman. She gestures to Anh with the handle. "Anh, you can't stop."

Anh continues to stare mutely toward the hock area, where everyone else is busily back at work with a tiny bit more room per person. Agnes puts the knife into Anh's gloved hand, closes her hand around it, and gently turns her back to face the boning table.

"You can't stop." Agnes sighs and looks in my direction, then picks a piece of meat up off the belt and places it in front of Anh. Anh looks down at it, and cuts.

The guy is back on the line two hours later. I go into autopilot for the rest of the day. I'm no longer slicing meat, I'm fashioning a simple, elegant wedding dress out of peau de soie, an A-line with pleats that run from the waist to the feet. No frilly train, but a subtle band of patterned lace around the waistline. Sleeveless, though not low-cut, with thin straps. Pretty yet unassuming. And the sheerest, most delicate bridal gloves. No fancy patterns, basic white, and they cut off just before the elbow.

The day ends. I hope Anh comes back tomorrow. We need the extra hands at the boning table. I head for the locker room. Pushing my way numbly through the all-female mass, I reach my locker and pause. My lock's been snipped with a bolt cutter. I remove the severed combination lock and pull it open.

The severed head of a dead calf lolls lazily on the top shelf of my locker. Most of its hair has been shaved off, but tufts still cling to its floppy, oversized ears. Both lips have been removed, exposing its skeletal teeth. Its fat, amputated tongue has been stuffed back into its mouth, and it sticks out at an abnormal angle. It smells like vomit. The flesh around the base of the head is mottled and bloody. Along the hacked neckline, two flies sit and feast.

Fucking gross. I slam the locker door shut with all my strength. It bounces back open, forcing the raunchy odour back in my face. With the force of the jolt, the calf's head bounces and tips forward. It topples out of the locker and heaves onto my yellow rubber boot. With a fearful bolt of adrenaline, I kick it down the row of lockers. It comes to a stop at the other end of the hall, where a group of women are coming out of the showers. They stop en masse, emitting yelps and grunts of disgust, looking over at me and swearing. The calf's tongue came free of the head when I kicked it; it lies on the ground a few feet away. I crumple to the bench and find myself crying for the first time in years. I wish I were anywhere but here.

I step out of the women's locker room an eternity later. As I head for the exit, a deep voice calls out to me.

"Hey, slut." Karl Willson stomps my way with a crooked sneer on his lips.

I cross my arms in front of my chest. "What the fuck do you want?"

He answers in singsong. "Is Princess having a bad day?" Karl reaches forward with a start and shoves my crossed arms so hard I fall backward to the ground. He leans in and I cover my face quickly. He's yelling in my ear. "What? That black bitch show you what a fucking cow you are?"

I kick him in the shin, a glancing blow, and he steps back. I scramble to my feet. A dozen passersby have slowed or stopped. "What the fuck, Karl!"

"Kevin told me what you did last night, you fucking whore."

The crowd begins to filter away. Another lover's spat. Happens all the time.

"Those people believe in revenge. You better watch out."

"Karl, you're full of shit."

He spits in my face and walks away. Two women's voices approach, not speaking English. I climb to my feet, recognizing Agnes's voice.

She wears a white blouse, acid-wash jeans, and a faded denim jacket. Next to her stands a tall woman with a pretty face marred by dark circles under her eyes. A dark-green, patterned scarf covers her hair and drapes across her shoulders, underneath which she wears a simple white dress. I notice the slight curve of her belly. Makok's wife.

"Wanda, this is my friend, Mende."

I glance downward then look up at her, my face flushed. "How are you, Mende?" I manage.

"It is nice to meet you." Her heavily accented English is stilted and formal.

Agnes turns to me. "We're going to church. There are things we need to speak to the pastor about . . . maybe you'd like to come with us."

"I'm sorry, Agnes. I need to go make dinner for my father." I look at my feet, and back at the two of them. Mende appraises me.

"I heard what happened, Wanda. I thought some spiritual guidance might be a help."

I pause. "You know what happened?"

"At your locker."

I exhale. "A stupid prank. Some joker from the kill floor."

"I believe things happen for a reason, Wanda. If you don't want to come now, you could attend our Sunday morning service." She touches Mende's arm before adding, "It can help when troubling things happen."

I decide something. "Agnes, I'd join you but I'll be packing. Dad and I are moving to Vancouver. We leave Monday."

Agnes breaks into a sudden grin. "I can't believe you didn't tell me!"

"No one knows."

"It's time you saw the world." Agnes came from Africa and had lived in Newfoundland for years before coming here. "What are you going to do in the big city – work in a butcher shop?"

"I'm going to be an apprentice to a dressmaker." I realize this by saying it aloud for the first time.

Mende appears distracted, but offers Agnes a confused look. Agnes speaks to her quickly, pointing to me several times. I realize she's translating the conversation we just had. Karl lied – I doubt he could have communicated anything to Mende. He must've snuck in when the locker room was empty and busted into my locker himself. Whatever.

I embrace Agnes. Mende turns to me and says, "Good luck." The two of them walk away. Men and women stream past in the opposite direction by the dozens, on their way into the plant for B shift.

Better get home and tell Dad. I exit the building and walk alongside the chain-link fence that leads from the plant to the parking lot. I can't remember where I parked my Civic. I scan the sea of parked cars, and nothing looks familiar.

FRAN KIMMEL

PICTURING GOD'S OCEAN

We were on that beach in Florida when I caught a pervert snapping photos of my little girl.

I was dumping the leftover fries into the garbage can by the busy road; Becky and Lora were close to the water. Becky hopped up and down in front of her mother, hairless and naked and milky white, while Lora worked the sand out of her bathing suit.

The guy looked like any other local, with a year-round tan, orange shorts, and a T-shirt that came from a closet not a suitcase. But there was a hunger in the way he leaned forward, the way his finger eagerly snapped. When I whirled around to take in his telephoto's view, it was pointed right at Becky.

He bolted just before I reached him. I chased him through the tunnel that ran under the main drag and into the state park. We sprinted past the visitor centre and the circle of covered picnic tables, trampled across a burst of plastic-like flowers, and landed along a nature trail. He pounded through the forest, fast at first, flinging his camera into an island of tangled mangroves. I kept losing sight of him as we snaked through the trees. He made it to the parking lot before me, where he fell down on all fours and puked into the gravel. When I caught up, I decked him in the head, hard, and then I fell down too. A lady with an enormous yellow hat was close by, lugging stuff from her trunk and fumbling with a cellphone from her beach bag. She yelled into the phone: . . . *his head's bleeding real bad, the guy's gonna kill him.* It took me a minute to figure out I was the guy.

———

The holiday was Lora's idea. She wanted Becky to see the ocean – to find real seashells. We'd never even been on a plane before.

"Lake Winnipeg can be like the ocean," I offered. "It's a lot closer."

Lora pretended not to hear. She was filling in Becky's passport application. Next of kin. Who to call in case of emergency. The colour of her eyes, her hair. How much weight she took up in this world.

The passports cost $67 a piece. We had eleven days until payday. A carton of milk in the fridge. A couple of whitefish in the freezer. A mounting stack of bills from every quack we could find this side of the border. Tibetan herbalists. Homeopathologists. The oxygenated water man.

These were our dark days.

"We could go to those little cabins at Gimli," I tried. "Becky loves it there."

"In winter, Michael? So she can stand on the beach in her snowsuit? Nothing's open."

"I meant in the summer. We can take Becky next summer."

When Lora finally looked up at me, I'd become a stranger. Her eyes saw just another someone who couldn't comprehend how far away the summer was.

————

Two cops – a large white guy and an even larger black woman – appeared out of nowhere. Me and the pervert were still down on the ground, panting. After I choked out my side of the story, the guy muddled through his. He was just taking a few beach photos for his wife's scrapbook was all. He blubbered the words in fits and starts, like a four-year-old getting jabbed with needles.

"So why'd you dump the camera then?" the lady cop asked. Officer Jarvis. I still don't know her first name. She answers her phone like a man. Jarvis, she barks, in a deep, no-nonsense, get-to-the-point kind of way.

The guy shook his head from side to side, mumbling how there was a crazy man chasing him through the trees.

She followed me back to the mangroves and we rooted around in the muck.

"That's a nasty cut," she said, her giant hand pointing to my shoeless foot.

Blood gurgled from between my toes and puddled on the wet ground.

I found the camera wedged between the folds in a mossy log. The lens cap had sprung loose, cracked in two. Jarvis pushed me aside effortlessly, brushed off the ants, and lifted it by the strap.

I wanted to know what they could do to a pervert in the US of A. If they could shackle his wrists and throw him in a cell with carjacking types who had little girls of their own.

Her expression remained hard, but her voice seemed to soften. "Let us worry about the details, how about? You give us your information and we'll let you know."

————

Lora's church paid for our airfare. I didn't want their charity – I didn't even know those people – but their gesture made Lora cry. I vaguely remembered meeting Danny the Preacher in the meat section of Sobeys. He seemed more a John Lennon than a Jerry Falwell type. I imagined him sitting beside my wife, one empathic palm lightly patting her knee, while she poured out the details of our whole sad story. I hated that picture in my head, but it was those kinds of intimacies that allowed her to go on. And she had to go on or I was done for.

In the beginning, I tried to do the right thing. I'd usher our ragged family back to the house from the latest ordeal with the god-like Dr. Arnold. We'd throw in the *Land Before Time* video for Becky, and Lora would go into the bathroom to scrub away the hospital stink, and I'd move from room to room, fixing the sticky window and cracked tiles, rechecking the furnace filter, re-sorting the paint cans under the stairs. I'd grind the coffee beans when the church people arrived, bow my head and wait silently when they offered their prayers, hold back Becky's hair when she vomited into the pail. Throughout it all, I'd keep saying to Lora, over and over, "Becky's gonna be okay; we're gonna be okay."

That was in the beginning. Lora finally told me to shut up and spare her my empty, godless assurances. I felt relieved to not have to speak the words. After that, we spent our days dancing around the elephant, waiting for night, barely clinging to respectability until Becky had been tucked away. Then we came together like animals, my wife and me, clenching and pounding and clawing through the darkness. I did nothing to stop it. I let the anger wash over me like a scalding shower, not much caring if I tore her in two. In the mornings, Lora dressed in the closet behind the closed door so I wouldn't see her purpled skin.

———

When Officer Jarvis and I got back to the parking lot the other cop stood post by the police cruiser, arms crossed, yawning. The pervert slumped in the back seat. I walked up to the car and glared through the glass at his sweaty face. A blood-soaked gauze square had been taped to the gash above his right ear. He stared past my hip at the camera swinging below Jarvis's fist. Then he put his unshackled hands to his face and rocked back and forth. I almost felt pity. Not for the man, but for what a man can be reduced to.

Jarvis handed me a pen and a clipboard and told me to use the cruiser's hood for a desk. She said I should write down everything from when I first saw the suspect to when she and her partner showed up. "Stick to the facts," she warned. "Leave your emotions out of this."

I stared at the form for a long time, emotionless, trying to remember the facts. We wanted to give Becky everything. That was a fact. But when that wasn't enough, we brought her to the ocean instead. Lora and I set up camp on the beach, closer to the water than the rest. "Look, Becky, look at the huge waves." We watched as our daughter listlessly filled her pail with the heavy, wet sand. "Where are the shells, Michael?" Lora kept asking. "There's just these tiny broken bits that could be anything. Washed up cardboard pieces or oyster turds."

"I'll get rid of the lunch garbage." I walked away from them, turning back once. I remember trying to muster a little enthusiasm for Lora's sake, making some stupid remark about blowing up the beach ball, a soccer game, girls against boys. Lora nodded absently, not taking her eyes off Becky.

The cameraman stood beyond the garbage cans. Click. Click. Click. I thought maybe it was dolphins, or a pelican skimming the water's surface, so I turned around too. That's when I saw what he saw. I was overcome by such a profound and utter misery my knees buckled out from under me. The top of Becky's head was as smooth as a snow globe, her stick of a leg needle-bruised from knee to thigh. Click. Click. Click. She could have been a war refugee, a skeleton child with an unspeakable past. Lora kept thrashing Becky's bathing suit with her open palm, as though it were filled with stinging bees and if she just kept pummelling, she could kill them all. Click. Slap. Click. Slap.

I scribbled out the story about my chasing the bastard. First we ran here, and then we ran there. I left out the part about my needing to run away from that scene on the beach.

Officer Jarvis read over my account while her partner leaned

into the car door and examined the group of bikinied girls
that had gathered a few cars down. Jarvis must have been satisfied, because she initialled the statement and told me to go
back to my family. Before she let me go, she folded at the
waist and looked down at my congealing toes. "Get that
checked out," she ordered. "You should probably get a tetanus
shot. No telling what you stepped on."

Then she flicked a dismissive wrist at her partner and they
both got in the car and drove away with the pervert in the
back.

———

By the time I limped back to the beach, Lora was frantic.
Becky had fallen asleep in her arms under the shade of the
rented beach umbrella. Where had I disappeared to? How
could I just leave them like that? What happened to my foot
for God sakes?

I stuck to the facts, while Lora's eyes darted back and forth
looking for terrible things against the concrete wall that held
back the road. Then we packed up the umbrella and the towels
and pails and the ball-still-in-its-bag and trudged through the
tunnel and back to our motel.

Lora wanted me to go to emergency for my foot, but I
couldn't face another hospital, so we stayed in our shabby
room the rest of the day. She filled the bathtub and I soaked
my foot until the yellow water turned pink, and then she
wrapped my toes in overpriced gauze strips from the motel's
gift shop. We ordered takeout Chinese that came in those
house-shaped cardboard boxes you see on TV. Becky ate part
of a dumpling. We threw the rest away.

"I want to go home, Michael," Lora whispered. "There's no hope here." Our daughter lay between us on the motel bed, oblivious to the ocean we'd brought her to on the other side of the closed curtains.

———

Becky slept the entire flight home and all through that night too. The next morning she wolfed down a man-sized heap of Shreddies. Dr. Arnold told us this might happen and that it would be a good sign. When Becky held out her bowl for more, Lora kissed her forehead and said, natural-like, "Sure sweetie. Of course. As much as you want," as if her asking was a regular thing. But when Lora tried to pour the milk, her fingers shook so badly I had to cover her hand with mine and steer the carton to the bowl.

I couldn't bear that scene – my daughter asking for more, like a normal kid, my wife wanting so badly to pour life back into her she was trembling like a bird. I left them in the kitchen and climbed into my truck and drove past every house in the neighbourhood. I couldn't think of where else to go, so I headed to the job-site. I was supposed to be at the beach, taking care of my family. Nobody expected me back for days. But then that's the thing, isn't it? Life's surprises. Nobody expected to find monsters under the bed either, waiting to prey on their little girls.

———

"We're not out of the woods yet," Dr. Arnold told us. This was at our last consultation. "But I'm optimistic," he added at the end. Sneering, I thought. Lora said it's just the way his mouth moves when he tries to smile. I suppose I should feel grateful to the man. But he makes it sound like we've been on a camping trip together, sharing the same tent. Who is he to think he can dole out hope like ice cream scoops? When I picture all the times his rough, clammy hands have been on my daughter, poking and prodding, oblivious to her tears, I want nothing more than to punch him in the mouth.

But hope is slippery. Becky's grown an inch these past few months, the top of her new reddish curls reaching the sixth ladybug on her growth chart. I'm afraid to blink in case I miss something.

———

Lora hasn't confessed to her church about the wasted there-and-back airfare. I haven't confessed to Lora either. She has no idea about the kind of thoughts that were chasing me on that beach and ever since. My wife believes I'm a man she can count on. I've overheard her tell her friends as much when she's talking on the phone.

A few weeks after we got back from our trip, she sent a card to Preacher Danny, which we both signed. He posted the note on the vestibule's bulletin board. She wrote: *We can't thank you enough for your prayers. Your generous gift gave our family God's ocean.* She says God will forgive her for omitting the details.

Officer Jarvis says it's all in the details. The pervert was a city worker, a member of the Coconut Creek Scratch Bowling League. His digital images were just a low-grade ranking of kiddy bum shots and side views. There were twenty-two such pictures on his memory stick – no coercion or enticement or children posed in sexual acts. There was no proof of distribution, either, nothing to warrant more than a slap on the wrist from the pornography police.

I should have thought to kill him when I had the chance. I have this weird little recurring daydream where he hangs himself in his wife's laundry room. It comforts me, his dangling head swinging back and forth inside mine.

———

The summer's come fast. My wife and I have a new routine these sweltering nights. We lock the screen door and turn out the porch light, and then we sneak into Becky's room to listen to the sounds of her little girl snores. Lora sometimes takes my hand. Or she stands on her toes and brushes her cheek against mine. Or she rests against me like I'm her rock. She does these things so tenderly I can hardly catch my breath. Somehow she's forgotten how we were, back when we had a dying child. We've never once spoken about the marks we left on each other. I want to ask for forgiveness, but I don't have the courage.

I bought a bag of seashells at the airport. This was just before we pushed through the same boarding gate we'd stepped out of twenty-eight hours earlier. It was one of those rare last-minute ideas that turned out right. Lora buries the shells in the backyard sandbox, and she and Becky go beach-combing before the sun gets too hot.

On Saturday mornings I crack a beer, stretch out on the grass, and watch my girls. Mostly I watch Lora. There'll be something about the way she tilts her head back and smiles at the sky that makes me believe the damage can be reversed.

She's long since erased the dirty pictures. I wish I could follow her path, dive into the place where she goes inside, but I don't know how. Where she's able to see the goodness of her God working alongside the terrible things that happen to people, I still see the terrible things. I see Becky tethered to the hospital bed, Becky inside his camera, Becky in the evidence file. I see Lora struggling underneath me, my fingers clamped over her throat or digging into the flesh of her perfect white arms. Sometimes, I wake up from a dead sleep and feel my lungs exploding, like I've been running across a beach of broken glass, trying to get away.

Officer Jarvis says to stop calling. She says the case is closed, and there's nothing more to discuss. I think about what it takes to see what she sees each day and still keep going. To get out of bed, get your shirt buttoned right, act like you're normal.

There's a pea-shaped lump between my toes that throbs from morning to night. I don't pretend to understand what I stepped into on that beach. All I know is I have my girls back, and I'd be hard pressed to run anywhere again. It's a fair trade no matter which way you slice it. If Lora knew the whole story, she'd say her God thinks so too.

DANIEL GRIFFIN

THE LAST GREAT WORKS OF ALVIN CALE

found out because of a dream. In this dream I was speaking to my son and asked how he was. "I'm skinny," he said. "Really skinny."

"How skinny?"

A long sandy silence followed. "Really, really skinny."

"Why?" I said, and he paused again, long enough that it built a pressure inside me. Something awful waited.

"I've just become too skinny," he said at last.

That pulled me to a shallow wakefulness and I tossed and turned a while. When the clock said five, I got out of bed, made coffee on the propane stove, and sat in the withering darkness. Although Alvin lives only a few hours south of me, we've whittled our connection thin and I hadn't seen him in almost three years.

I should have made my way into town and phoned him right then, but instead, once daylight held a steady grip on the land, I picked up my rucksack and a small canvas and went out to paint.

There's a cluster of giant firs I love – a cathedral that blots out the sky and encloses the forest floor. I set my stool in a well-worn spot in a bed of needles among the ferns and propped the blank canvas in front of myself. The painting consumed me as it always does, the physicality of the work, the concentration required to transfer life through my eyes and through the brush onto canvas. A day of work beat away the voices that dream had awoken. A week later, though, I dreamed about Alvin again. He said he wished he wasn't so skinny. Pain and suffering lurked among those words. I was up early enough to watch the sun rise, but this time, once that ball of fire was clear of the trees, and its rays cut deep into my cabin, I walked out to the logging road, got in my truck, and headed for town. The nearest phone's at a Petro-Can on the Pacific Rim Highway. I plugged in a quarter. Alvin's phone rang almost a dozen times. I was ready to hang up when Sandy answered.

"Hi," I said. "It's Skylar."

"Oh my God. Skylar." The way she said that set off a depth charge within me. "It's your dad," she said to Alvin.

"Sorry if I woke you. If it's a bad time . . ."

And then my son was on the line. "I was wondering when you'd call."

I didn't recognize Alvin's voice at first. He was six weeks into an experimental treatment for a stage-four tumour in his sinuses. His nose had started to collapse from the radiation and it gave his voice a high edge.

"Alvin?" I said. "What is it? What's going on?"

"Oh God, Dad. Oh Jesus. Didn't you get my letters?"

———

I live in a cabin in the bush year round with no electricity and no phone. It's crown land and it was once a commune of sorts. This story truly starts there almost thirty years ago. I was drawn to the west coast by what Emily Carr had done, what Jack Shadbolt and Sybil Andrews were doing, and what I thought I could do. I was pulled into the bush by the dark, rich colours of the earth, the filtered light and ancient trees. Alvin's mother and I built the cabin I live in now. At its peak we were a community of a dozen souls – a draft dodger, his wife and their baby, a former math professor, a communist from the north of England, and a pair of sisters, one of whom had adopted a son. Curious locals joined us off and on. And starting in the summer of 1978, a girl from Quebec named Sylvette Turcotte. I met her on a rainy day outside the Co-op. She had a striking face – deep-set eyes, big and open. She'd travelled west with a boyfriend who now worked in a logging camp.

For almost three years Sylvette was my model. She was the source of the best work I've done in over forty years of painting. She had an elastic body, graceful and elegant in every posture. She had skin that picked up dimples of sunlight, a figure that cast shadows upon itself. There are models who contribute to figurative work on levels beyond shape and form, and she was one. Even today I believe her body enabled me to see the human figure in a new way.

People in town called us hippies. They talked about free love. There was love, but it was never free. My wife left me a year after Sylvette arrived. Alvin stayed. He was sixteen by then and had begun to sketch Sylvette while she posed for me. Like Picasso, Alvin never drew as a child draws. He was proficient and precise from the day he began. Standing beside me in that cabin twenty-some years ago, he captured her with simple strong lines, bold gestures with charcoal, pencil, and eventually paint.

In 1981, Sylvette left and Alvin left with her. Sylvette was two months pregnant. She and Alvin lived together on Galiano Island and then on Salt Spring. This was the early eighties. I was lost in a short flash of fame built on those paintings of Sylvette. My only works in the National Gallery are of her.

Eventually Sylvette returned to Quebec. She still lives there, in Montreal. She has a daughter I've never met. The year Alvin found out about his cancer, the year I had those dreams and drove down island to be with him, this girl Lysanne had just turned twenty-three.

———

Alvin's wife, Sandy, is short with a roly-poly beauty – a plump frame, big cheeks. She met me at the door, opened it wide. "How are you doing?" I said.

Sandy backed off a step and raised the cigarette in her hand. "Started smoking again."

Alvin was on the sofa at the far end of their loft. The TV cast a trembling glow across his blanketed body. I wanted to walk straight over, but something held me a moment – a cocktail of anxieties: the possibility he was asleep, fear of what I was about to see, and the years of muck built between us, a weight like undigested meat in the belly.

Sandy led the way and Alvin turned to face us. His nose was wounded, red and bloody-looking. A gauze patch covered his right eye. The skin of his face, leathery and thin, looked ready to break apart.

I sent out a hand, but wasn't sure where to lay it. Eventually Alvin raised his own hand, embraced mine. "It's good to see you," I said.

He coughed, and it moved his whole body. He coughed again – took several attempts to get up the phlegm, and then he rested. He didn't speak, but he looked at me, that one eye red-rimmed, worn and droopy. I could feel my own eyes fill with tears and finally overflow. I've lived a long life. I've stilled my heart more times than I can count, but here was my son, my only son, the child I raised. It took a moment to pull myself into control. "Today was a radiation day," Sandy said. "We just got back from the hospital. It's been a hard day for him."

Alvin turned his head, looked up at the ceiling. I glanced around the loft. Three walls were filled with paintings. It was all his work, but I only recognized one – a painting of Sylvette lying supine, face turned away. I knew it because he'd painted it standing beside me in my cabin over twenty years ago. It had a raw, fleshy power, a bold weight in colour and composition – amateurish, but strong and fresh in his interpretation of the body.

The day he began this painting is marked in my mind so clearly I can recall the canvas I was working on. I never finished it. I set it down as though it were somehow tainted by the power of the painting emerging beside it.

Pablo Picasso's father, Jose Ruiz, was also an artist. He taught the young Picasso for years, but they fought bitterly. They had a falling out. The exact cause isn't recorded, but Picasso began signing his paintings using his mother's maiden name. Ruiz set down his brushes, gave painting up altogether in the shadow of his teenage son's brilliance.

———

Alvin noticed me looking over his paintings. He raised a hand. "Old work." It was a croak of a voice. He took a deep breath, spoke again. "Hung for a party ages ago."

Sandy backed off a step. "I'll make tea. Just sit with him. He'll like that."

I took the rocker at the near end of the sofa. A newscast flickered across the TV, pictures of soldiers in desert fatigues. The volume was off. "The body's a miraculous thing," I said. "You'll see. Your body will amaze you."

Sandy returned with the tea. "He needs distractions," she said. "Made me get him a TV. We keep the volume off sometimes so I can hear him." She handed me a mug, sat at the far end of the sofa, and lifted his feet onto her lap. "He listens to books on tape from the library. And we get a lot of movies. Plus he sleeps a lot. Especially after the treatments." She patted his feet. "He's so glad you've come. We've been waiting, hoping you'd get his letters."

"Don't go into town much these days. Sometimes forget to check my mail."

Sandy turned her attention to the TV, finished her cup of tea, then left to go grocery shopping. Alvin snored faintly. I sat alone with him, took his hand, dry and chapped, skin brittle from years of oil paints and turpentine.

In the early evening, Alvin awoke. He looked around. "I'm here," I said. "Right here." After a silent moment, he closed his one eye and slept again. He was like this as a boy – a fitful sleeper. He'd call out, his mother or I would come in, and he'd roll over and sleep again.

When Alvin next awoke, I lifted Rilke's *Letters to a Young Poet* from where it was face down on the coffee table and offered to read. He held up a hand to stop me. A moment later he said, "I'm trapped in my mind. Not enough energy to do anything, but my mind still churns." It was nine at night. He'd slept about six hours. "I drift through anxieties and worries, dwell on unsettled business. Probably all these drugs I'm taking."

"Worry never helped anyone."

"Remember how I wanted to live in town, wanted to go to school, have friends?"

I nodded and he raised his hand to his face, explored a moment. "I wanted a TV and a record player. I wanted to be a regular kid. Go to school. A locker. Remember how much I wanted a locker?"

"Could have got you a locker if you'd just said."

"You and Mom were in la-la land. She was stoned or drunk and you were painting or dilly-dallying with someone or other."

"Oh for God's sakes, Alvin."

He turned his head to look up at the ceiling. "After you moved us up there, I mostly hated you. I thought I hated the painting too. Until Sylvette arrived. Although for a long time I just did it so I could see her naked."

"Why are you talking like this, Alvin?"

He shook his head and maybe he shrugged.

"You're going to pull through this –"

"Dad," he said.

"Your doctor's good? I mean, you're happy with your treatment, your oncologist?"

"Sandy thinks I should try something more natural. Diet-based. Fighting fire with water not with fire."

"Sounds oversimplified."

"The work was flying out of me just a few months ago. I was exhausted, sleeping twelve hours a day, and painting the other twelve. Thought it was the work draining me. And then I started getting these headaches. For a month or two I assumed it was the turpentine. Tried different products, the fumeless stuff. Looking back there were six months of warning signs before I went to the doctor. That's what would have made the difference. Catching this six months earlier."

On one of the first days I was there, I came upon Sandy in the kitchen staring out the window with her hands in the murky dishwater. She didn't turn around but seemed to sense my presence. "Had my hair done today," she said.

"Looks nice." I'd already done the dishes. I wasn't sure why she had her hands in the sink.

"I wanted a baby," she said at last. "Everyone looks at us and says it's so tragic. Alvin. Cancer."

She turned toward me, clasped her dripping hands. "I've left him three times because he didn't want kids. Each time he'd somehow pull me back, say he was ready. Never happened though."

She was waiting for me to say something. I took in a breath, but before I could speak, she said, "He can be a selfish bastard."

"Most artists are."

"So self-absorbed. He chose painting instead. Muck-covered canvases instead of a family, instead of a child to love."

"Some people aren't cut out to be parents."

"It's not that I don't love him, Skylar. But I'm forty-one, for God's sakes. I've spent ten years waiting for him."

"He's not much older than you, and he's fighting to live."

She nodded, shifted back a little, leaned against the counter. "See, I can't even explain it to you."

"He's my son."

"I'm in mourning already for a life I'll never have. He won't even let me try in vitro. I'd be willing to do that, you know. Happy to do it even if he weren't around for the baby."

"You shouldn't say things like that. Him not being around, I mean."

"Forget it. Just . . ." She turned and set her hands back into the dishwater.

———

They had visitors. The woman who lived downstairs popped by that afternoon with her twin boys, creating a short-lived whirlwind of activity in the loft. While Alvin, Sandy, and the mother spoke, the twins chased each other and squealed. One rattled a toy car in circles on the hardwood. Both started tossing paper airplanes about the room. I sat in the corner and watched.

Later in the week there was a man with long matted hair that he pinned in a pile on top of his head. He didn't say much. He just sat drinking tea with Alvin. Mostly, that's what I did too. I sat by him and drank tea. I read aloud from *Letters to a Young Poet* once in a while. When he was up for it, we talked. One morning out of the blue he said, "I wrote to Sylvette. And to Lysanne."

"Didn't realize you were still in touch."

"We are and we aren't."

"Good. I'm glad."

The morning sun threw a great box of light into the loft, revealed dancing particles of dust around us. "Do you think it's odd we never talked about this?" Alvin said. "About Sylvette?"

"These things happen between men and women."

"Not that. I mean, not just that." He wiped his forehead with the palm of his hand. "I knew you were sending her money. Maybe because of that, all involved were just as happy to let you think Lysanne's your daughter." I could feel him looking at me, but I didn't meet his gaze. "She's not though."

"I know, Alvin. I put two and two together over the years." I didn't want to go down this road with him, didn't want a tour of the past. For me every moment but now is best sealed in a box and left to gather dust. Maybe that's one of the reasons I paint. It's the very essence of living in the moment. I turned my attention to a still life hanging on the far wall, a bright tapestry of flowers and vases and gourds.

"Maybe because you thought she was yours –"

"Don't know that I ever thought that." I managed a chuckle, eyes focused on the still life, hoping we could just leave it at that.

"I sometimes allowed myself to think she wasn't mine. Or at least not to take responsibility."

"Now you're trying to blame me."

"I have a daughter I don't even know."

"Jesus Christ, Alvin." The strength of my own words propelled me from the rocker. I took two paces and turned. "It was a piece of generosity I could little afford that went largely unrecognized. Unappreciated."

"No need to blow a gasket, Dad. I'm sure it was appreciated."

"Just to be clear here, I never claimed her. I never offered her my name. I simply sent some money. Truth is I've never seen her. Not since she was a baby. There was plenty of time for you to take some responsibility."

Alvin was suddenly sweating, drops beaded on his narrow forehead. He noticed me watching. "It's the medication," he said and wiped the sweat away.

I looked back at the painting. "That still life has a nice balance. It's well composed."

"These are all old. Hung them for my birthday. Been meaning to take them down."

"For Christ's sakes, Alvin, take a compliment."

"I spent my life trying to capture the truth of the world only to realize it's impossible."

"You set your sights too high. Always have."

"I heard you and Sandy last night. Talking about kids and all. I guess I am a selfish bastard." He licked his lips and resettled his head. "Have you gone up to the studio?"

"Not yet."

"You know, this last creative spurt started with her, with Sylvette. Painting the memory of her."

"Will she come? Sylvette?"

"Don't know."

"Would it help if I phoned?"

"Doubt it. I've written to so many people without hearing back. Suppose I've pushed everyone away over the years. Just like you did."

"Who else did you write to? Besides me, I mean."

"Mother."

"Alvin. How –" I cut myself off. "She's been dead five years, Alvin."

"What am I saying? I mean –" He looked like he was forcing himself to smile. "Oh God, I don't know what I mean. I'm just so tired I can't think straight."

"Rest," I said and crouched by him, pulling up the blanket. "Just rest."

———

If he hadn't mentioned Sylvette, I might not have gone up to his studio. And if I hadn't seen those paintings before he died, I might have left them as they were and gone on painting in obscurity the rest of my life. But that's not how it happened.

In the morning with the brightness of early sunlight, I pulled paintings from slots, removed drop cloths, set canvases around the room. They were paintings of pain and suffering – fire, bodies, war, and destruction. These were paintings of death and Armageddon in the hazy colours of dawn and dusk – figures melting into shapes and colours, an energetic blending of figurative and abstract. They were painted with wild brushstrokes, a firm, ambitious movement on every canvas. They were a horror story of a mind that seemed rawly touched by death. And I couldn't take my eyes away.

In most, the figures were unrecognizable, but there was a series of small portraits of distorted and blasted faces. Sylvette was a mere memory on the canvas, but I knew it was her.

For almost an hour I looked over the paintings, not as a critic, nor painter nor father. They connected beneath that, connected with the human through the primordial visual – the sense that travels directly to the soul and can make it shudder.

When I returned to the loft, the man with the dreadlocks piled on his head was sitting in the rocking chair. I lingered at a distance, waited until he was done with his tea then walked him out. At the door, he said, "Think positive thoughts. Give him your positive energy. It's making a difference already."

When I returned, Alvin was asleep. I rocked by his side while images from those paintings coursed through my mind – the burning colours, the lopsided composition, the twisted faces, figures sprawled across canvases. When Alvin finally awoke, I took his hand. "They really are quite good," I said after a moment.

His one eye focused on me, bloodshot and red-rimmed; it was hard to return his gaze. "If it weren't for the fact they're in my studio, I wouldn't be sure they were mine."

"They're an achievement," I said. This was another understatement, and I knew I should have said more, but I didn't have the generosity at hand.

"Just before you called last week," he said. "I went up there. When I looked at them, even with just one eye, I could see that I was dying."

"Don't say that, Alvin."

"I'm fighting this, Dad, but I'm just saying."

———

The next day, I drove back to Tofino, back to my cabin and the bush. I arrived at dusk and slept. In the morning I began to paint. The only cabin I use is one large room with windows facing every direction and a bedroom loft above the little kitchen. The rest of the space is studio – floor spackled with paint, two easels in the middle of the room alongside a large white mobile wall. I use a narrow counter at one end of the room as a pallet. The other side of the room is racks and slots for paintings. Space is so tight I've removed most older canvases from their frames and rolled them.

That morning, I began from the bones of abstract work I'd done off and on the past two years – a dozen paintings that were not yet realized. My best work comes from painting over an existing piece, starting again without starting again.

For eight solid hours I worked with brush in hand. Painting is physical and draining, but I worked on three different canvases before I lay down and slept. Over the next five days all I did was paint, sleep, and eat. I pushed until this old body teetered on the edge of collapse. And then I went into town. It was Tuesday, two days after Alvin's second-to-last radiation treatment. Someone should have been home, but I called all day without getting through. I left two messages and then checked at the post office for any general delivery mail. There was a card from Alvin postmarked in May. "I have stage four cancer. I'd like to see you. I'm writing because I don't know how else to get in touch. Will you come?" Some words were scratched out. At the bottom he signed it only with an *A*.

The card was two months old and although I told myself that, I couldn't help but read it as today's news. My body slumped against the post office wall. The clerk stepped from behind the desk, but I waved her off and managed to stand.

I returned to the cabin to sleep that evening. The last quarter-mile along the ridge that leads to my house was a struggle. My legs were watery weak. Twice I had to rest where I wouldn't normally even pause.

I spent the next day in bed, didn't return to town until that Thursday. Sandy answered the phone. "They've stopped the radiation." That was the first thing she said. "They found more cancer. In his brain."

"I'll be right down. I'll come tonight."

"We're leaving this afternoon. There's an alternative treatment centre in Tijuana. We've been considering it for a while. Sort of famous for holistic treatments."

"And they say they can help?"

"They're willing to try."

"Sandy, it's a long way for him –"

"Let me put Alvin on. Hold on a second."

Alvin grunted into the phone. "So she won that battle," I said, meaning it to be a light-hearted comment though I knew it didn't sound that way.

"There's only one battle here, Dad, and we're all on the same side."

"I know. I'm sorry."

"So am I."

"If these are your last days, Alvin, don't spend them in Mexico. You could paint. We could paint together."

"I've lost one eye. I'm half-blind in the other. I'm just trying to live, Dad."

"Do you want me to come with you?"

"I don't know."

My fingers ran down the pad of buttons on the phone, touching but not pushing. "I've been working since I saw those paintings of yours. They've travelled with me. They live in my mind. Best things you've ever done."

"I know. Even when I was working on them I knew. It was like I'd channelled something, brush guided by a force beyond me, as though the paintings weren't even mine."

"You said you'd written to your mother. Who else did you write to?"

"My mother? Dad, I didn't –"

"Never mind. Forget it. I'll see you when you're back. You hang in there, okay?"

———

It took me an hour to walk the path back to my cabin. I had to rest at every chance. It took two days before I could pick up my brushes. Even then, all I could do was stand and stare. All my life I've thought I had something to say. Pile all my paintings end to end and they couldn't whisper a word of comfort now. I set down the brushes, looked out the windows – out over the ocean, across the great expanse of grey that meets the sky in a fine, thin line. I can stare out there for hours, watching the weather change, watching distant boats, mind racing out over the Pacific, out toward Japan and China.

That weekend I bought a roll of quarters. At the library, I wrote down every number for a Sylvette or Lysanne Turcotte in Montreal. I called them all from the pay phone outside the Co-op with no luck. When I was done, I called Alvin's neighbour for an update.

"What am I supposed to know?" Sue said. "What am I supposed to tell you? They just left."

Back in my cabin, I set those abstracts in storage slots and worked in the garden. I harvested my marijuana crop, carried it into town. I called Sue again. She said they were giving him some tests. That was all. No other news. I spent the rest of the week putting frames together. I gessoed them, then drove back to Victoria.

I used the key they kept under a flower pot. Up in Alvin's studio, I lay the paintings out, drank from them again, then gathered together the half-dozen smallest canvases, the portraits I believed were of Sylvette – her face melting away into abstract forms. These I took with me.

In my studio the next morning, with those portraits of Sylvette arranged behind me, I raised my brush and stared again at a blank canvas, bent close until I could make out its dimpled skin, could smell the dried gesso. At the bench, where all the colours of God's prism are squeezed in drips and drabs, I touched my brush to the azure blue of a summer sky. Standing at the easel, I turned slowly and faced Alvin's paintings. I crouched by the first – a rich vision of a face turned raw and bloody across the top of the painting. It was as though the skull had been sliced open and the top lifted off. The face itself was green, grey, and blue, and I brought my brush so close to the dark shadow of the nose that it might have touched. I backed away, dropped the brush, and for a moment paced the room. I walked end to end, looked out at the ocean, but not even that could hold me. At last, I returned to the painting. I raised my brush and this time it did touch.

In the early 1900s, Chaim Soutine used to send an assistant to buy paintings from hawkers on the banks of the Seine. He'd use these as a base. He'd begin from them. I'd done similar things throughout my career, although never with a painting of my son's. In one way or another every artist works from the paintings of others. We all stand on each other's shoulders, we all take and we all give. It's the cycle of art.

———

Next morning I returned to town and called Sue. "They're coming home," she said. "But it's not good news. They're going from the airport straight to the hospice."

My body went slack. I leaned against the phone booth to stay upright. My mind had formed a scale from worst news to best and this was as close to the worst as I'd allowed myself to consider. I managed a few words of thanks into the receiver, backed out of the booth and walked away.

The Sooke Hospice is a quiet retreat in the hills – a peaceful place where people go to die. I arrived in the evening after a rain. The earthy smell of a warm, damp garden was rich in the air. A woman in a black leather coat stood smoking under the awning. I walked past her and through to reception where a nurse led me down a short hallway. Alvin was propped up in bed, ashen and gaunt – the withered branch of an ancient tree. Sandy was curled in the chair beside him, and my entry woke her. She rubbed her eyes, and Alvin turned my way. He seemed to smile as he raised a hand. He said something, but it was just a croak.

"Lysanne," Sandy said. "She arrived last night." And then the woman in the leather coat was at the doorway. Her stringy black hair fell over her face, but even through that veil she looked like her mother – the strong jaw and muscular face, shoulders set at attention. This could have been Sylvette walking into our lives twenty-some years ago.

Sandy stood. "Lysanne, Skylar."

Lysanne stepped forward. "How do you do?" She rose to her toes and kissed my cheek. "I do not speak English well." She flashed a wide, embarrassed grin, almost giggled.

"Welcome," I said. "It's so good. I mean." I turned to Sandy unsure of what Lysanne could understand. "You should have said. You should have told me."

Alvin raised his hand for Lysanne. He spoke little above a whisper, and she leaned close to listen. She nodded as though she understood, although the language barrier must have prevented him from getting words across. When she backed away, Alvin managed to sit up, and with our help, he stood. He posed for a photograph with me and Lysanne. We rang for the nurse. She took another, which included Sandy, then one of just Alvin and Lysanne, one of him with Sandy, and finally one with me – the two of us trying to smile, my arm around his bony shoulder.

Alvin slept and Lysanne went out to smoke again. Sandy joined her. I watched Alvin, his rib cage barely registering each shallow breath – every one a labour to produce. His face, once round and full, had been chiselled away. It was now just bone and skin.

Sandy returned and I listened as she made herself comfortable. "So?" I said after a while.

"So," she said.

"Lysanne."

Sandy nodded, gestured outside. "She's talking to someone on the phone."

"I didn't mean that. I meant –"

"I know what you meant."

I stretched out my legs.

"He's happy," Sandy said. "It's made him happy." She leaned her head back and for a moment I thought she was going to sleep. "Months ago, when we first talked about going to Tijuana, it seemed so expensive. In the end, the money was nothing. It was the cost in time. It really just exhausted him. He could have spent a few more days with Lysanne. A few more days at home."

"I know."

"It feels like it's been so long, but really it's only been three months. Hardly a beat of time." She raised her head, opened her eyes, and looked at me. "Sometimes I wonder if all this effort to prolong life was more for me than him."

"Have you talked to him about this?"

"In a way."

"Now's the time. I mean, if it's important, don't let him go without talking this through."

She snorted. "That's rich, you telling me I need to communicate. The things the two of you need to talk through could fill a book."

I did my best to smile, but I knew it wasn't coming through. I turned back to Alvin, still and peaceful-looking. "Maybe that's it. There's so much there's effectively nothing."

"That's one way to look at it."

"We connect through our work."

"That's a bullshit answer."

"What do you want from me, Sandy?"

"I don't want anything from you. Maybe Alvin does though. Maybe you do, but can't see it."

"I believe it's possible to connect through the paintings, that our shared endeavour brings us together on a different level. I know you'll never understand, but it's true."

———

We sat with him through the night, the three of us, his witnesses, alternately holding his hand, brushing the sweat from his forehead, and rubbing his bony feet. In the morning, he asked for more morphine. Sandy climbed into bed with him, curled against him while the nurse increased the dose in his IV. That evening he died – a last quiet breath and then nothing. Stillness. Peace.

"Will you leave me with him?" Sandy said. "For a while."

I led Lysanne into the damp night, into the rich, earthy smell of summer. The moon was full, leaden in the sky, hanging there heavy and white, ready to fall earthwards. We got into my truck and I drove us into town.

I switched on all the lights in the loft and took Lysanne to the sofa where Alvin had spent so many of his last days. The canvas that hung above it was the only painting of Sylvette left in the house as far as I knew. Lysanne gazed at it and nodded. "Sylvette," I said. "Alvin. He was little more than a child. So was your mother."

I went to prepare the bed for her and when I returned, she was sitting on the sofa, arms folded, alone in her thoughts. I sat and took her hand, squeezed it, this soft, still hand of the only child of my only child.

From the moment I'd stepped into the loft, I could feel my son's paintings. They called to me, the last great works of Alvin Cale. Although I sat with my granddaughter, my mind was already heading upstairs, and although I told myself I wouldn't take them, I knew it was a lie. I knew that before the next day passed all those canvases would be in my truck. This knowledge, wrapped tight in shame, ate away at me while my granddaughter wept.

ABOUT THE AUTHORS

Jesus Hardwell's short fiction has appeared in *The Dalhousie Review*, *The Windsor Review*, *Front & Centre*, and *Exile*. Hardwell recently completed a volume of stories entitled *Bloodgroove* and is currently at work on a number of plays as well as a vocal chamber drama, *The Star-Knot Variations*. He lives in Guelph, Ontario.

Daniel Griffin's previous appearance in *The Journey Prize Stories* was in 2004. "The Last Great Works of Alvin Cale" was one of five stories he published in 2008. His work was also highlighted in *Coming Attractions 2008*. Griffin lives with his wife and three daughters in Victoria, B.C., where he is completing a collection of stories about fathers, brothers, and twenty-first-century family life. You can read more of his work at www.danielgriffin.ca.

Paul Headrick's first novel, *That Tune Clutches My Heart*, was published by Gaspereau Press. "Highlife," which appeared in *Event*, is part of *The Doctrine of Affections*, a collection of stories on musical themes forthcoming from Freehand Books. Headrick teaches English and Creative Writing at Langara College and lives in Vancouver with his partner, novelist Heather Burt.

Sarah Keevil has published short fiction and poetry in *CV2*, *Descant*, *filling Station*, *Kiss Machine*, and *Room*. She has degrees in English and Creative Writing from Concordia University and was the winner of the 2004 Irving Layton Award for Fiction. "Pyro," which first appeared in *Event*, was also nominated for a National Magazine Award. She currently lives in Toronto, where she is at work on her first novel.

Adrian Michael Kelly is the author of a novel, *Down Sterling Road*. His short stories and essays have appeared in *Queen's Quarterly*, *Best Canadian Stories*, *Canadian Notes and Queries*, *The New Quarterly*, and *Prairie Fire*. He currently lives in Calgary, where he is completing a collection of short stories to be published by Biblioasis.

Fran Kimmel is an Alberta lifer who recently moved from Calgary to the rural community of Lacombe. Her short fiction has appeared in *Grain Magazine*, *Prairie Fire*, *The Fiddlehead*, and *filling Station*, and she has won both CBC Anthology and Write for Radio awards. She writes extensively for the corporate sector and is working on a collection of interlocking stories.

Lynne Kutsukake's short fiction has appeared in *Grain Magazine*, *The Windsor Review*, *Ten Stories High Short Story Anthology*, and *Ricepaper*. Another story is forthcoming in *Prairie Fire*. She has studied in the Creative Writing Program at the University of Toronto's School of Continuing Studies and attended the Writing with Style Spring 2008 Program at the Banff Centre. As well as writing fiction, she has translated modern Japanese literature. Kutsukake lives in Toronto and is currently working on a collection of short stories.

Alexander MacLeod lives in Dartmouth, Nova Scotia, and teaches at Saint Mary's University. His short stories have appeared in many Canadian and American journals, and his first collection will be published by Biblioasis Press.

Dave Margoshes is a Regina writer whose stories and poems have appeared widely in Canadian literary magazines and anthologies, including the *Best Canadian Stories* volumes. He's published three novels and five collections of stories; the most recent, *Bix's Trumpet and Other Stories*, won two prizes at the 2007 Saskatchewan Book Awards, including Book of the Year. "The Wisdom of Solomon" is the latest in a series of stories based on the life of his father.

Shawn Syms's fiction, poetry, essays, and journalism have appeared in the *Globe and Mail*, *PRISM international*, *The Danforth Review*, *Quill & Quire*, and twenty or so other publications. He's in the final stages of writing *Human Forces*, a short fiction collection.

Sarah L. Taggart's story "Deaf" won *The Malahat Review*'s Jack Hodgins Founders Award. Taggart was born in Calgary and is hopefully almost done her Master's in Publishing from Simon Fraser University. She might live in Montreal.

Yasuko Thanh has lived in Germany, Mexico, and Central America, and currently resides in Victoria. Her stories have been published in *Prairie Fire*, *Descant*, *Fireweed*, *The Fiddlehead*, *PRISM international*, and *Vancouver Review*. Her non-fiction has appeared in publications as diverse as the

Vancouver Sun, Island Parent Magazine, Speak, and *subTerrain.* She was a finalist for the Hudson Prize, the Millennium Prize, and the David Adams Richards Award. She is at work on a novel and a short story collection called *When You Get Where You're Going.*

ABOUT THE CONTRIBUTING JOURNALS

For more information about all the journals that submitted stories to this year's anthology, please consult *The Journey Prize Stories* website: www.mcclelland.com/jps.

The Dalhousie Review has been in operation since 1921 and aspires to be a forum in which seriousness of purpose and playfulness of mind can coexist in meaningful dialogue. The journal publishes new fiction and poetry in every issue and welcomes submissions from authors around the world. Editor: Anthony Stewart. Submissions and correspondence: *The Dalhousie Review*, Dalhousie University, Halifax, Nova Scotia, B3H 4R2. Email: dalhousie.review@dal.ca Website: www.dalhousiereview.dal.ca

Event is a celebrated literary journal in which readers encounter new and established talent – in fiction, poetry, non-fiction, and critical reviews. The journal thrives on a balance of both traditional narrative and contemporary approaches to poetry and prose. *Event* is home to Canada's longest-running annual non-fiction contest. It is our goal to support and encourage a thriving literary community in Canada, while maintaining our international reputation for excellence. Editor: Rick Maddocks. Managing Editor: Ian Cockfield. Fiction Editor: Christine Dewar. Poetry Editor: Elizabeth Bachinsky. Submissions and correspondence: *Event*, P.O. Box 2503, New

Westminster, British Columbia, V3L 5B2. Email (queries only): event@douglas.bc.ca Website: www.event.douglas.bc.ca

Exile: The Literary Quarterly is a distinctive journal that recently published its Anniversary Special 30 Volumes/120th Issue, featuring new work from, among others, those who appeared in the first issues (Margaret Atwood and Marie-Claire Blais), the middle issues (Austin Clarke and Susan Swan), and those who continue to carry on the tradition (Priscila Uppal, a finalist for the 2007 Griffin Poetry Prize, and Matt Shaw, winner of the 2006 Journey Prize). With over one thousand contributions since 1972, *Exile* has become a respected forum, always presenting an impressive selection of new and established authors and artists, drawing our material (literature, poetry, drama, work in translation, and the fine arts) from French and English Canada, as well as from the United States, Britain, Europe, Latin America, the Middle East, and Asia. Publisher: Michael Callaghan. Submissions and correspondence: Exile/Excelsior Publishing Inc., 134 Eastbourne Avenue, Toronto, Ontario, M5P 2G6. Email (queries only): exq@exilequarterly.com Website: www.exilequarterly.com

Grain Magazine, a literary quarterly, publishes engaging, surprising, eclectic, and challenging writing and art by Canadian and international writers and artists. Published by the Saskatchewan Writers Guild, *Grain* has earned national and international recognition for its distinctive content. Editor: Sylvia Legris. Fiction Editor: Terry Jordan. Poetry Editor: Mari-Lou Rowley. Submissions and correspondence: *Grain*

Magazine, P.O. Box 67, Saskatoon, Saskatchewan, S7K 3K1. Email: grainmag@sasktel.net Website: www.grainmagazine.ca

The Malahat Review is a quarterly journal of contemporary poetry, fiction, and creative non-fiction by both new and celebrated writers. Summer issues feature the winners of *Malahat*'s Novella and Long Poem prizes, held in alternate years; the fall issues feature the winners of the Far Horizons Award for emerging writers, alternating between poetry and fiction each year; the winter issues feature the winners of the Creative Non-Fiction Prize; and beginning in 2010, the spring issues will feature winners from the Open Season Awards in all three genres (poetry, fiction, and creative non-fiction). All issues feature covers by noted Canadian visual artists and include reviews of Canadian books. Editor: John Barton. Assistant Editor: Rhonda Batchelor. Submissions and correspondence: *The Malahat Review*, University of Victoria, P.O. Box 1700, Station CSC, Victoria, British Columbia, V8W 2Y2. Email: malahat@uvic.ca Website: www.malahatreview.ca

The New Quarterly is an award-winning literary magazine publishing fiction, poetry, interviews, and essays on writing. Now in its twenty-eighth year, the magazine prides itself on its independent take on the Canadian literary scene. Recent issues include the Montreal Issue (in both English and French), our Salon des Refuses, and Last Poems (the end of poetry and the poetry of last things); upcoming is an issue on Lists as both a thematic and a formal element, and a series on the role of the critic. Editor: Kim Jernigan. Submissions and correspondence: *The New Quarterly*, c/o St. Jerome's University, 290 Westmount Road North, Waterloo, Ontario, N2L 3G3. Email: editor@tnq.ca, orders@tnq.ca Website: www.tnq.ca

Prairie Fire is a quarterly magazine of contemporary Canadian writing that publishes stories, poems, and literary non-fiction by both emerging and established writers. *Prairie Fire*'s editorial mix also occasionally features critical or personal essays and interviews with authors. Stories published in *Prairie Fire* have won awards at the National Magazine Awards and the Western Magazine Awards. *Prairie Fire* publishes writing from, and has readers in, all parts of Canada. Editor: Andris Taskans. Fiction Editors: Warren Cariou and Heidi Harms. Submissions and correspondence: *Prairie Fire*, Room 423–100 Arthur Street, Winnipeg, Manitoba, R3B 1H3. Email: prfire@mts.net Website: www.prairiefire.ca

PRISM international, the oldest literary magazine in Western Canada, was established in 1959 by a group of Vancouver writers. Published four times a year, *PRISM* features short fiction, poetry, creative non-fiction, and translations by both new and established writers from Canada and around the world. The only criteria are originality and quality. *PRISM* holds three exemplary competitions: the Short Fiction Contest, the Literary Non-fiction Contest, and the Earle Birney Prize for Poetry. Executive Editors: Nadia Pestrak and Dan Schwartz. Fiction Editor: Rachel Knudsen. Poetry Editor: Elizabeth Ross. Submissions and correspondence: *PRISM international*, Creative Writing Program, The University of British

Columbia, Buchanan E-462, 1866 Main Mall, Vancouver, British Columbia, V6T 1Z1. Email (for queries only): prism@interchange.ubc.ca Website: www.prismmagazine.ca

Vancouver Review is an iconoclastic, irreverent, and wholly independent cultural quarterly that celebrated its fifth anniversary in 2009. *Vancouver Review* focuses on B.C. cultural, social, and political issues, and publishes commentary, essays, and narrative non-fiction, as well as fiction and poetry in every issue. With its Blueprint B.C. Fiction Series, launched in the summer of 2007, it explores the zeitgeist and geographic implications of the province through illustrated stories by first-time and established authors. Editor: Gudrun Will. Fiction Editor: Zsuzsi Gartner. Poetry Editor: Caroline Harvey. Submissions and correspondence (email submissions preferred): *Vancouver Review*, 2828 West 13th Avenue, Vancouver, British Columbia, V6K 2T7. Email: editor@ vancouverreview Website: www.vancouverreview.com

Submissions were also received from the following journals:

The Antigonish Review
(Antigonish, N.S.)

The Claremont Review
(Victoria, B.C.)

dANDelion Magazine
(Calgary, Alta.)

Descant
(Toronto, Ont.)

The Fiddlehead
(Fredericton, N.B.)

FreeFall Magazine
(Calgary, Alta.)

Geist
(Vancouver, B.C.)

Maisonneuve Magazine
(Montreal, Que.)

Matrix Magazine
(Montreal, Que.)

The New Orphic Review
(Nelson, B.C.)

On Spec
(Edmonton, Alta.)

*The Prairie Journal of
Canadian Literature*
(Calgary, Alta.)

Queen's Quarterly
(Kingston, Ont.)

Ricepaper Magazine
(Vancouver, B.C.)

Soliloquies Anthology
(Montreal, Que.)

subTerrain Magazine
(Vancouver, B.C.)

Taddle Creek
(Toronto, Ont.)

This Magazine
(Toronto, Ont.)

The Windsor Review
(Windsor, Ont.)

PREVIOUS CONTRIBUTING AUTHORS

* Winners of the $10,000 Journey Prize

ᴬᴬ Co-winners of the $10,000 Journey Prize

I

1989

SELECTED WITH ALISTAIR MacLEOD

Ven Begamudré, "Word Games"

David Bergen, "Where You're From"

Lois Braun, "The Pumpkin-Eaters"

Constance Buchanan, "Man with Flying Genitals"

Ann Copeland, "Obedience"

Marion Douglas, "Flags"

Frances Itani, "An Evening in the Café"

Diane Keating, "The Crying Out"

Thomas King, "One Good Story, That One"

Holley Rubinsky, "Rapid Transits"*

Jean Rysstad, "Winter Baby"

Kevin Van Tighem, "Whoopers"

M.G. Vassanji, "In the Quiet of a Sunday Afternoon"

Bronwen Wallace, "Chicken 'N' Ribs"

Armin Wiebe, "Mouse Lake"

Budge Wilson, "Waiting"

2

1990

SELECTED WITH LEON ROOKE; GUY VANDERHAEGHE

André Alexis, "Despair: Five Stories of Ottawa"

Glen Allen, "The Hua Guofeng Memorial Warehouse"

Marusia Bociurkiw, "Mama, Donya"

Virgil Burnett, "Billfrith the Dreamer"

Margaret Dyment, "Sacred Trust"

Cynthia Flood, "My Father Took a Cake to France"*

Douglas Glover, "Story Carved in Stone"

Terry Griggs, "Man with the Axe"

Rick Hillis, "Limbo River"

Thomas King, "The Dog I Wish I Had, I Would Call It Helen"

K.D. Miller, "Sunrise Till Dark"

Jennifer Mitton, "Let Them Say"

Lawrence O'Toole, "Goin' to Town with Katie Ann"

Kenneth Radu, "A Change of Heart"

Jenifer Sutherland, "Table Talk"

Wayne Tefs, "Red Rock and After"

3

1991

SELECTED WITH JANE URQUHART

Donald Aker, "The Invitation"

Anton Baer, "Yukon"

Allan Barr, "A Visit from Lloyd"

David Bergen, "The Fall"

Rai Berzins, "Common Sense"

Diana Hartog, "Theories of Grief"

Diane Keating, "The Salem Letters"

Yann Martel, "The Facts Behind the Helsinki Roccamatios"*

Jennifer Mitton, "Polaroid"

Sheldon Oberman, "This Business with Elijah"

Lynn Podgurny, "Till Tomorrow, Maple Leaf Mills"

James Riseborough, "She Is Not His Mother"

Patricia Stone, "Living on the Lake"

4
1992
SELECTED WITH SANDRA BIRDSELL

David Bergen, "The Bottom of the Glass"

Maria A. Billion, "No Miracles Sweet Jesus"

Judith Cowan, "By the Big River"

Steven Heighton, "A Man Away from Home Has No Neighbours"

Steven Heighton, "How Beautiful upon the Mountains"

L. Rex Kay, "Travelling"

Rozena Maart, "No Rosa, No District Six"*

Guy Malet De Carteret, "Rainy Day"

Carmelita McGrath, "Silence"

Michael Mirolla, "A Theory of Discontinuous Existence"

Diane Juttner Perreault, "Bella's Story"

Eden Robinson, "Traplines"

5
1993
SELECTED WITH GUY VANDERHAEGHE

Caroline Adderson, "Oil and Dread"

David Bergen, "La Rue Prevette"

Marina Endicott, "With the Band"

Dayv James-French, "Cervine"

Michael Kenyon, "Durable Tumblers"

K.D. Miller, "A Litany in Time of Plague"

Robert Mullen, "Flotsam"

Gayla Reid, "Sister Doyle's Men"*

Oakland Ross, "Bang-bang"

Robert Sherrin, "Technical Battle for Trial Machine"

Carol Windley, "The Etruscans"

6

1994

SELECTED WITH DOUGLAS GLOVER;

JUDITH CHANT (CHAPTERS)

Anne Carson, "Water Margins: An Essay on Swimming by My
    Brother"

Richard Cumyn, "The Sound He Made"

Genni Gunn, "Versions"

Melissa Hardy, "Long Man the River"*

Robert Mullen, "Anomie"

Vivian Payne, "Free Falls"

Jim Reil, "Dry"

Robyn Sarah, "Accept My Story"

Joan Skogan, "Landfall"

Dorothy Speak, "Relatives in Florida"

Alison Wearing, "Notes from Under Water"

7

1995

SELECTED WITH M.G. VASSANJI;

RICHARD BACHMANN (A DIFFERENT DRUMMER BOOKS)

Michelle Alfano, "Opera"

Mary Borsky, "Maps of the Known World"

Gabriella Goliger, "Song of Ascent"

Elizabeth Hay, "Hand Games"

Shaena Lambert, "The Falling Woman"

Elise Levine, "Boy"

Roger Burford Mason, "The Rat-Catcher's Kiss"

Antanas Sileika, "Going Native"

Kathryn Woodward, "Of Marranos and Gilded Angels"*

8

1996

SELECTED WITH OLIVE SENIOR;

BEN MCNALLY (NICHOLAS HOARE LTD.)

Rick Bowers, "Dental Bytes"

David Elias, "How I Crossed Over"

Elyse Gasco, "Can You Wave Bye Bye, Baby?"*

Danuta Gleed, "Bones"

Elizabeth Hay, "The Friend"

Linda Holeman, "Turning the Worm"

Elaine Littman, "The Winner's Circle"

Murray Logan, "Steam"

Rick Maddocks, "Lessons from the Sputnik Diner"

K.D. Miller, "Egypt Land"

Gregor Robinson, "Monster Gaps"

Alma Subasic, "Dust"

9

1997

SELECTED WITH NINO RICCI; NICHOLAS PASHLEY

(UNIVERSITY OF TORONTO BOOKSTORE)

Brian Bartlett, "Thomas, Naked"

Dennis Bock, "Olympia"

Kristen den Hartog, "Wave"

Gabriella Goliger, "Maladies of the Inner Ear"**

Terry Griggs, "Momma Had a Baby"

Mark Anthony Jarman, "Righteous Speedboat"

Judith Kalman, "Not for Me a Crown of Thorns"

Andrew Mullins, "The World of Science"

Sasenarine Persaud, "Canada Geese and Apple Chatney"

Anne Simpson, "Dreaming Snow"**

Sarah Withrow, "Ollie"

Terence Young, "The Berlin Wall"

10

1998

SELECTED BY PETER BUITENHUIS; HOLLEY RUBINSKY;

CELIA DUTHIE (DUTHIE BOOKS LTD.)

John Brooke, "The Finer Points of Apples"*

Ian Colford, "The Reason for the Dream"

Libby Creelman, "Cruelty"

Michael Crummey, "Serendipity"

Stephen Guppy, "Downwind"

Jane Eaton Hamilton, "Graduation"

Elise Levine, "You Are You Because Your Little Dog Loves You"

Jean McNeil, "Bethlehem"

Liz Moore, "Eight-Day Clock"

Edward O'Connor, "The Beatrice of Victoria College"

Tim Rogers, "Scars and Other Presents"

Denise Ryan, "Marginals, Vivisections, and Dreams"

Madeleine Thien, "Simple Recipes"

Cheryl Tibbetts, "Flowers of Africville"

11

1999

SELECTED BY LESLEY CHOYCE; SHELDON CURRIE;

MARY-JO ANDERSON (FROG HOLLOW BOOKS)

Mike Barnes, "In Florida"

Libby Creelman, "Sunken Island"

Mike Finigan, "Passion Sunday"

Jane Eaton Hamilton, "Territory"

Mark Anthony Jarman, "Travels into Several Remote Nations of the
    World"

Barbara Lambert, "Where the Bodies Are Kept"

Linda Little, "The Still"

Larry Lynch, "The Sitter"

Sandra Sabatini, "The One With the News"

Sharon Steams, "Brothers"

Mary Walters, "Show Jumping"

Alissa York, "The Back of the Bear's Mouth"*

12

2000

SELECTED BY CATHERINE BUSH; HAL NIEDZVIECKI;

MARC GLASSMAN (PAGES BOOKS AND MAGAZINES)

Andrew Gray, "The Heart of the Land"

Lee Henderson, "Sheep Dub"

Jessica Johnson, "We Move Slowly"

John Lavery, "The Premier's New Pyjamas"

J.A. McCormack, "Hearsay"

Nancy Richler, "Your Mouth Is Lovely"

Andrew Smith, "Sightseeing"

Karen Solie, "Onion Calendar"

Timothy Taylor, "Doves of Townsend"*

Timothy Taylor, "Pope's Own"

Timothy Taylor, "Silent Cruise"

R.M. Vaughan, "Swan Street"

13

2001

SELECTED BY ELYSE GASCO; MICHAEL HELM;

MICHAEL NICHOLSON (INDIGO BOOKS & MUSIC INC.)

Kevin Armstrong, "The Cane Field"*

Mike Barnes, "Karaoke Mon Amour"

Heather Birrell, "Machaya"

Heather Birrell, "The Present Perfect"

Craig Boyko, "The Gun"

Vivette J. Kady, "Anything That Wiggles"

Billie Livingston, "You're Taking All the Fun Out of It"

Annabel Lyon, "Fishes"

Lisa Moore, "The Way the Light Is"

Heather O'Neill, "Little Suitcase"

Susan Rendell, "In the Chambers of the Sea"

Tim Rogers, "Watch"

Margrith Schraner, "Dream Dig"

14

2002

SELECTED BY ANDRÉ ALEXIS;

DEREK MCCORMACK; DIANE SCHOEMPERLEN

Mike Barnes, "Cogagwee"

Geoffrey Brown, "Listen"

Jocelyn Brown, "Miss Canada"*

Emma Donoghue, "What Remains"

Jonathan Goldstein, "You Are a Spaceman With Your Head Under the
Bathroom Stall Door"

Robert McGill, "Confidence Men"

Robert McGill, "The Stars Are Falling"

Nick Melling, "Philemon"

Robert Mullen, "Alex the God"

Karen Munro, "The Pool"

Leah Postman, "Being Famous"

Neil Smith, "Green Fluorescent Protein"

15

2003

SELECTED BY MICHELLE BERRY;

TIMOTHY TAYLOR; MICHAEL WINTER

Rosaria Campbell, "Reaching"

Hilary Dean, "The Lemon Stories"

Dawn Rae Downton, "Hansel and Gretel"

Anne Fleming, "Gay Dwarves of America"

Elyse Friedman, "Truth"

Charlotte Gill, "Hush"

Jessica Grant, "My Husband's Jump"*

Jacqueline Honnet, "Conversion Classes"

S.K. Johannesen, "Resurrection"

Avner Mandelman, "Cuckoo"

Tim Mitchell, "Night Finds Us"

Heather O'Neill, "The Difference Between Me and Goldstein"

16

2004

SELECTED BY ELIZABETH HAY;

LISA MOORE; MICHAEL REDHILL

Anar Ali, "Baby Khaki's Wings"

Kenneth Bonert, "Packers and Movers"

Jennifer Clouter, "Benny and the Jets"

Daniel Griffin, "Mercedes Buyer's Guide"

Michael Kissinger, "Invest in the North"

Devin Krukoff, "The Last Spark"*

Elaine McCluskey, "The Watermelon Social"

William Metcalfe, "Nice Big Car, Rap Music Coming
   Out the Window"

Lesley Millard, "The Uses of the Neckerchief"

Adam Lewis Schroeder, "Burning the Cattle at Both Ends"

Michael V. Smith, "What We Wanted"

Neil Smith, "Isolettes"

Patricia Rose Young, "Up the Clyde on a Bike"

17

2005

SELECTED BY JAMES GRAINGER AND NANCY LEE

Randy Boyagoda, "Rice and Curry Yacht Club"

Krista Bridge, "A Matter of Firsts"

Josh Byer, "Rats, Homosex, Saunas, and Simon"

Craig Davidson, "Failure to Thrive"

McKinley M. Hellenes, "Brighter Thread"

Catherine Kidd, "Green-Eyed Beans"

Pasha Malla, "The Past Composed"

Edward O'Connor, "Heard Melodies Are Sweet"

Barbara Romanik, "Seven Ways into Chandigarh"

Sandra Sabatini, "The Dolphins at Sainte Marie"

Matt Shaw, "Matchbook for a Mother's Hair"*

Richard Simas, "Anthropologies"

Neil Smith, "Scrapbook"

Emily White, "Various Metals"

18

2006

SELECTED BY STEVEN GALLOWAY;

ZSUZSI GARTNER; ANNABEL LYON

Heather Birrell, "BriannaSusannaAlana"*

Craig Boyko, "The Baby"

Craig Boyko, "The Beloved Departed"

Nadia Bozak, "Heavy Metal Housekeeping"

Lee Henderson, "Conjugation"

Melanie Little, "Wrestling"

Matthew Rader, "The Lonesome Death of Joseph Fey"

Scott Randall, "Law School"

Sarah Selecky, "Throwing Cotton"

Damian Tarnopolsky, "Sleepy"

Martin West, "Cretacea"

David Whitton, "The Eclipse"

Clea Young, "Split"

19

2007

SELECTED BY CAROLINE ADDERSON;

DAVID BEZMOZGIS; DIONNE BRAND

Andrew J. Borkowski, "Twelve Versions of Lech"

Craig Boyko, "OZY"*

Grant Buday, "The Curve of the Earth"

Nicole Dixon, "High-water Mark"

Krista Foss, "Swimming in Zanzibar"

Pasha Malla, "Respite"

Alice Petersen, "After Summer"

Patricia Robertson, "My Hungarian Sister"

Rebecca Rosenblum, "Chilly Girl"

Nicholas Ruddock, "How Eunice Got Her Baby"

Jean Van Loon, "Stardust"

20

2008

SELECTED BY LYNN COADY;

HEATHER O'NEILL; NEIL SMITH

Théodora Armstrong, "Whale Stories"

Mike Christie, "Goodbye Porkpie Hat"

Anna Leventhal, "The Polar Bear at the Museum"

Naomi K. Lewis, "The Guiding Light"

Oscar Martens, "Breaking on the Wheel"

Dana Mills, "Steaming for Godthab"

Saleema Nawaz, "My Three Girls"*

Scott Randall, "The Gifted Class"

S. Kennedy Sobol, "Some Light Down"

Sarah Steinberg, "At Last at Sea"

Clea Young, "Chaperone"